TAO OF LOVE

TAO OF LOVE

THAMES RIVER PRESS
An Imprint of Wimbledon Publishing Company Limited (WPC)
Another Imprint of WPC is Anthem Press (www.anthempress.com)

First published in the United Kingdom in 2011 by

THAMES RIVER PRESS
75-76 Blackfriars Road
London SE1 8HA

www.thamesriverpress.com

© Leda Joandaughter, 2011

All rights reserved. No part of this publication may be reproduced
in any form or by any means without written permission of the publisher.

The moral rights of the author and the translator have been asserted
in accordance with the Copyright, Designs, and Patents Act 1988.

All the characters and events described in this novel are imaginary
and any similarity with real people or events is purely coincidental.

A CIP record for this book is available from the British Library

ISBN 978-0-857283-54-2

Typeset by Tetragon

TAO OF LOVE

LEDA JOANDAUGHTER

THAMES RIVER PRESS

To my husband, my angel, John

1

Dawn came, initializing the morning, punctuated by sunbeams and crisp autumn air.

Annabelle dressed quickly as usual, periodically calling across the hallway to her daughter: "Hurry up, Sarah! What are you doing in there?"

Annabelle mumbled to herself: *I don't know... I just don't know why.*

It was another day, starting up again: good suit, new stockings, sensible shoes, burgundy lipstick.

Sarah burst out of her room, wordless, backpack on already.

"Have you had breakfast?" asked Annabelle.

"Yes."

Together they hastily descended the short set of creaking stairs into the dining room of their small rented shanty where a man was sitting, reading a newspaper amid stacks of cardboard boxes.

"Any jobs there, Dennis," said Annabelle. It was a question but she intoned it like a statement, flatly anticipating his negative response.

"Nothing good, no," he said without looking up, "but thanks for asking. Bye Sarah."

Wordless, Annabelle and Sarah hurried outside to a wood-veneer station wagon parked in front of the shanty, then drove through five narrow blocks of quaint New England houses amid pockets of children walking with their assorted book bags.

Annabelle stopped the car in front of a two-storey, red-brick elementary school and said, "Have a good day."

"You too, Mom," said Sarah, slamming the car door behind her.

At first Annabelle drove in silence, carefully avoiding the children hurrying off the sidewalk all around her. Soon she was heading south along the beach road, her windows down, her lungs filled with salty air. She turned on the radio and listened to NPR news: commentary on the recent strikes in Poland... safety concerns about oil-rig platforms following the huge explosion in the North Sea two months earlier...

Eventually she skimmed the dial until she heard a familiar voice crooning a song her mother used to play. She paused, unable to move past it – a silly song about falling in love at first sight. *Right. Like that ever really happens.*

Yet she started singing with it, unconsciously, automatically, loudly, and so entirely alone.

The tune soon ended but Annabelle's voice continued, as she switched off the radio and sang ballads she'd long ago memorized, about torment, desolation, sinking ships and despair. These were not the happy songs she shared with Sarah, but the lamentations she reserved for solitude. She sang until her eyes welled with tears, which she immediately laughed off as indulgence: admittance of sorrow, the relief of release.

> It is better not to cry
> Because the well is too deep.
> Remember that.
> It is better not to eat
> Because eating inspires hunger,
> Memories of candy mom gave me
> To ease it all
> Along with too much TV...
> No tears, little food.
> Act smart.

She shook off the poem she was forming during the meditative state of driving, having arrived at the city and being now stuck in a line of traffic crossing the General Edwards Bridge. While inching forward with the other cars she sensed herself as some strange fish, stuck in a school above a river, mourning this necessary migration towards her place of business, wishing she could be home with Sarah, singing and dancing, twirling away the traumas that haunted her.

Finally she reached a five-storey garage, carefully parked her conservative vehicle, and headed towards a high-rise across the street from MIT. It was a good idea to walk quickly and not look around until reaching the well-travelled street, the secure corporate elevator, her office door, which she relished in closing behind her, shutting out unnecessary glances and conversations.

At lunchtime she faced the beverage dispenser and tried to choose among soft-drink brands. She'd started this job two weeks earlier and was attempting to appear professional at all times. But she was acutely self-conscious, even here, alone with these vending machines.

The year was 1988. Annabelle Bonney, aged thirty-three, was divorcing her husband, Dennis, finally. That decision made smaller ones impossible.

She was still living with Dennis but they hadn't slept together in months. His touch made her break out in hives.

It was a sign.

She'd signed a lease for a new apartment and would be moving out the following weekend. He wasn't moving yet. He had said he would move to California. He hadn't said when that would be. She didn't know how he'd keep up the rent on the shanty until then, but that wasn't her business. She was taking their child, Sarah, with her. Sarah was used to it, they had moved before, often every year, sometimes more.

Annabelle was still wearing her wedding ring at work, hoping to avoid questions, personal interactions. During the interview with her new boss, Annabelle had mentioned Dennis. She wasn't sure why because even then she was planning to leave him. She would have to figure out how to gradually work the separation into casual conversation. That morning Daryl, the other lead writer, mentioned he was getting divorced so Annabelle empathized, revealing she was going through the same thing. She told Daryl in confidence. She had to tell someone.

Suddenly she wasn't alone. Someone was standing beside her. She quickly pressed the cola button, attempting to mask her indecisiveness.

"Are you new?" said the person.

She intended to glance at him but his eyes caught her and she could not look away. He was the best looking man she had ever seen. He was bathing her in the longest, most arrogant gaze she'd ever encountered from anyone.

1. *I am going to marry him.*
2. *Do not be insane! Be rational.*

She strove to remain professional.

"Yes," she said, "I'm Annabelle Bonney. Are you an engineer?"

He had the demeanour of a software engineer, a cerebral snob.

He paused, turned away, slipped some coins in the candy-machine slot, pressed a button, looked back at her, and held out his hand. She shook it, mechanically, shocked by the moist warmth of his huge palm.

"Yeah," he finally said, "I'm Eddie. What do you do?"

She studied this miracle: nearly seven feet tall with shoulders of a god, clear skin, high cheekbones, broad smile and round brown eyes that glued her like flypaper until she toddled from one foot to the other, nearly tottering but nevertheless professional.

"I work as a tech writer," she said.

His long, straight brown hair was tied back in a ponytail. His T-shirt had an acupuncture graphic depicting key body-penetration points. His khaki shorts revealed long legs, all muscle, entirely frosted with masses of curly brown hair.

1. *He's only a child.*
2. *He can't be older than twenty-five.*
3. *I'm too old for this.*

Eddie nodded, reached into the candy machine, and pulled out a Mars bar. Annabelle realized the papers she'd been holding in her left hand were dangling over her left fingers, hiding her disingenuous wedding band. She smiled at Eddie and blushed. He nodded again and walked away.

1. *He must think I'm a fool.*
2. *Am I a fool?*

She made her way to the women's bathroom, removed the thin gold band from her left third finger, and washed her hands twice.

Afterwards she stood back and stared at the huge utilitarian mirror. Her face was aglow, her cheeks still red, throbbing with longing that she wanted to deny.

Annabelle's face was a curious mixture of beauty and impishness with a sober, sad edge. Her long hair was thick, auburn, streaked with grey wisps, and tied in a ponytail falling just below her waist; this hair, so defiantly long, was the last remaining outer vestige of her nonconformist soul.

She was also tall, slender and completely flat in the chest.

Her tailored suit was hazel green, matching her eyes, creating a stunning effect. She didn't know that, having purchased the suit at discount, at an upscale consignment shop. It was practical, effective for its purpose. The fact that it made her eyes shine, radiant, was lost to her; as far as she was concerned, her eyes were the colour of mud.

The red in her cheeks refused to fade. She could still smell him, his faint sweat scent. She splashed cold water on her face and looked up again, her face now wet as well as red.

Finally she ventured into the hallway, conscious of dampness all around her. While turning the corner by the snack-food alcove she discovered his office, his nameplate, Ed Wright, his enormous form silently perched before a video-display monitor. He didn't look up. She hurried past.

Her office was one floor above. She took the stairs instead of the elevator. With each step she paused, shaking her head as if unable to comprehend the recent encounter that had startled not only her consciousness but also her tightly wound body.

Back at her desk she typed at her keyboard and periodically closed her eyes, reviewing his image in her mind. Was he actually a giant? Why had he perused her like that? Why should she care?

This was not the time to start feeling attracted to anyone, especially someone so young and overwhelming, so confidently and organically musky.

Reasons to Avoid Eddie:

1. *Divorce initiated because Dennis is so immature. Eddie appears to be very young, probably immature.*
2. *Dennis only recently agreed to the divorce. Not a time to get confused by hormones. Just keep a clear head, free and clear of all men. Celebrate freedom; enjoy independence.*
3. *Men are too dangerous now, sex with someone new is life-threatening. Forget about sex.*
4. *Men do not believe in love, all they want is sex; don't confuse hormones with love.*
5. *Eddie might be married or gay. He's probably not available anyway.*
6. *Office romances are extremely unprofessional. Never have an office romance!*
7. *Eddie has long hair. Sarah would think he was strange.*

The seventh point was the momentary clincher. Annabelle couldn't picture Eddie around opinionated, literate, precocious Sarah. Astute criticism came easily to Sarah, a trait that made her seem older than eight.

Later that afternoon Annabelle returned to the seventh floor. Eddie was still at his desk. She glanced in his office window. He glanced at her. Neither smiled. She hurried past. He didn't look up when she walked by again. She couldn't help spy his immense knees, bent at thirty-five degrees. *Those knees.*

I can't keep doing this, she told herself while climbing the stairs. *Stop this right now.* She replayed her reasons to avoid him, adding new points, and although she went on like this for the rest of the day, some voice in her head kept repeating "Eddie."

She left work at five to reach the after-school programme by six-thirty. Although she spent every night on her modem, completing her tasks, she worried about not being able to stay at the office longer, like the DINKs who populated most of her company. DINK is an acronym for double income, no kids.

Once past the rotary in Medford, while heading north towards Route 1, she turned on the car radio.

"Dear Holy Mother," she said, "I need a sign."

The only song she knew with the word "Eddie" in it was 'Eddie's an Angel' – a fairly remote oldie.

She said aloud, "If this person Eddie who I met today is the right man for me, then please let me hear the song 'Eddie's an Angel' before I get home tonight."

For years she'd been asking for signs such as this. She'd never gotten one. It was an easy way to make decisions, like the narrator of Poe's *Raven*, obsessively asking a bird if his lover would return when all that bird can say is "nevermore", although he'd go on asking anyway. *Ridiculous*.

At the next light she slammed on the brakes, skidding towards the car in front because the song 'Eddie's an Angel' had started playing on the radio.

"I'm losing my mind," she whispered, "I actually am."

That night she dreamt of Eddie kissing her: long vivid kisses.

For the next month she never ran into him, never encountered him at the soda machine, never had a chance to talk. Sometimes she'd see him when passing his office for a snack, but she forced herself to look away fast, trying not to look in there in the first place. Sometimes they'd pass in the hallways but she refused to catch his eye. Once she accidentally did look at his face but he was talking to someone else and seemed not to notice her.

Yet during all the moving and settling into the new apartment across town, Eddie's image repeatedly appeared, always at night, an image she could not and did not want to suppress, impressed before her eyes whenever she fell asleep.

> You strange man
> about whom I know so little
> you show up in my dreams
> like some storm at sea,
> sudden as night clouds
> over the moon.
> In daytime
> I catch glimpses

of your fleeting shape;
my spirit shifts to accommodate:
I watch, wound tight
as wind through a blocked tunnel.
I hear you tick,
I unscrew your screws,
I enter the night;
the storm. I watch.
I wait.

Despite the dreams, each morning arrived like clockwork, repeating the same routine. Annabelle would shake off the memories of Eddie stored from sleep, full of resolve to ignore any potential office interaction, until the cycle would sweep back to night, with newer, deeper dreams of him.

Annabelle lived in Gardenia, Massachusetts, twenty miles north of Boston, along the Atlantic coast. When she and Dennis separated this time, she wanted to move closer to work, but was determined to stabilize the situation for Sarah as much as possible, by not making her have to change schools again.

Gardenia was tiny and safe, populated primarily by wealthy people with yachts. It had clean parks along the ocean and most of the stores sold pottery, dried-flower arrangements, and crystal jewellery. There were few apartments; Annabelle had rented the least expensive one she could find. It had only one bedroom, which she gave to Sarah. Annabelle slept in what was intended as the dining room.

Annabelle worked in Cambridge, Massachusetts, for Mastersview Inc., or MVI, as most people referred to it. MVI was the largest software company in the world. Her division, MFI, redistributed financial databases and developed searchware for Wall Street analysts.

MVI prided itself on its social conscience: it actively recruited ethnic minorities and women, promoted gay rights, and hosted a large multicultural daycare centre.

For years Annabelle had been intrigued by MVI's reputation. Although there was only one female vice president and no woman had ever sat on the Board of Directors, it was still the most flagrantly liberal Fortune 500 company she'd ever heard of. The VP of marketing at the company she'd just left once spent an entire divisional meeting describing MVI's successes and its vast cash resources. Annabelle decided then that someday she'd work there – work for the best.

Technical writing had never been her ambition. She'd majored in English in college, focusing on poetry and drama, hoping to teach someday. But the computer profession allowed her to support Sarah. With bone-chilling Reaganomics afoot, there was no other way.

To compensate for her prostitution of the writing vocation, Annabelle always tried to compose thought-provoking documentation. She would carefully contemplate the right words to describe exactly how to create script files, alter printer configurations and query databases. If an example required a proper name, she'd supply an obscure poet.

It had been a gruelling day, devoid of joy. Annabelle fussed with her pillow, punching it like a loaf of bread; one more kneading would fix it.

She closed her eyes and prayed to the Holy Mother that all would be right: the circle, Sarah, her life, her mother Mary, the apartment, the car.

The dream began where her mind left off: the circle grew to include MVI and Eddie. Images flashed, recurring totems, animals. As fast as they came they made sense. A giant brown bear stood before her, its massive arms around her. Colourful prayer flags flew from its hands. The bear became a beautiful wrinkled woman with a multicoloured striped apron.

"I love you," said the old woman.

"I know," said Annabelle, handing the woman a basket of fresh dinner rolls, adding, "These are for you. Sarah saved them for you."

The old woman paused to appreciate the gift. "My child," she said, "long ago I saw your pain. But I was helpless to touch your wound. Through the years of prayer I have guided you to this moment." She paused again while staring into Annabelle's reflected eyes. "Still," she continued, "I cannot hand you that which you seek. You must not die too early or fall victim to the ordinary. Your spirit is strong and will hold for a bit longer. Do nothing more."

Suddenly the basket of dinner rolls became a large white cake.

White light filled the dream space. Annabelle woke – cold – her pillow wet with tears. *I can't do nothing! Just another cosmic busy signal. What kind of spirit message is that?*

She opened a dresser drawer to expose candy bits, a habit she'd inherited from her mother. She unwrapped an old molasses toffee and chewed, waiting for her mind to come back on, to return to worries about work and the divorce.

That afternoon she went with the rest of her documentation group to a routine going-away party for someone she didn't know in the division.

Eddie was there, across the room, continually circling the area circumference, maintaining his distance but seemingly keeping one eye on her at all times, even while laughing with other people.

She became feeble-minded around him, lost all trains of thought, and wondered what he was saying. She imagined him privately telling everyone at the party how awkward she was.

Finally, while she was standing next to the cake, he came over to get a piece. For a moment they looked at each other but neither smiled or said anything. Then he left the room.

On the way out of the party, she passed Gail Greene's office. Gail was a product manager with whom she'd had friendly discussions at the water cooler. Annabelle glanced in and saw Eddie in there talking to Gail. Both Eddie and Gail looked at her and stopped talking.

1. *That's it: he's definitely talking about me.*
2. *He must think I'm ignorant because I'm so nervous.*
3. *That's it. Forget it. That's it.*

Annabelle's boss abruptly left the company and Daryl was promoted to take her place. Once Daryl became manager, Annabelle became the sole senior writer.

The other two writers in the division were non-technical and inexperienced. They worked on the MFI text-manipulation software, which Annabelle thought was so simple it didn't even need manuals. But they took their jobs very seriously and she only ran into them at the weekly documentation meetings, which Daryl disbanded as soon as he became manager.

Besides Daryl, Annabelle's only other writing colleague was her editor, Patty, an earthy consultant who worked at home three days a week because she had a toddler.

So Annabelle was alone most of the time, occasionally meeting with the hardware technicians who'd designed the system installation procedures.

Daryl seemed pleased with his sudden authority and immediately assigned Annabelle to work on the division's most complex new product: MVI Access.

"Can you get started on it tomorrow?" he asked, standing in the threshold to her office. She glanced out her eight-foot plate-glass window with a panoramic view: Medford, the Bunker Hill Monument, and a thin slice of Boston. Some golden autumn leaves were fluttering around outside, against the high-rise glass, as if confused: an example of nature tricked by architecture.

"Sure," she said, distracted by the leaves, which belonged in a poem.

"Good," he said. "The kick-off meeting is tomorrow at ten in room 7024. Do you know any of those guys?"

She shook her head.

"Arthur Ziminski, Bob Thomas, Ed Wright, Josh Margolis, and ummm, Tam Jacobson. Arthur is leading the project and he'll start mailing you specs soon. Like right away, today."

Annabelle shook her head again, hearing his name, Eddie's name.

"What's the problem?" said Daryl. He leant against her door, his trim body seeming subtly seductive. His face was boyish, his hair grey. She would have thought he was in his early forties if he hadn't told her about his two children, out of college, in their twenties.

Once again, Annabelle shook her head.

"There's no problem," she said.

"Why are you shaking your head?"

"I don't know."

"OK," he said, shrugging, walking away.

1. *Don't jeopardize professionalism for the sake of Eddie. Just go to the meeting and pretend he's not there.*
2. *Don't act weird in front of Daryl.*
3. *Don't act weird in the meeting.*
4. *Eddie is just an engineer; he probably can't even spell.*

Annabelle had trouble sleeping that night. Her dreams were thickly coated with incorrect answers and conference tables seeping bitter coffee, congealed cream.

In the morning she arrived promptly at ten but Eddie never appeared. The marketing and engineering strategies were outlined and the technical specifications, or specs, were reviewed. The next meeting was set for the end of the month, to give all the players a chance to become fully acquainted with the scope of the project.

Annabelle remained intently focused and took copious notes.

After lunch she passed Eddie's office on the way to the snack-food alcove and paused. A child was in there, a boy, about Sarah's age.

Could he be Eddie's child? With such short hair? Eddie is too young to have a son that old; he must be a nephew or something.

Eddie glanced through his hallway window and smiled at Annabelle. The smile seemed deliberate, as though intended for an old friend. Then he looked back at the boy who sat perplexed in front of the computer, his plump hands running through his short hair. Annabelle hurried past and glanced over her shoulder to see to whom that smile had been aimed. She was alone in the long corridor.

The next day, Annabelle waited by the soda machine for more than twenty minutes, pretending to be indecisive. Eddie finally walked by on his way to the bathroom.

"Hi," she sputtered, "I noticed a child in your office yesterday." She felt anxiety beaming from her forehead.

Eddie backed up to the wall and leant against it. *He's meek. How odd for such a huge man.*

"That's my little boy," he said in a quiet voice. "He visits my office on Wednesday afternoons."

"Oh," said Annabelle, "I have a daughter about that age. Are you teaching him about computers?"

"Yeah," said Eddie. "How old is your daughter?"

"Sarah's eight."

"Oh. Dan is nine."

They both paused.

"I'm planning to buy my daughter a computer for Christmas," said Annabelle. "Do you have any suggestions on what I should get?"

"You could call the Somerville Computer Exchange," he said. "That's where I got the Apple. It has good games for kids that age. Do you have specific applications you want?"

"Well," she said, "I'd like to do some of my own writing with it. So I need a good word processor. But if I had all the money in the world to spend I'd buy a Next machine."

"Did you know that MVI's going to be developing on the Next soon?" asked Eddie.

"No," said Annabelle, slowly.

1. *This man has a son and probably also has a really beautiful wife.*
2. *He must think I am pathetic.*
3. *I've got to end this obsession.*

All was quiet.

"See you later," Eddie said eventually, heading for the bathroom.

That night, Annabelle dreamt she was in a meeting with Eddie and everything was business as usual except she was wearing a leopard-print string bikini.

Annabelle had hoped life would be serene with Sarah in the new apartment, free from the arguing that commenced whenever Dennis was around. Yet arguing continued anyway, between mother and daughter, endlessly, about shoes, the weather, television. Annabelle interpreted this as Sarah's attempt to preserve her absent father's combative spirit, taking his place, maintaining a sense of loyalty, and so, in kind, Annabelle reluctantly retaliated the way she always had with Dennis, dissolving in silence until Sarah, desperate for attention, would acquiesce. Then they would make up and be friends for a few days before starting up a new round.

Despite this, Sarah shared her mother's interests; they both wrote fiction and poetry and were ardent vegetarians.

Responding to Sarah's unfailing interest in dinner preparation, Annabelle always tried to teach her the importance of balancing beans and grains, citing examples of each: green peas with brown rice is fine, black-bean chilli with some oatmeal bread, pasta and navy beans, all good combinations.

Annabelle usually let Sarah help in the kitchen: washing squash, draining and crumbling tofu, or setting the table. She didn't give her any dicing jobs, however, since Sarah had trouble handling sharp knives and always cut towards herself, towards her own heart.

Throughout early autumn, Annabelle spent her lunch hours at the Cambridge Court House, researching divorce agreements. Years earlier she had worked as a paralegal and was determined to save money by processing the divorce herself, *pro se*. On alternate weekends, when Sarah was with Dennis, Annabelle painstakingly drafted an agreement and gave it to Dennis to sign on the Sunday before Thanksgiving.

"I'm not signing that," he said after paging through the document, straining to read it in the dim twilight.

They were standing in the vestibule of Annabelle's apartment building, a small house with two flats on two floors. The top floor was currently unoccupied.

The wood floor glistened; clamshells were stencilled along the wall, two inches below the ceiling. Annabelle studied the ceiling. *Strange, the things one notices while feeling adversarial*. Clamshell stencils abounded in the town, along with lobster doorknockers, conch ashtrays and anchors on lawns.

Dennis had just dropped off Sarah after spending a Sunday with her. Sarah had gone inside and turned on the television without saying a word to Annabelle.

Annabelle had been trying to whisper but Dennis was making no attempt to lower his voice; she sensed one of his episodes coming on, and leant against her apartment door, ready to rush inside and bolt him out if the need arose, for once wishing someone lived upstairs.

"Why won't you sign it?" whispered Annabelle, "What's wrong with it?"

"Oh, it's a great agreement; I mean you've really covered everything. That's nice, you do good work, I always said that. But I'm not signing it." He was wearing a suit and tie, as usual. He was four inches shorter than Annabelle, had short brown hair, big blue eyes and big bones.

"Well, exactly what is wrong with it?" repeated Annabelle, trying to control her impatience.

"I said it's a great agreement, but I'm not divorcing you."

"Dennis," she sighed, "you told me that you are moving to California. You agreed to this divorce. I've spent all my free time the last two months working on this when I really wanted to be volunteering for Dukakis. You need to take this seriously."

"Well, I guess you wasted your time, didn't you. And Dukakis would have lost anyway."

"Dennis. Why won't you sign it?"

"I changed my mind. I'm staying in town. I don't want a divorce now."

"But we can't live together. You know that."

"We don't have to live together to be married," he said.

"Dennis," she said, her voice rising as it tended to in all conversations with him, "you have never behaved like a married person. It's as if we've never been really married. This is not a real marriage."

"Sure it is," said Dennis, calmly. "And I'm not divorcing you because I don't want Sarah to have the stigma of a broken home. I don't want her parents to be divorced."

"That is ridiculous. For us to go on like this would be the most confusing thing for her."

"No, what it is, is that you're too selfish to think about what's best for Sarah. All you care about is what would make your life the most convenient."

"That is patently not true. All the time we were separated you never even bothered to call Sarah – and you never once paid me a penny of child support. And soooo many times you insisted that I lend you money that you never paid back. I've been raising her in spite of you – you just want the privileges of marriage with none of the responsibilities—"

"I'm not signing the fucking papers," he shouted, tossing the stack in the air, where it exploded, and the pages scattered, slowly settling on the polished floor while he turned and slammed the hard oak door behind him.

Annabelle knelt and gathered the papers, trying to organize them, sifting the pages like coupons to freedom. Sarah joined her as the evening darkened.

"You were fighting again, weren't you," said Sarah.

"Your father and I are having trouble reaching an agreement," sighed Annabelle.

"Daddy said he doesn't want the divorce. He said it's bad when parents get divorced."

Sarah had large blue eyes that were squinting in anger; her curly, strawberry blonde hair was matted from the wool hat that Annabelle insisted she wear outside to protect her ears. Over and over Sarah pulled her fingers through that hair, then down her neck, which was thick but not fat. She was sturdy, like Dennis.

Annabelle was still trying to organize the page numbers, wondering where page eight went. "Sometimes it's the best thing for everyone when parents get divorced," she said, "it's not good for parents to fight all—"

"But Liza Macall's parents got divorced and I hate her!" screamed Sarah. "I'm not going to be like Liza Macall!"

Annabelle shook her head. "It's time to get ready for bed. You need a bath."

While the tub ran, Sarah wrote in her math notebook, then tore out some pages and thrust them in Annabelle's lap.

"That's a story I'm writing," said Sarah, tugging off her sweat socks and running towards the bathroom.

Annabelle read Sarah's story:

> Once upon a time a king and queen had a little girl. The king did not have money so the evil queen made him leave the little girl. She was very evil to do that and then the king died.

2

The next day, while reading through her electronic mail at work, Annabelle encountered a message from "EWRIGHT":

Via: 1
To: ABonney
From: EWRIGHT
Subject: NEXT

>As per follow up of our last discussion...
> MVI now has a NEXT machine over in the resource room at the main devl bldg. And it's open to public use.
> Eddie

She stared at the words on her screen. *Eddie. The* Eddie. It had been more than a month... maybe two months since they'd had the conversation about the computer. *How had he remembered that? How had he remembered my name?*
She spent long minutes composing a careful response.

Via: 1
To: EWRIGHT
From: ABonney
Subject: NEXT

>Hi, thank you for the information about the NEXT machine. I heard

that MVI was going to have a presentation and a video by Steve Jobs. I couldn't go, but did you make it?

I bought Sarah a PC for Christmas; now I need to find some good computer games. Can you suggest any good PC games for an eight-year-old kid?

Thanks,

Annabelle

All afternoon she checked her interoffice mail for a response, then left without receiving one, ruminating throughout the long drive to Gardenia.

1. *I waited… But I never counted on you.*
2. *I watched you… but never too closely.*
3. *I tried to ignore you.*
4. *You were a dream.*
5. *I got an electronic message from a dream?*
6. *Dreams can't write. Dreams can't dream.*
7. *What exactly does this mean?*

That evening, Sarah sat at the kitchen table, writing out her spelling words, chewing the eraser end of her pencil.

"Please don't chew your pencil," said Annabelle, preparing dinner, hastily dicing some mild cheddar cheese.

Sarah ignored her.

"Sarah, I read what you gave me to read last night and I've been thinking and thinking about how to respond. Did you write that about your father and me? Do you think I'm like the evil queen because I left your father?"

Sarah looked up. "No. I guess I sort of felt that way last night. When I'm with Daddy I sometimes feel like that. He gets so sad and then I feel sad." She looked back at her spelling book.

"Are you sad now?" asked Annabelle.

"No," murmured Sarah, the eraser tip protruding from her lips.

"Do you understand why we're getting divorced?"

"No," said Sarah, still looking at her book, "but I didn't understand why you were married, either. I don't really want to talk about it, Mom."

1. Sarah shares her father's ability to ignore me.
2. Sarah, I love you so much... but I wish it was easier for us to talk. It's getting hard already and you're not even a teenager.
3. Or maybe it's the only way you can deal with all the adjustments you've had to make.
4. You don't understand the divorce, but you never understood the marriage either, because it wasn't really a marriage.
5. And it just isn't fair that such an unreal marriage requires a real divorce.

After Sarah was asleep, Annabelle covered the kitchen table with a green linen cloth and placed candles at each corner: white at the east, red at the south, blue at the west, green at the north. In the centre she set a small iron kettle filled with potting soil and a thin white candle; then she scattered some sliced geodes, agate, seashells and peppercorns on the cloth and stood in silence.

She turned to the east and used her right hand to outline a star, imagining airborne creatures, the mind: the domain of that direction.

She turned to the south, outlined another star, and envisioned flames, the beating of the heart. Next, to the west, a star, water and soul; at last the north, the North Star, the body, the earth.

Then she lit the white candle in the centre of the kettle and stood back, staring at the table, set with holistic affirmations, like a psychic buffet.

"Dear Heavenly Mother," she whispered. "Dear Great Spirit... Dear Holy One... if it is Your will... if You will true love for me, then please... please... may it be."

A new interoffice electronic message came in the morning.

To: ABonney
From: EWRIGHT
Subject: NEXT and PC Software

> No... I decided to skip both the presentation and the video.
> How much hardware is enough? I'm reminded of the Zen story about the master archer and his pupil. The one where the Master

tells his fully trained pupil to put away his bow and do something else, because the bow was only the tool and not the way.

When does one just listen to sound of wind or of falling snow or just play a game of hearts on a rainy Sunday afternoon?

As per PC games again I direct you to the resource room at the main devl bldg. It's a strange place filled with hundreds of programs (organized by vendor name). I'd love to walk over there with you and play with the software.

Now that you own a machine are you going to become a hacker, adding memory, writing TSRs?

Peace,
Eddie

Annabelle reread the fourth paragraph several times. He said he would "love" to walk over there with her. He would love to be with her. He would love her.

She felt a strange, foreign, giddy sensation, which she controlled by drafting installation instructions for a new machine, installing adapter cards and trying to figure out which dip switch setting went where.

Potential Responses to Eddie's E-Mail:

1. *Talk about computers.*
2. *Talk about children.*
3. *Talk about MVI?*
4. *What does he want?*

At lunchtime she wrote back:

To: EWRIGHT
From: ABonney
Subject: Good Day!

I liked your e-mail. Are you a poet as well as a computer wizard? I'd like to join you on a trip to explore the NEXT machine and the resource room. Any day is fine with me as long as I don't spend too much time there. I have a Christmas deadline on the install notes I'm writing right now.

Now that we have the computer at home (which I haven't installed yet and have to keep secret because it will be a gift from Santa to Sarah) I'm hoping to use it for some of my writing as well. I'm planning to write a novel for my mother (she has Alzheimer's disease). I wrote my first novel a few years ago; you can read it if you're at all interested (I'm always looking for an audience).

So long,
Annabelle

She stared at the message for several moments, debating whether or not to send it. She could escape out of it. She watched her fingers press the keys: <ALT> <FILE> <SEND>. Too late, it was gone, he would get it.

She would have to wait for him to get it. She had accepted his invitation, they were making a date.

Why did I offer to let him read my novel? Now he's really going to think I'm strange, begging for an audience...

The novel was her pride and scourge, unpublished, unruly. She'd written it in a state of frenzy, a study in madness, a thinly masked epitaph to pain: her impossible marriage to Dennis, her abused childhood, a long poem, a livid artery. She had never let Dennis read it, even when they were living together.

In the novel her name was Germaine, Sarah was Eleanor, and Dennis was Richard: all allegorical allusions to the involvement of King Richard and Queen Eleanor with Germany but she was sure nobody would recognize that.

The manuscript was stored in a box in her closet. For five years an author's agent had represented it, claiming it probably wouldn't sell but he wanted to promote it anyway because he felt it was a "literary masterpiece". It "haunted" him. She didn't argue.

Later the agent said it wasn't category, brand name, or schlock, so it had no market and he gave it up. She decided he was going through a midlife crisis, abandoning his idealistic visions. She wondered why college English departments didn't offer courses in schlock writing, since it is such a lucrative revenue generator.

1. *Why did I offer to let Eddie read it?*
2. *My subconscious must want to test him.*

3. He probably won't even want to read it so this whole issue is just moot.

She brought the manuscript with her to work the next day. After logging in she checked her mail every five minutes for his response, which appeared just as a light rain started.

To: ABonney
From: EWRIGHT
Subject: Writing, Computers, and Field Trip

Good Morning,
   Writing: Sometimes I write poems. Mostly I throw them away because they don't make much sense.
   Computers: I'm a hired man, in the old New England tradition of farming families and hired men drifting in and finding work. There are few of us here on the 7th floor who have a clear vision of how best to use computers. (They don't belong in supermarkets.) When a process is computerized much of the spirit of the thing is lost and unfortunately not redistributed somewhere else.
   Art: My spirit is dying here. High-tech wizardry for all its glitz is void of life. Every once in a great while I allow myself to play with stained glass or pottery.
   Field trip: Any warmish sunny afternoon would be a good time. Anytime is OK. I also have show and tell in my office in the form of an Apple. You might be interested in the series of programs which are written for children. My son Dan likes their word-processing package.
   Working mothers with spare time: Is this an anomaly? And yes, I would like to read your novel.
   Peace,
   Eddie

She held her breath and carried her manuscript down the steps to the seventh floor.
   Eddie wasn't in his office. She paused by the door. People would wonder why she was standing outside an empty office.

Self-consciousness drove her in; she crept to his chair and examined his desk, his walls.

He had books on DOS, C and yoga. He had a small yoga poster on the wall. Taped above his monitor was a bumper sticker that said "Free Tibet". *Yes, he has a social conscience! Good! Good! He is sensitive.* Intimacy overwhelmed her. She fingered the back of his chair. This was where he sat.

She looked for pictures, faces important to him. Leaning along the corner of a bookshelf ledge, near the window, was a photograph of a child, the one she'd seen in his office. The child was alone in the picture, smiling, holding something up to the camera; she couldn't see what it was. She looked for other pictures, anything with a woman in it, some hidden wife, the significant other. None appeared to be there in the tidy room. *Just one child, much yoga, and a good bumper sticker. Ah, a book on Judo. He must be in a meeting.*

A wave of panic swept over her. They hadn't been face to face for more than a month. Now she was dropping her soul in his chair with a yellow sticky note stuck to the top. The note said "Eddie – here's my novel, *The Unlikely Child*. I hope you like it. Be honest. Annabelle."

Returning to her office she spent several minutes trying to refocus, comparing her personal apparatus to his: she had one framed school photograph of Sarah and a few wind-up toys. Wind-up toys are not unprofessional; all geeks love windup toys.

By noon, she felt courageous enough to return to Eddie's office, but her telephone rang first – the nurse at Sarah's school: "Sarah is quite ill; she has a high fever and a sore throat."

"Are her cheeks bright red?" asked Annabelle.

"Yes," said the nurse. "Do you want me to give her some acetaminophen?"

"No, I'll leave right now to pick her up."

Annabelle self-studied homeopathy, made annual appointments for herself and Sarah with Marija, a homeopathic practitioner, and guessed, from the brief description the nurse gave, that Sarah needed Belladonna, because Marija had cured Sarah before with this remedy when she'd presented the same symptoms. But Annabelle didn't dare ask whether the nurse had any Belladonna on hand.

"What do you mean?" the nurse would probably say. "Do you mean deadly nightshade?"

"It's a natural remedy derived from that, yes," Annabelle would have to reply, assured of zealous reproach.

She sent an e-mail to Daryl, explaining she was leaving early because Sarah was sick, wishing him a happy Thanksgiving.

At home, after Sarah had chewed up her remedy, Annabelle helped her settle comfortably in bed. The telephone rang. Dennis was on the other end, irate and snappy, a good candidate for homeopathic Hyoscyamus, although he never would swallow anything she'd try to give him.

"So what about tomorrow," he said. "My family's expecting you for Thanksgiving."

"Dennis, I don't think divorced people tend to spend Thanksgiving together."

"We're not divorced!" insisted Dennis, laughing.

"We will be soon," said Annabelle.

"You always came to dinner before. What about Sarah? Can she come to Thanksgiving with me? Are you going to deny her the only fucking family she has?"

"Sarah's sick," sighed Annabelle. "But if she's feeling better tomorrow, I guess she could go with you."

The following morning Sarah's fever was gone; she looked strong and healthy, and said she felt perfectly fine, so Annabelle allowed Dennis to take her to his mother's house, while Annabelle went to visit her mother, Mary, in the nursing home.

They sat in the cramped activity room where Mary took sporadic bites of mushy turkey and potatoes. The tray was barely warm. Annabelle cringed at the uninhibited chewing, everyone eating with the TV set on, vacantly watching tempestuous soap operas. All the residents looked ancient except Mary, who glowed with the ironic vibrancy of youth.

"Happy Thanksgiving, Mom," said Annabelle, several times.

Mary stared ahead.

"Do you remember me?" Annabelle asked after a time, the question she always tried not to ask, always asked anyway.

Mary smiled. "Annie?"

Annabelle laughed and nodded.

"Annabelle Lee," said Mary.

"Yes!" said Annabelle.

"The child by the sea," said Mary. Then she paused. "Did he do that?"

"Do what?" said Annabelle.

"Over there," said Mary, not pointing to anything, not indicating any direction.

Annabelle shook her head and said, "I don't know what you mean."

"Don't let it smash you," said Mary.

"What?"

Mary looked at her fingers. "Here," she said, "right here," shaking her head.

"I don't know what you mean, Mom."

"Did my mother die?" asked Mary.

"Yes, I'm sorry… She did. She died years before I was born," said Annabelle.

"Did my father die?"

"Yes," said Annabelle, holding the spoon to Mary's lips, urging her to try the wax beans.

"And Uncle Vince?"

"Yes."

"I don't want any more," said Mary, pushing away the spoon.

Annabelle's mother had vanished years earlier; now she was Mary, a sweet lady Annabelle could visit and bring flowers to, a visual reminder of someone she once knew, still loved.

Annabelle drove home, forcing away old tears.

1. Maybe if she'd gotten rid of her aluminum cookware earlier and hadn't eaten all those antacids.
2. I learnt about homeopathy too late. But as Marija said, it may not even be Alzheimer's; Mary's had progressive memory loss since I was seven, when she had that ear surgery and came home from the hospital with half her face coloured purple. It could have even been a lobotomy. Am I crazy to think that?
3. Is it any coincidence that the surgeon who operated on her ear was on the board of directors of my father's company?

4. *If only my goddamn father hadn't driven her crazy. That's the only thing I know for sure. He drove me crazy too, but I hide it pretty well.*
5. *No. Don't allow him that much power. I'm not crazy. I've just lived through too much paternal insanity and violence. And he is no longer part of my life.*

The apartment seemed treacherous without Sarah on Thanksgiving. Annabelle checked the windows and back door several times to make sure they were all securely locked.

In the past she would go with Dennis to his mother's house, even when they were separated, for Sarah's sake, so there would be family to share turkey with, a fowl both she and Sarah always refused to eat.

Annabelle sat in silence for a long while.

Eddie's Potential Reactions to the Novel:

1. *He won't like it.*
2. *He'll say he likes it but he won't actually read it.*
3. *He may just say it's interesting.*
4. *He'll say he likes it just to be nice.*

Dennis called in the evening, saying, "Sarah's going to stay here until Saturday. My mom has some extra clothes for her."

"You should have discussed this with me before making that decision, Dennis."

"Sarah wants to stay here. Is that all right?"

"Let me talk to her."

Annabelle waited several minutes for Sarah to come to the phone, out of breath and full of the affected chatty voice she always wore at Dennis's mother's house.

"Can I stay until Saturday, Momma?"

"If you want to," said Annabelle.

"Good. I want to. Bye—" sang Sarah, petulantly; then the phone dropped and the dial tone returned.

The next day, MVI was closed but Annabelle went there anyway to catch up on her deadline. She walked by Eddie's vacant office on the way to the soda machine. The box containing her novel was perched on a shelf above his desk. A blue folder covered the box. She paused, staring through his office window, saddened that he hadn't brought the manuscript home with him, that he'd placed its priority below whatever work the blue folder contained.

On Saturday evening Dennis left Sarah at the apartment door wearing a dress that had been left at his mother's house, a dress she had outgrown. It was pink, smocked at the bodice, intended for a younger child. Sarah sauntered around the living room while Annabelle folded laundry. Finally Sarah announced, "Everyone was asking why you didn't come to dinner."

"When mothers and fathers get divorced, they don't often have Thanksgiving dinner together," said Annabelle, trying not to sound impatient.

"But Daddy said you're not getting divorced," beamed Sarah, "he promised that would never ever happen."

Sarah smiled while Annabelle held her tongue, bit the inside of her cheek, tempted to explain vicarious sentiment, tempted to describe codependency, tempted to say that Dennis had never loved her, that he didn't want the divorce because it would force him to grow up.

"Sarah," sighed Annabelle, "it will happen. We are getting divorced."

Wordless, Sarah flicked on the television set.

Monday's Objectives:

1. *Find a way to get Dennis to sign that agreement.*
2. *Finish the cabling configuration section in the install reference.*
3. *Stop sending e-mail to Eddie for a while; at least wait until the divorce papers are filed in court.*
4. *Stop obsessing over Eddie; if he didn't even bother to bring my manuscript home with him, then he must not be interested in me.*

On Monday morning Annabelle took a break to get another cup of tea. It was quiet, and she had writer's block. When she returned to her office, her manuscript was in its box on her chair, with a blue folder on top.

She opened the folder. It contained poems:

Twelve Roses for Germaine

A rose for no reason.
A rose for bowing before the storm.
A rose for crying.
A rose for walking in the bleeding darkness.
A rose for forgetting.
A rose for the dark time.
A rose for the waking dreams.
A rose for remembering.
A rose for challenging the doctors.
A rose for writing out the feelings.
A rose for finding Eleanor.

The twelfth rose was painted at the bottom: pink with a thornless black stem. The poem was signed "Gen (Eddie)".

She wrung her hands and began perusing the fifteen pages that followed: poems for Eleanor, poems from "Joe Six-Pack", poems "by" Richard, and poems about angels, Hiroshima, Dan and Sam.

Acorn Game

As Eleanor hides the acorns (in plain view)
We share in their invisibility
Our spirits free

Dan's Gen

No pain greater than the tears of my son
As he reads of Hiroshima
His heart broken.

Dad's Words

Roosevelt's spirit got tired so his assistant
(a less skilled man) had to take command.
President Truman had gotten Stalin's promise
for the Russians to enter the war against Japan.
But Truman didn't trust the Russians
and dropped the bomb without their help
because when the war was over, Truman
didn't want those Russians anywhere near Japan.

TAO OF LOVE

Just between you and me
I think Truman never played "go"
so he didn't understand how winning is losing
and the other way around.
The bomb's flash created forty years of darkness.
The leaders of the dark times are now grandparents
and are beginning to see with regret
just how foolish they have been.
They're beginning to hide their acorns
in plain sight
playing again with their childhood dreams
of love and peace on the green planet.

Notes from Hell #1

Hell takes no prisoners
Death, suffering and renewal
Are all one.
Each new day brings sunshine.
"Good Morning" New Day.

Notes from Hell #2

Dear Poet,
Your poem "Notes from Hell #1"
Is bullshit!
Stop denying how you really feel.
You're fucked and it's time
for you to feel the pain.
Sincerely yours,
Joe Six-Pack

Notes from Hell #3

It hurts too much to write any more.

Notes from Richard #1

For your book to sell
You must make me real.

Notes from Richard #2

Boy have you changed.

Notes from Richard #4

Please forgive me when
Your being a fucking bitch really turned me off.
Do you see now
That boys playing at manhood
Are not allowed to bow before womanhood?
It's only in drunken failure
In the company of other men
That we can feel.
And then it's Damn those Red Sox!
And jeez look at Kojak.
Nothing really heavy.
Why can't women understand our rage?
That our proud actions are greater
than their mere routines?
We are killers
Born with arrogance
To leave the softness
Of our mother's pen
In favour of our father's fist.

Notes from Richard #5

There was nothing written
On this can
To tell me
Just how hard life would become.
I am sorry for failing
You
And the kid.
P.S.
Excuse #4

Notes for Germaine #1

Seek the bear
Tell her your dreams
Her heart is very big
She will guide you
Past the sins of man

Past the pain of your earth's welcome
To woman's power
There not to rest but to return
For the wheel's calling
Is never-ending, even for the bear
And her friends.

Notes for Germaine #2

Earth angels are given Zen begging bowls
And told to go among the mortals
To help with their evolution.
These angels often get bloodied
Because their work is hard
And they're not very good at defending
Themselves.
Sometimes they help little children
Win at hearts
Or just hang around ashrams
Where it's warm.
Sometimes they go for walks with old people
To help them with their arthritis.
A lot of the time they end up
On the wrong end of cannons
Or starving
In famines.
Why does God send them
When She knows that this is so?
It's just how love works.

Annabelle gathered the poems together, slipped them in the folder, hugged the folder and left for the seventh floor, silently rehearsing a response.

Eddie was standing at his whiteboard writing an algorithm when she arrived. He turned to her, then wrote something else, then sat down. He didn't smile. He gestured to a chair by the office window. Annabelle sat trembling, clutching the folder. She smiled but his face remained sombre.

"Are these poems from you?" she asked.

He nodded.

She wanted to reach for his face, touch his skin, lay down her cautious heart – lie down with him.

"I liked your poems," she said.

"Thanks," he said, "your novel really touched me. It inspired me to write. I couldn't stop writing."

"Why did you sign your name 'Gen'?" she asked.

Eddie paused and took a deep breath. "Gen is this little boy whose family gets blasted into oblivion in Hiroshima... in a comic book. I felt sad for him. I liked the name. Sometimes I call myself Gen."

"Oh. Well... I loved these. I really did." She sifted through the pages and brought one to the surface of the stack.

"Here's one. This is wonderful." She began to read aloud: "THE REAGAN YEARS. Sammy has won the lottery. Ten whole dollars. With the money he's bought a bottle. It's OK Sam...' That's just great... Brautigan-esque."

Eddie nodded.

"Who is Sam?" she finally asked.

"Sam's my brother. He's my room-mate."

"Oh. I see." She looked back at the stack of poems. "What are 'Notes From Hell' about?"

"My divorce. I'm divorced. I figured I'd have to feel the pain before I could get over it. That's what those poems are about."

"Oh," she whispered. "I'm in the process of a divorce myself."

Eddie didn't respond and they were both silent for several more minutes. The space between them throbbed.

1. *I ache.*
2. *I am lovesick.*
3. *Oh no.*

"I've got to get ready for a meeting," Eddie said at last, standing up.

"OK," said Annabelle, "Thanks for the poems."

She stood up and walked to the door.

Eddie said, "I'd like to get to know you."

Then he turned his back to her and continued writing on the whiteboard.

3

Arthur Ziminski sat at the southern head of the conference table and Brian Anderson sat at his polar north. Between them sat a few middle managers, software engineers, quality-assurance testers, phone support, and Annabelle, representing documentation.

"OK folks," said Brian, the senior product designer in charge of MVI Access, "any problems?" He had an angular face, pointed nose, short blond hair, and a small mouth crammed with sharp yellow teeth.

Arthur, the burly engineering project leader, sighed. "We've been looking into the expanded memory problem," he said. "There's a bug in some 80286s at Shawsson with addressing and math-coprocessor problems. Bugs in the optimizer version that the debugger can't find. Some overlay and memory thrashing... Floating-point rounding, editing calculations, database-pricing problems."

The door burst open and Eddie sauntered in. Everyone, except Annabelle, looked up. Eddie rolled an upholstered chair to the table and sat directly across from Annabelle, who remained intent on Arthur's large face, red beard and balding curly hair.

"Problems with the new graphics drivers," continued Arthur. "Printer font and page-sizing problems. Mullainn gave us a tape four days late with values out of range and missing CUSIPs. Calculostat sent a tape with duplicate CUSIPs and tickers with negative prices." Arthur stopped and glared at Brian.

"Is that all?" said Brian.

Everyone laughed, except Arthur.

Annabelle glanced at Eddie whose eyes were fixed on her. He grinned and waved across the table. She looked at her notes, then back at Arthur.

"Are you following this, Ed?" said Brian, looking at Annabelle.

"Yeah, yeah," said Eddie, smiling at Annabelle. "The floating-point problems are due to the NA values being used by the database library – they're getting sucked into the calculations and screwing up the averages—"

"Should we set up a task force to address these problems individually?" asked Brian, interrupting Eddie.

"Until we find a decent candidate for QA director, that might be prudent," said Arthur, his face nearly as red as his beard. "My team can't lead QA and code at the same time."

"I guess Daryl's not here today," said Brian, ignoring Arthur's comments. He turned to Annabelle. "Any problems in doc?" he said.

Eddie was still grinning at her. Annabelle shook her head, unable to concentrate.

"You have all the specs you need?" said Arthur.

Annabelle nodded.

"Moving along," said Brian, "what does phone support need in order to prepare for beta?"

After the meeting, Annabelle skirted the conference-table corner, away from Eddie, and hurried to the elevator.

To: EWRIGHT
From: ABonney
Subject: Notes for Gen

I was a little unnerved at the meeting today. Daryl had asked me to represent doc and I get very nervous when I have to speak in front of a group.

Thanks again for the poems. Please keep writing to me.

Your poems made me think of when I was 14 – I angrily told my father that our country never should have bombed Hiroshima and my father insisted that if we hadn't, he would have been on the front line of the invasion of Japan and if that had happened he surely would have been killed, and, therefore, consequently, I never would have been born. So all through my adolescence I believed I was personally responsible for the bombing of Hiroshima.

I love your poem about angels. If you'd like, I'll lend you some of Rainer Maria Rilke's poetry; he envisioned himself as a Russian monk and wrote from that point of view. He also wrote a lot about angels. (My only problem with Rilke is that he used masculine pronouns to describe God.)
Annabelle

To: ABonney
From: EWRIGHT
Subject: Thoughts from Gen

Your father's attempt at justifying Hiroshima bothers me. Birthing is not as linear as he would have liked you to believe. I choose to believe you would have been born anyway, even if differently.

No, I haven't read any Rilke and Yes please do lend me his book.
Peace,
Eddie

To: EWRIGHT
From: ABonney
Subject: Thoughts for Gen

I stopped by your office but you weren't there so I left a book of Rilke's poetry on your chair.

I'm feeling kind of lost today. All these changes are hard on Sarah. She doesn't really understand the divorce, but Dennis keeps telling her that divorce is totally horrible and terrible so she thinks it's terrible... Of course it is by nature terrible, but Dennis is determined to make it as difficult as possible. Maybe she senses that. When I try to talk to her about it, she tells me she doesn't want to talk about it.

How old was your son when you got divorced? Was he sad

about it? What did you tell him? Sarah's father (Dennis) keeps telling me that we should just separate and not get divorced because he says that Sarah will have the stigma of "being from a broken home". (In other words, it's already broken, but don't tell anybody.) So we've separated five times already, and this time I just want it to be over for good. (But I wonder, is Dennis right, am I being selfish?)

(Let me know what you think of Rilke's poetry. If you like it, I'll bring in more.)

Do you still want to go to the resource room with me sometime?
Annabelle

To: ABonney
From: EWRIGHT
Subject: Notes from Gen #2

Barbara and I met in college. After graduation we were married. We both worked as teachers in an elementary school. Six months into this experience I left the relationship, telling Barbara that our marriage had been a mistake and I wanted out. I retreated to the woods and began to live as a hermit. Later we both agreed that I had been rash so we got back together. We moved to Stockbridge. It was to be a new beginning. It was in Stockbridge that our relationship grew, lived, and died. It died because we were too young, I didn't love Barbara enough, and I was being too much like my father (the only real model I had at the time). I left again when Danny was four. To this day I don't think he has any real sense of why I left. He still asks for me to come back. For a while he would invent machines that would make me come back. For a while he invented machines to kill me. He believed that he was the cause of our divorce. (This is normal.) He believed that I had lied to him, that he had been betrayed. When I left he was too young to articulate a lot of this. He feels that I have made a very bad mistake. (Nine is a very righteous age.)

It's fair to say that Dan hasn't "gotten over" the divorce. But I don't think anyone really gets over anything. One simply goes on (often with a little limp). One carries the life experiences both good and bad for ever. Perhaps that's what dying is for.

What to tell Sarah? Is the truth as you understand it, over and over and over for a very long time. With lots of love from you and Dennis, all will go well.

I do not know very much about you or your situation, but here is my advice: Find a warm place for you and Sarah. Be careful to keep as much as possible constant. Take the extra effort necessary to reach out to those who can help you. Rest. When spring comes it will become warm again. The waves of the divorce will be less frequent and life will become easier. (This is in no way a suggestion to deny any of the current waves of feeling. These you must always face, sooner or later.)

I have spent my years since the divorce doing what I call "getting off the wheel" – avoiding meaningless things. I try to be with people in a very open and honest way and I love each day as if it were the last. I have learnt to breathe. I have learnt to meditate. I have learnt to cry, to love, and to feel better than I used to.

Thank you for the Rilke poetry book. Will you be my teacher and show me the ways of reading and writing good poems?

Yes... We're still on for our field trip to the resource room. How about Friday 11:30?

Peace,
Eddie

To: EWRIGHT
From: ABonney
Subject: Re: Notes from Gen #2

I don't think I can teach you how to write good poems because you're already writing great poems. (Maybe you can teach me how to write good poems.)

I love Rilke for the Deity he describes; it's very personal to me. I don't belong to a church but I have a deep longing to embrace faith.

I guess I'm just feeling sad right now... Every year I feel this grief. It's been about eight years since John Lennon was murdered. I remember it so clearly. It was right after he and

Yoko had released a new album and they were becoming politically active again. I was so happy about that, hoping their activism would somehow prevent Reagan from ruining this country... because so many people listened to Lennon... and he and Yoko cared so much about peace and about the poor... Then he got killed. Don't let me get started on my conspiracy theories. But it is very interesting that his killer just sat there afterwards, in a daze, confused by what he had done. And because he admitted to what he did, no real investigation was ever conducted. And his killer's father had worked for a major oil company, and if what I read is correct, that company signed an agreement with the Shah of Iran. (Could there be a connection between that and the President Elect's former occupation as head of the CIA? The CIA and oil? What an interesting, volatile mixture!)

I keep thinking that if John were still alive, the world would be so different now. Now all we really have to look forward to is the rich getting richer, the poor getting poorer, and the US becoming a full-fledged military-industrial complex.

Nobody else is brave enough now (or popular enough or loud enough) to say what John would have said if he'd lived.

So it makes me sad.

Yes, Friday at 11:30 would be fine.

Annabelle

To: ABonney
From: EWRIGHT
Subject: Thank you

Thank you for the tears
  Which just fell
  on my printout
  slowing my use of
  Bob's new function "extern int menu_get_iteminfo()"
  ...It's been a while.
  Peace,
  Eddie

On Friday, just before noon, Eddie knocked on Annabelle's office door.

"Ready?" he said.

She nodded, grabbed her coat and purse and followed him down the hall, trying to match his long strides. They rode the elevator with a few other people from the eighth floor: finance types. Nobody spoke. Annabelle hastily donned her black shawl coat, checking the mirrored elevator door to see if her front was evenly buttoned, glancing at the mirrored ceiling as she pulled her black beret over her left ear.

Once on the street Eddie slowed down and they strolled together through Kendall Square, across raging traffic.

"So what brought you to MVI?" Eddie suddenly asked.

"I used to work for a competitor," she said, "I worked on spreadsheets and products just like MVI Access. Touchy-feely stuff."

"You mean you were hired to fill a rec? Did you go through a headhunter?"

"Yes. Is that unusual?"

Eddie whistled. "Very unusual. Most recs are filled within. MVI hates to pay recruiter's fees. You must be good."

They turned the corner by First Street, past another parking lot.

"How do most people get hired?" she asked. "From within? How do they get in to begin with?"

Eddie gave her a long look. She glanced away.

"MVI likes to buy up little companies and gobble them alive. That's how I got here. I was working for a little startup in Woburn called Osirhys. We redistributed small financial databases on PCs. Our head honcho, Les Marin, cut a deal with Timothy Zimman and that was that. MVI came over with a whole case of fancy champagne, Brie, and their best engineers. We all got pretty drunk celebrating our proud future. That's about it. They tore apart our prototype and proceeded to buy up another company in Danvers. Texxtpoint. What a dog of a product they had! But their management was nastier than ours and took over the show. So what you see as the MFI division is really the gruesome marriage between Osirhys and Texxtpoint. Almost everyone we work with came from one or the other. You're an anomaly, being neutral."

"Where did Daryl come from?" she asked.

"Well Daryl and a few others are refugees from MVI proper. He used to work on MVI's word-processing package. But most of the people I work with are from Osirhys. Most everyone on the other side of the seventh floor is from Texxtpoint. All of upper management – Dan Neece, Brian Anderson, Susan Cox, Janette Fuller, they all came from Texxtpoint. You've met some of the Osirhys survivors. Like Ted Aaron, Frank Marks, Arthur Ziminski. My boss, Bob Thomas. Gail Greene. Bob and Gail are lovers."

Annabelle glanced at him. He smiled, unabashed. Open office romance. She blushed.

"Anyway," continued Eddie, "the Texxtpointers are all technical airheads."

"Then why are they managing the projects?" she said, sceptically.

"They have this uncanny inbred business savvy. Like battery acid. They suck up other people's ideas and regurgitate them as their own. Zimman just eats it up."

They arrived at the huge main development building. Annabelle followed Eddie through the lush brick lobby with high walls generously clothed in oil canvases: paintings of diverse ethnic faces.

"You've seen the rotating politically correct art gallery, have you?" he asked.

She nodded, stepping onto the elevator with him. Several other people joined them: a man in a blue suit; a woman with a pink leotard and sheer flowered skirt; two androgynous people in jeans.

"MVI does have some advantages," continued Eddie, uninhibited by the other elevator occupants, "you should see the parties. Zimman likes to do it up in a big way. It almost makes you forget about the sloppy spaghetti code and ego problems." His voice faded as they stepped off the elevator. Annabelle trailed his heels until they arrived at the resource library.

The NEXT machine was in use when they arrived so they stood back and watched from the hallway.

"Isn't it remarkable?" whispered Annabelle. "A CD-ROM drive is actually part of the system. Who would be able to afford such a machine?"

"They're being used mostly by universities," said Eddie. "I heard they're putting whole encyclopedias on ROMs. It is amazing."

They remained hushed, watching, in awe.

Eddie turned to Annabelle. "The other interesting thing about them is that they're going to be hooked up to incredibly wide area networks so that people can send electronic mail to each other all over the world – just like we do on our MVI network. It will make sending electronic-mail messages as easy as making phone calls."

"Wow," whispered Annabelle.

Eventually they returned to the aisles of computer programs. Annabelle gleefully found a book she'd written stored with the stacks of competitor's documentation.

"I wrote this," she exclaimed, handing the book to Eddie. He opened it and looked at her.

"Maybe I'll break the programmer's first rule and actually read the doc. As long as you wrote it." He smiled. Annabelle looked away.

Soon Annabelle realized that everywhere they went women seemed to be ogling Eddie. *I'm not the only one obsessed with those eyes and shoulders and knees.*

Eddie led Annabelle to the cafeteria. She found a container of peach yogurt and a small bag of popcorn.

"Let me pay for that," he said as she stood in the cashier line.

She shook her head, embarrassed, saying, "Really, no."

They sat by a huge window overlooking the Charles River. Eddie consumed a plate of ziti and leant back between mouthfuls. Annabelle quietly ate her yogurt, tried not to choke on her popcorn, then spoke nonstop, attempting to mask her nervousness.

"I'm glad you liked the Rilke book," she said. "He really defines the great Deity for me. He talks about people who try to hold God – possess God – and how that isn't possible. God can't be owned."

Eddie nodded, smiling.

"And you'd like Neruda too. There's one sonata especially; it's one of my favourite poems ever, about forgetfulness. And how there are some things we'd like to forget. I'll bring it in for you; it's in a book of Neruda translations by Robert Bly. Have you ever heard of Bly?"

"No." Eddie shook his head, his elbows resting on the table, his brown eyes aimed at Annabelle.

"Well, you ought to read some of his stuff too. You ought to go see him speak, I mean because from what you've told me, you seem to be the kind of man he talks about; the kind of man who could use his help."

"What do you mean?" Eddie frowned.

Annabelle awkwardly laughed. "When you got divorced," she said, "it sounds like you gave up a little more than you should have. All the men's-movement stuff might help you – you know – there's this concept called the 'soft male'." She paused, shocked by what she had just said. Eddie stared at her. She nervously looked at her hands and stammered, "I'm sorry. I mean I just think you'd enjoy learning more... about that..." She stopped speaking and looked out the window.

It started snowing on their return trip. They took side streets where rubbish-laced chain-link fences surrounded small biology companies. The air was grey. Eddie was quiet. Annabelle sensed his warmth beside her and tried not to stumble for want of the sight of him.

When they arrived at their building, Eddie left for a meeting. Annabelle didn't hear from him again before leaving work for the weekend.

She put down her sewing needle and answered the ringing telephone. Annabelle had been sewing Sarah's costume for the school play, a week away.

"Annie," said Dennis, "I'm sorry about what I did."

She waited for him to continue.

"I'll sign anything you want," he said.

"Good. I'll put the agreement in the mail tomorrow. You need to have it notarized."

"OK. How're you doing?"

"Fine. I'll see you. Bye."

"Can I take you out to dinner?" he asked.

"What? You have money?"

"We could go get a pizza."

"You could help pay for a new coat for Sarah. She really needs a new one. The green one is getting frayed and I'd like to get her a nice down one. It would keep her a lot warmer than that green one."

"Sure. Can we have dinner?"

"No, but you can help with the coat."

"I just miss you. I miss being a family."

"Oh give me a break. I'll send the agreement off tomorrow."

"I know I fucked things up," he said, "I know it was all my fault. They just screwed me out of my job, you know that. That's why you left."

"That wasn't the only reason."

"It was the main reason."

"There were hundreds of main reasons. Enough. OK? I'll see you."

"We could just get one little pizza. Have you eaten yet?"

She hung up. The telephone rang again. Twenty-seven times. She disconnected it.

Resolutions:

1. Do not have dinner with Dennis. Do not give him another chance. He's already had at least six chances.
2. Keep this resolution.
3. Get clear with Eddie. He could be a good friend. He's very nice. When men turn into lovers they stop being nice.

The problem with the third resolution was the intensity she felt while with him. She practised thought-stopping techniques to repress that excitement but that night she dreamt of him and woke up weeping, repeating, repeating, repeating his name – Eddie's name.

To: ABonney
From: EWRIGHT
Subject: Gen's newest poem

>Bye. Like falling leaves
>Bye. Like running water.
>Bye. Like early dawn.
>Can I see you in the spring?

She read it and read it and read it again. It was Monday morning; she had to hurry to a design meeting. Eddie had mailed the message on Friday afternoon, after their walk. He was saying goodbye. In just one date, one slip of the tongue about the soft male, one walk down the street, she had made him say goodbye.

To: EWRIGHT
From: ABonney
Subject: Re: Gen's newest poem

> I don't understand your poem. Is it directed towards me? If yes, OK; otherwise, OK.
>   Annabelle

"What do you think?" asked Frank Marks, looking at Annabelle.

Frank was a boyish blond man with a beaming grin who'd just been demonstrating the new MVI Access Help system to the small group of techies and middle managers assembled in his cluttered office. Annabelle was still ruminating over Eddie's e-mail, holding her head high, trying not to cry, and attempting to appear professional, unable to focus on the demo. She pooled the correct words that kept swirling away.

Before she could answer, Susan Cox, a tiny woman in a red silk suit said, "It's clunky. Can't you make it at least a little bit interactive?" She stressed the words "a little bit".

Frank laughed. "You don't call this interactive? See, you press the down arrow and look at all your choices!" He pressed the down arrow key several times and watched the screen cursor jump from one topic to the next, in a vertical line.

"No, I wouldn't call that interactive," insisted Susan. "It's slow, it's counter-intuitive." Her chin rested on her fingertips, which she'd pointed together to form a pyramid. Her face was pinched and white except for pink eyeshadow painted on swollen lids.

"And it's based on your design!" laughed Frank again, winking at Annabelle. "Besides, that's what we have writers for. I can speed it up, but I'm sure Annabelle here will make it useful, right?"

Annabelle blushed, opened her mouth, and Susan spoke again, "Well, Annabelle is going to have a fucking hard time making this piece of shit useful for anyone. And this is NOT how I designed it."

Susan left the room. The meeting ended.

To: ABonney
From: EWRIGHT
Subject: Gen's bye poem explained

> The moment it tries to describe was the feeling I had watching the elevator doors close. The feeling of sadness. And so, the rather soulful "bye".
> I had wanted to hold your hand as we walked but felt too shy to ask.
> How was your weekend?
> How is Sarah?
> How are you feeling?
> Would you like to go to one of the Christmas ballets with me?
> Peace,
> Eddie

Annabelle read Eddie's message and shook her head. *Now what should I do? He's so nice. God I have to be careful.*

To: EWRIGHT
From: ABonney
Subject: Re: Gen's bye poem explained

> I just came from a very strange design meeting... but I'll spare you the details.
> Thank you for the ballet offer but it would be awfully hard for me to go anywhere these days. I appreciate your kindness. Usually I try to avoid relationships with men as friends, because some have been dishonest about it – pretending they just want friendship, then demanding more later, and telling me we can't be friends any more. Do you understand? I like you very much and want to stay your friend. And if you ever want to hold my hand, you may.
> I've been talking and writing to you about some pretty heavy things. I do not want to become an emotional drain on anyone, especially you.
> Do you play a musical instrument? I used to sing at coffeehouses and anti-nuclear benefits and such. For a while I wanted to study voice at Eastman. This weekend I was thinking

I'd like to find people to jam with. Do you play the guitar or something? – maybe that would give me the incentive to go back to music.

Sarah is fine, I think. I'm trying to be very gentle with her while she acts out her anger.

How is Dan? Do you spend Christmas with him and Barbara? (If not, does he want you to?) Dennis's family invited me to their annual Christmas Eve party but I won't be going; Dennis will take Sarah. So I'm planning to bring my mom home and spend a quiet day with her (light some candles, drink some eggnog, answer the same questions over and over). She usually asks if her mother died and how did she die; if her father died and how did he die; and she asks whether I'm Annie. (I went by the name Annie until I turned 30, then I decided to reclaim my true name, Annabelle, which nobody ever called me as a child unless they were angry with me.)

Anyway, my mom's very sweet. I love her. She loves me (she does remember how to do that; sometimes that's the first thing they forget how to do – but she never will).

OK. I'll let you get back to work. I brought you some bubbles. I'll drop them by.

Annabelle

To: ABonney
From: EWRIGHT
Subject: Re: Gen's New Bubbles

I think I can understand your experiences with men in relationships and I'm truly sorry you have been so hurt. Hidden in all our modern dramas are the experiences of our forebears. Men are stuck on Gilligan's Island reliving the Greek tragedies.

Right now, your feelings for men are secondary to caring for Sarah, getting food, shelter. This is as it should be. It really is OK to do nothing.

Please know that you have found a friend in me; someone you can lean on, someone who doesn't mind getting heavy or caring for someone else's needs. Can you give yourself permission to ask? It's OK.

Sam (my brother) is the family musician (not me). He teaches it at a school in Brighton. I'm sorry that I don't know how to play much beyond a flute or recorder (and have always had difficulty reading music). Would you like to share some of Sam's CDs? (He wouldn't mind.)

Danny gets nervous around Christmas because he equates gift-giving with love, and being rather insecure, gets worried that he won't get any presents, i.e., will be unloved.

THANK YOU SO MUCH FOR THE BUBBLES. It's a real gift. Bring the corners of your mouth close to your ears (smiling instructions) and know that I have showered my co-workers with many bubbles.

Peace,
Eddie

Annabelle had to leave for home before she could respond. While cooking dinner she processed a mental list.

New Resolutions:
1. *Buy a bigger wok.*
2. *Help Sarah with her spelling homework after dinner.*
3. *Figure out this relationship with Eddie or Gen or whoever he is. a) He is so nice; so far no evidence to the contrary. b) He is willing to share his feelings. c) His temperament appears to be very even. d) He may be seeking physical involvement.*
4. *Do not get physically involved with Eddie under any circumstances.*
5. *Be prepared to end all contact with Eddie.*
6. *End all contact now. It will make the inevitable ending less painful in the long run.*

4

After Sarah fell asleep Annabelle sat at the kitchen table, listening to the refrigerator humming, staring at the worn linoleum. She thought about her performance review and anticipated Daryl's comments:

Oh, she's a fine writer but she has this obsessive-compulsive problem. Gets involved with large engineers and spends too much time writing friendly electronic messages. Has slightly better than rudimentary knowledge of the stock market; could be developed but she hates Wall Street, wishes all those fat dogs would roll over and die.

Writes quickly, meets or exceeds all deadlines. Uses names of obscure poets in all examples requiring proper names. Doesn't talk at meetings. Just works for the money, doesn't stay late because she has a young daughter. Gets emotional because she's in the process of a divorce but hides it well. Wears nice clothes.

A lump welled in her throat. She began shaking her head.

One More Set of Issues to Resolve:

1. *Become more professional!*
2. *Read more books on the stock market.*
3. *Start talking in meetings. Talk louder.*
4. *Try not to—*

The telephone rang. It was 10:30 p.m. She hesitated, and then answered it.

"Hellloow," he slurred.

She said nothing.

"Annie," he said, "I have to talk to you. It's important."

"I'm sorry Dennis but I can't talk right now."

"We have to talk."

"You need to sign the papers in front of a notary. Have you done that yet?"

"What you been doing?" he said.

"I'm going to bed now. Goodnight."

"I'm coming back, Annie. I need you."

"Stop this. OK? Just stop this!"

"I know you want it. Just give it up, all right? I know you better than anyone. I'm coming over."

Annabelle hung up. The telephone rang again and she disconnected it.

Advantages to Relationship with Eddie:

1. *Eddie is a foot taller than Dennis.*
2. *Eddie is twice as strong as Dennis.*
3. *Eddie knows Judo.*
4. *Eddie could protect me from Dennis.*

Arguments against Advantages:

1. *Not fair to involve Eddie in this.*
2. *Eddie deserves friendship, not exploitation.*

Resolutions:

1. *Do not accept Dennis's bullying.*
2. *Do not discard Eddie's friendship.*

To: ABonney
From: EWRIGHT

Snow dream…You and Sarah are running around and around waving your hands catching snowflakes on your tongues.
   Peace,
   Eddie
   P.S. Lunch today! Please!

She closed her office door, then swivelled her chair so that she could face Eddie. She had turned off her computers and sounds from other offices muffled in.

Eddie opened a plastic shopping bag and pulled out a sandwich. Annabelle's sandwich was neatly arranged on a plastic plate on her desk.

"What kind of sandwich is that?" asked Annabelle.

"Alfalfa sprouts and mayonnaise," he said.

"Really?" She laughed.

"Yes," he smiled.

"So is mine!" she said. "I never met anyone else who ate plain alfalfa sprout sandwiches before!"

"Neither did I," he said, taking a bite.

Annabelle paused.

1. *Eddie doesn't seem to think the coincidence is a big deal.*
2. *I have to stop looking for signs.*

They chewed for a while. Both sandwiches were made with light rye bread.

"When I met you I thought you were about twenty-five," she said, having eaten quickly, trying not to talk with her mouth full. "How old are you?"

He laughed. "I'm thirty-five. I'll be thirty-six in June."

"You're two years older than me! I guess it's your long hair. It makes you look very young."

"I always wanted long hair, but if you don't like it I'll get it cut."

Annabelle stared at him. "Why would I ask you to do something like that?" she said, carefully wiping her hands with a white paper napkin, then pulling a wad of red satin out of her briefcase.

"I don't have time to finish this at home," she explained, starting to sew gold sequins on the collar. "This is Sarah's costume for her play Friday night. She's going to be an elf."

As she sewed she spoke, picking at threads of a long story.

"Dennis called again last night. I wish he'd just sign the papers... as he has promised... so many times..."

Eddie frowned at her.

"You said you met Barbara in college?" she asked.

Eddie nodded.

"I met Dennis in college. But I guess it was different from your situation."

"How so?" he murmured.

"It really was a lot like my novel, you know. Having read that, you already know some of the story."

The room was quiet. Annabelle sewed.

"What was the story?" said Eddie, finally.

"Oh, you know, I was falling apart emotionally then; all that stuff from my childhood kept surfacing. So I ended up moving in with Dennis and getting a job doing house-cleaning. That helped me pull myself together. I mean it enabled me to suppress a lot so that I could keep going." She looked at him again.

"So moving in together led to getting married?"

"Well, yes. We got married because of Sarah but it's not fair to blame it on her."

She looked up and saw Eddie staring at the palms of his massive hands, curled on his lap.

She continued sewing. "Well, OK, you know how in my novel Germaine bled so much as a child because she was abused? Well… that was autobiographical. And when I was a teenager my mother said a doctor had told her I wouldn't have children. So I always thought I'd never have them. Dennis certainly didn't want children, and I thought it would never happen." She shook her head and stared into space. "But then, when I actually did get pregnant, it was just this miracle! And there was no way I could even consider an abortion. So because he couldn't convince me to have an abortion he insisted that we get married and I agreed. Can you believe how ridiculous we were?"

She glanced at him again, self-consciously searching his face for a response. He nodded.

"And then what?" he asked.

She paused, poking the needle through another tiny sequin eye, "I don't mean that I regret having Sarah – I've never regretted that – Sarah is the light of my life! I just never should have married Dennis. It would have been easier to be a single mother. All my friends said it would be a marriage made in hell. He's just so incredibly irresponsible. It was like I had two children instead of one."

She stopped. Now Eddie was staring out the window. He tilted his ear towards her, whispering, "That must have been hard."

"I really started to hate him." She stopped, surprised by her words.

"I mean," she quickly added, "it was hard to be married to someone I had to take care of, who didn't help with anything. So he'd leave me and I'd leave him. I kept moving from one apartment to another because of that and even though we were legally married we rarely spent any time together... Then, about three years ago, we separated and didn't see each other at all. He didn't bother to see Sarah. He never called her or anything. So I thought that was it, we'd finally get divorced."

She paused and let out a long sigh, glancing out her window at thick winter clouds. "But then things got really complicated. My sister asked me to take care of my mother for a few weeks but that turned into two years. My mom has Alzheimer's disease... uh... or something like that... but that's another story. Anyway, when she came to live with me I was in denial of all that. I just figured she couldn't remember things because she was dealing with all the years of stress... all the years of stress created by my father. My father is not a kind man. But I ended my relationship with him many years ago."

Eddie was looking out the window. She sighed again. "Yeah. So... We were living in an old slum apartment then and I was always worrying. There was no place for my mom to go during the day, she couldn't go to school with Sarah or to work with me and there were no elder services in the town where we were living, so I'd write notes and tape them all over the walls."

Eddie nodded. Annabelle smiled and paused, shaking her head, remembering.

"I wrote notes about everything – where to find food, arrows to the bathroom... warnings about using the stove... I always worried that someone would come to the door and she'd let them in while I was out. I used to call her from work about five times a day to check in."

"That was tough," whispered Eddie.

"Oh, it got worse. Then some truly horrible people moved in upstairs and I was just beyond terrified all the time about that... then Dennis started calling me again. I was so lonely – and scared

– that I started seeing him again. Because… I felt we at least had some protection with him around. And of course I didn't think twice about lending him a lot of money again… and I finally decided to give it one more try so we rented a little shanty in Gardenia… probably the only low-budget housing in town… But a few weeks after we all moved in together my mom started wandering and I had to find a nursing home for her. That was unbelievably hard. I hated to have to put her there but I had absolutely no other choice. And then, of course, Dennis took up all his old habits."

"So that's when you filed for the divorce?"

She examined the shiny satin and started sewing again.

"Well, I'm still trying to file for divorce. He just won't sign those papers. But there were so many events leading to it… Finally he told me he was moving to California, so I said OK, I'll file for divorce and he said OK. So I found the apartment I live in now, but now, of course, he won't sign the agreement and says he doesn't want to move to California, and doesn't want a divorce."

She lowered her voice: "In the past, whenever I'd ask for a divorce he'd threaten to fight for custody of Sarah. He doesn't have any grounds to stand on, but the thought of a custody battle just terrifies me… How did I get started telling you all that?"

When she looked up from her work, Eddie was looking down. Annabelle thought about ladies' sewing circles and how gossip starts. *It's so darn easy to talk and sew. Why did I tell him all that?*

"I know a great therapist you could see," he said, "I saw her during my divorce from Barbara and she helped me a lot."

Oh God, now he really thinks I'm crazy.

"Oh, I'm OK," she insisted, "I'm sorry I bothered you with all this. I really shouldn't have told you all that."

"No, that's OK; I just think she could help you. I'll get you her number."

Annabelle hesitated. "Well, how much does she charge for a visit?" she asked, picking up her needle again, trying to evade the subject.

"Don't worry about that. I'll pay for it."

Annabelle looked up from her sewing.

"Um. I can't possibly ask such a thing," she said, shaking her head.

"Well," said Eddie, still looking at the carpet, "I can't counsel you because I'm so madly in love with you."

Annabelle stared at him and tried to form words. Finally he got up and left her office.

She waited for him to return. Then she folded the costume, stuffed it in her briefcase, and walked down the hall.

Daryl's door was open. She knocked on it.

"Do you have a minute?" she asked.

"Sure," he said, "come on in."

She closed the door behind her.

"What's up?" said Daryl, motioning for her to sit down.

"Daryl," she said, slowly, sighing and sitting, "Ed Wright just told me that he's madly in love with me."

Daryl paused. They were both silent.

"Well," Daryl suddenly said, "he never told ME that! And I've been working with him a lot longer than you have!"

Annabelle smiled and shook her head while Daryl chuckled.

Finally Daryl said, "The rumour mill has it that you and Ed have been floating around together. You've been seeing him for a while, have you?"

"No. We've been sending each other electronic-mail messages for a few weeks. I let him read my novel. We've had lunch a few times. So this is pretty sudden."

"Is this a problem?" asked Daryl. "Do you like him?"

She touched her fingers to her lips. "Um. I just love him," she heard herself whisper.

"So what's the problem?"

"What do you mean? I'm still trying to get divorced."

"I've worked with Ed off and on for about four years now and I can tell you that he's one of the most decent, good natured human beings I've ever met. He's got a great attitude about life. If he says he loves you and you love him, then that's not a problem. You could do a lot worse!"

Annabelle smiled and sighed. "Believe me, I know about doing worse. But how can he just come out and say that, just like that?"

"I guess he loves you so he told you. I guess that's part of why he has a great attitude about life. I know I'd never be that impulsive with anyone. And I also know that I need an attitude adjustment."

Annabelle continued smiling, continued shaking her head.

1. Here I am, having an intimate conversation with my new boss about a mutual colleague.
2. How did this happen?

"You think it's OK?" she asked eventually.
"You don't need my permission," he said.
Annabelle returned to her office and read her new electronic-mail messages.

To: ABonney
From: EWRIGHT
Subject: Untitled

> I am sorry that
> I hurt your feelings when
> I told you that
>
> I loved you.
> It is raining.

To: ABonney
From: EWRIGHT
Subject: Untitled

> It's still raining
> the pine cone has refused
> to speak with the bonsai tree
>
> It was God
> that made me
> leap naked, young again
> into the brook
>
> Splashing! Cold water
> Clear sandstone and blue sky.
>
> Will you forgive me?
> Or do I have to move to Idaho?

To: EWRIGHT
From: ABonney
Subject: Untitled

> oh my goodness.
> Idoloveyou
> so much
> but i am afraid
>
> i want to be with you
> please don't go to Idaho

"Did you get my response to your poems?" she asked, holding the telephone's receiver in her quivering left hand.

"Yes," he whispered, "I read it."

"Can you walk with me to my car tonight so we can talk?"

"Yes."

At five they met by the elevator on the eighth floor; neither spoke until they were sitting in Annabelle's station wagon. She moved the front seat back to accommodate Eddie's long legs.

"Um. What do you want from me?" she finally said.

"I don't want anything," he said.

He reached for her hand and held it. The moist warmth of his immense palm startled her. He leant over to kiss her. She backed away before his lips could reach her.

He looked out the window.

It had stopped raining. The December sky was black with streaks of azure, strange lines of blue madness. Rush-hour traffic hummed on the streets below the parking garage.

Eventually she forced herself to address her suspicion.

"Do you want to be my lover?" she asked, her voice breaking.

Eddie glanced at her and smiled.

"No," he said, "that's not it."

She was relieved and disappointed.

"Then what do you want?"

"Just walk with me."

"What do you mean?"

Eddie slowly breathed and sighed, "I just want you to walk with me. I want to give you the family you never had."

His response made her even more suspicious. He had briefly described his brothers and his parents, but he'd also mentioned an ashram in western Massachusetts and now she wondered whether he wanted her to join some kind of religious cult.

"What do you mean?" she repeated.

"I want to marry you," he said without hesitation, "I want to have children with you and marry you…"

Staring at the steering wheel, she quietly, nervously, inadvertently, sighed – a tiny half-laugh. Sarah had gone to a friend's house after school so she didn't have to hurry home as usual; she had a few minutes to spare.

1. *I always imagined that when the right man came along he'd do just this. No fooling around. He'd be decisive; he'd know what he wanted.*
2. *Eddie, even your name is right, Eddie Wright, the proverbial Mr Right. Am I really losing my mind this time?*

"But you hardly know me," she said at last. "How can you say you want to marry me?"

"Intuition." He paused for several moments. "I knew I wanted you the first time I saw you. I only loved one other woman before you and it wasn't my wife. It was a girl I went out with in college but she left me for God. She left me to become a nun. Maybe I could have stopped her but I didn't. So I married Barbara just because I liked the idea of being married and she was willing. She wanted to get married and we both wanted to have children. It was a counter-culture thing to do in those days because nobody was getting married then, especially not as young as we were. But I didn't love her and I married her anyway and we both suffered for it. I've had a few relationships since my divorce but I didn't love them either so I've spent more time breaking up than being in the relationships. Finally I decided that when I found the woman I wanted I would let intuition guide me and I would just tell her, without fooling around, and I would do everything I could to make her want me too. So that's what I did. I'm sorry if I upset you by telling you that I'm madly in love with you, but I am, that's all. I'm crazy about you Annabelle. That's all."

She shook her head again, wondering why he was crazy about her.

"I do want to have more children," she whispered. "You really want more children?"

"That's been my dream for years." He smiled.

"I have to go," she said. She turned her head, paused, then said, "I love you too," while looking away from him.

"Can I have a kiss?"

She shook her head. "I can't yet."

He nodded and got out of the car.

"I've been thinking it over," said Dennis, "and I'm not agreeing to a divorce, ever. I'm going to fight you all the way on this."

Gripping the receiver in her clammy left hand, Annabelle sighed.

"Dennis, you've been doing this for years. You abuse me then you say you'll fight the divorce after I leave you."

"I never abused you."

"I've made a 147-item list of what you've done to me. I'll submit it as an affidavit if I have to."

"You suck," he said, then paused, then continued. "You really fucking suck," he shouted, slamming down the phone.

Two hours later he called back.

"I'm sorry," he said.

Annabelle said nothing.

"Just have dinner with me."

"No."

"I'll do anything to make it up. I know the idea of moving to California was stupid. I like it here in Gardenia; I'm not leaving now. I could give up this place and move in with you and Sarah. Sarah needs to have her father around."

"What about all the years you weren't around? What do we do about those?"

"I'm sorry. I will change. I will. Let's just have dinner and we'll talk about it."

"No."

"Then I'm going to fucking run you through the wall!" he shouted and Annabelle hung up this time.

Sarah's sleeping breath sounded laboured but at least she wasn't wheezing. *It's just a mild cold.* Annabelle quietly stood and listened to the tiny night-time sounds, Sarah's breathing, and the furnace tapping.

Issues:

1. Yes I am. I am madly in love with Eddie. I am.
2. Eddie says he's madly in love with me.
3. I don't know what to do about this.

Resolutions:

1. *Avoid Dennis at Sarah's play.*
2. *Don't sit with Dennis and his family in the audience.*
3. *Pray.*

To: ABonney
From: EWRIGHT

I know it hurts a lot. The reality is that you're doing amazingly well. You're not being selfish. You're being clear with what you need. Please don't feel sorry about involving me in this stuff. It has become central to both our lives. Like it or not I'm sharing it with you. I want to hold you and make the pain go away.

I love you. I love you.

I
Love
You,
Eddie

5

To: ABonney
From: EWRIGHT

Walk today!!!!!!! Please, Please, Please

It was lunchtime, the Friday before Christmas. Eddie and Annabelle walked several miles along Memorial Drive, by the Charles River. The temperature just touched freezing.

They sat on a chipped park bench near the Harvard campus. Some sculls still floated with hardy rowers. The sky was sunny for a change.

"I'll miss you next week," Eddie said, "I wish I didn't have to go." His brown eyes mirrored the sunlight.

Earlier he had said it was his turn to be with his son for Christmas. They would be going to his parents' house in northern Vermont.

"I'll miss you too," she said.

"Can we talk on Christmas Eve? I want to know how you like the presents you're getting."

Annabelle's face remained blank. Eddie smiled. "I got you some presents. I'll bring them up before I leave today but you can't open them until Christmas."

She shook her head. "You shouldn't have done that. I've been so busy I haven't gotten you anything. Yesterday was the winter solstice and I didn't even celebrate that."

Eddie took her hand, which was dwarfed by his huge leather mitten, her fleece glove enveloped by his bear paw. They still hadn't kissed.

"What are you feeling right now?" he asked.

The sun was in her eyes.

Current Conflicts:

1. *Dennis's threats will never end.*
2. *Dennis will never agree to the divorce.*
3. *Dennis will retaliate with false accusations.*
4. *A multi-year legal battle will ensue.*

"I'm not really feeling anything," she said, her voice breaking.

"I won't ask you that again for a long time," he said, gently squeezing her hand, warming her, forcing her to feel something.

In the afternoon he brought a large shopping bag to her office. A hefty toy, a plush brown bear, weighted the top.

He closed her office door and pretended the bear was a baby, tossing it in the air, patting its back, hugging it. Then he leant over and hugged Annabelle. His touch shocked her. Never before had he come so close.

"I won't stay," he said, "I have a deliverable this afternoon. I have to get bar charts up and running before I can leave for Vermont. It's OK, I'm almost there."

He placed the bag in her hands. "There are some more presents in here. I want you to open these on Christmas Eve, OK?"

"I love the bear, but you shouldn't have given me all this. I wasn't expecting you to do this. I wish I had something to give you."

"You could give me a kiss," he whispered.

She paused, tilted her head towards his face, pressed her tight mouth to his lips, and quickly backed away.

"Well I guess that was a kiss," he said, smiling.

She had nothing to say. She was in love with a man she was afraid to kiss.

1. *That* AIDS *virus is so new. Nobody knows how many people are infected. Nobody knows if it can be transmitted via saliva. Has he ever been promiscuous, especially since* 1977?

2. Has he ever had a blood transfusion or shared a needle with anyone?
3. Does he have a tattoo?
4. Were his former girlfriends healthy?

Eddie was still smiling, waving goodbye.

"Merry Christmas," he whispered, closing the door.

"I love you," she said to the closed door.

After Sarah's play that night, Dennis confronted Annabelle in the crowd of parents rushing around the school looking for their children.

"I'm sorry about what I said," said Dennis, "I'll sign anything you want. Wasn't Sarah great?"

Annabelle nodded, trying not to stand too close to him.

"My mom will be crushed if you don't come to the party on Christmas Eve," he said.

"Um. I'm sorry. I can't be with you or your family for Christmas," she said, looking around for Sarah in the crowd, "I'm going to spend the evening with my mother."

"Well, you're invited."

"Are you going to sign the papers next week?"

"Yeah," he muttered. "Merry Christmas to you too."

Christmas Eve was an attempt to stay even on an ever-shifting platform. Sarah spent the afternoon with Dennis while Annabelle signed her mother out of the nursing home. Mary sat quietly in Annabelle's apartment, smiling, rocking in the cherry rocker. Her rocking had a halting quality, a random momentum.

"Merry Christmas, Mom," said Annabelle, handing her a large sugar cookie in the shape of a heart. That morning she and Sarah had baked four dozen cookies in various shapes: crescent moons, hearts and several types of stars.

Mary held the cookie and seemed to stare through it.

"The tree is pretty," said Mary.

Annabelle laughed. "Yes," she said. "It's Christmas!"

"It is?" said Mary.

"Yes!"

"It's nice. I'm nice."

"Yes you are," said Annabelle.

"Yes you are," repeated Mary. The cookie dropped from her hand and broke in two. Annabelle gathered the pieces of broken heart and residual crumbs in her warm hands.

"I'm here," said Mary.

Annabelle nodded.

"Did you?" asked Mary.

"Did I what?" said Annabelle.

"He didn't know. That would I and all." Mary shook her head and stopped talking, closed her eyes and soon snored.

Sarah's dress was sweaty, her face smeared with chocolate when Dennis dropped her off that evening. He was back in his car before Annabelle opened the door.

"You should see little Warren," said Sarah, "he's almost as big as me now!"

"Did you have fun?"

"Uh huh," said Sarah. "What did you do today?" She sat next to the tree, inspecting and shaking the few small wrapped parcels already there.

"Grandma came over and we sat and talked."

"What did you talk about?"

"I don't really know," said Annabelle. "What did you and your father talk about?"

"We didn't talk about you. That was good. We didn't really talk about anything. I just played with little Warren and Cindy."

Annabelle and Sarah ate cookies and drank cider, food in the living room, only on holidays.

"Is there a Santa Claus, Mom?"

"Yes."

"Sure there is," said Sarah, smugly, slowly nodding.

Annabelle was silent.

Finally Sarah said, "You know Mommy, when you and Daddy got back together the last time I knew it wouldn't last. You're much happier without him."

Annabelle looked at her.

"Daddy's not happier without you," continued Sarah, "but he wasn't happy with you either. He's never happy. That makes me sad."

"I'm sorry you're sad," said Annabelle.

"I'm not really sad," said Sarah.

After Sarah was asleep, Annabelle placed her presents under the tree, including the huge PC that had been stuffed in back of the mud-room closet.

Once Sarah's gifts were all set out, Annabelle retrieved Eddie's bag from under her bed.

Along with wrapped gifts, the bag contained an envelope with a little stick figure painted on the front. The stick figure had a cartoon balloon that said, "In silence, open me. Light enclosed candle."

She stuck the candle in an old empty jar, lit the wick, and turned out the lights.

There were two pseudo-Grecian pillars separating the living room from her bedroom; the redefined dining room. She silently sat watching the tree lights sparkling through a pillar, her bag of presents in hand. The only gifts Dennis had ever given her were paid for by money she had lent to him, money he never returned. He always ran out of cash before holidays.

Her childhood Christmas memories were no better. Her father and alcohol would mix and generate a wide variety of seasonal experiences, invariably explosive, ending in tears and violence.

Still, she kept a tiny crèche by the tree. The story of the nativity made her cry as a child, the simple story of Jesus. Like Buddha and others, he was God's son, she was God's daughter, everyone being either a son or daughter of God, God being female and male. *Goddess, God. Same thing.*

Finally she read Eddie's letter:

Dear Annabelle,

It's amazing how still life becomes in early morning. Today, the Friday before Christmas, will bring a very busy day. For me it also brings a parting between us, in which you will be sorely missed. I will miss not being able to go to work and see you there. I love you.

Before you are some Christmas gifts, each with its own story, and perhaps lots of fun. The bear was a marked-down orphan found huddled among other bears in a store in Boston. She is very soft and cuddly. Seemed to have your name on it.

> Read the Tao. It could help you.
> I found the necklace in Harvard Square. It was made in Czechoslovakia in the 1920s. It is made of pink aurora crystals. Pink is the colour that the renunciates wear at the ashram. (The renunciates are those who dedicate themselves to the yoga path.) And when set against the white outfits worn by everyone else, the pink is quite striking. I love the pink people for the courage and endurance they show on their path. So wear the pink as a great symbol of your path and your inner strength. I'm also fond of the aurora name. It suits you. Among other things, it means dawn. I love you.
> I hope you are warm and safe.
> I love you,
>   Eddie
>
> P.S. Perhaps we can learn to talk on the phone.

He listed his home phone number and the number at his parent's house in Vermont.

She began to unwrap the gifts: a Japanese book with blank handmade pages, a pen with a toy propeller for a top, a small box covered with a note that said "Open me last". She set it aside. More presents: a cube comprised of tiny magnifying glasses; some rough tumbled agate, jade, and tourmaline; a book: Tao-Te-Ching.

She opened the last box and gasped, tipping the candle from the side table, spilling a bit of hot wax on her arm.

The box contained a long necklace with multi-faceted pink crystals, the most beautiful bauble she'd ever seen. She peeled the wax from her skin, fingered a few crystals, and started a letter to Eddie.

> Eddie,
> It is Christmas Eve at 10:00 p.m. I followed your instructions and turned off my lamp, lit the candle, and read your letter. I wish I could be with you right now. Merry Christmas!
> I love all the presents, thank you so much, how could you? It is hard for me to receive these. I wish I had something for you.
> Years ago, I had a dream about the magnifying box you gave me – isn't that strange?

The crystal necklace is the most beautiful piece of jewellery I have ever seen. I got so excited when I saw it that I spilt hot wax on my arm! Pink. Yes.

I had a nice day with Sarah and my mom... but I also missed you.

I can't call you. This is due to my conditioning as a teenager, which mandates that because I'm female I should wait for you to call me. I know that's old-fashioned and irrational, but it's gotten integrated in my psyche, superstitiously, I guess. It's like my fear of walking under a ladder or spilling salt or buying something when the moon is void of course. And, also... I can't call you because I want to too much!

The telephone rang. *Eddie or Dennis.* She held her breath and took a chance.

"Hello?"

"Merry Christmas," he whispered.

She sighed. "I was just writing you a letter."

"Did you open your presents?"

Annabelle heard a voice say, "Dad. Daaaaadd."

"Hold on a second," said Eddie, muffling the phone. "Hi," he said again a few moments later. "That was Danny. I keep telling him to go to sleep but this is Christmas."

"I think Sarah's asleep because she's not making any noise. How are you?"

"I miss you. Did you open your presents?"

"Yes. Thank you so much. But you shouldn't have given me so much. I feel really bad that I didn't give you anything. I wrote you a letter."

"Do you want to read it to me?"

She read the letter.

"I'll be coming home on Friday morning," he said, "Can you come over for dinner that night?"

She paused. "If I can find a sitter."

"I love you," he said.

"I love you too." Her words were fearful, hesitant.

1. *How can anyone love someone this quickly?*
2. *Is this magic, is this a gift?*
3. *Saying I love you isn't enough. Words.*

They whispered good night, then Annabelle sat still, with visions of Eddie filling her head. At last she fell asleep, momentarily believing.

She spent Christmas morning setting up the computer.

Sarah used the word processor and tried out a video game, spending twenty minutes with the expensive machine. The rest of the day she played with her new Victorian paper dolls.

Early in the evening, Dennis called, chipper.

"I hope you had a nice day," he said.

"Yes," said Annabelle. "And you?"

"Pretty good. I missed you. Can Sarah stay with me this coming weekend?"

Annabelle paused, considering. "In the agreement I drafted she's to stay with you on alternate weekends, so… yes. That will be her weekend with you."

"Of course," he said. "Let's not talk about the agreement right now. OK?"

"Of course. Let's not talk about anything. I'll drop her off on Friday evening at six-thirty and pick her up Sunday morning at nine?"

"Yes, that would be fine. Merry Christmas."

"You too," she said, hanging up the phone.

Annabelle brought Sarah to work every day that week because school was in recess and she had no other childcare arrangement. The Gardenia elementary school was not equipped with holiday programme sessions, as most residents spent those vacations away, in places such as Aruba or Bermuda.

Sarah spent most of the week sitting under Annabelle's office computer table, reading from a series of children's novels about young babysitters. Each day at lunch they walked to the Kendall Square food court where Annabelle bought Sarah stuffed pizza and frozen yogurt with multiple candy toppings. It was the best vacation she could afford to give her daughter.

Sarah was used to it and had learnt how to acquire sweets and fun books in exchange for exhibiting unobtrusive, child-at-the-office, cute-but-quiet behaviour. Annabelle pre-approved each of Sarah's weekly visits, knowing her employers were willing to overlook the occasional child-in-the-office day or week in exchange for Annabelle's hyper-efficiency.

On Wednesday morning, while Sarah was consuming a box of chocolate-covered caramels, the telephone rang in Annabelle's office.

"I'll get it!" shouted Sarah.

"No, I will," said Annabelle, grabbing the phone from Sarah's sturdy, determined hand.

Sarah hovered while Annabelle spoke.

"Hello, this is Annabelle Bonney."

"Hi," said Eddie, "I love you."

"Oh, hello," said Annabelle, coldly.

"Who is it?" said Sarah.

"That was my daughter Sarah speaking," said Annabelle. "She's helping me out in my office this week."

"Oh," said Eddie, "hence the professional demeanour. I love you, I love you, oh I love you." He laughed.

Annabelle tried not to smile.

"What's so funny? Who is that?" said Sarah.

Annabelle held her hand over the mouthpiece. "Just someone I work with," she said.

"What does he want?" said Sarah.

"He wants to know how I'm progressing on a book I'm writing. Now would you please sit down over there? I can't focus on you while I'm working. Please?"

Sarah leant against a filing cabinet, loudly chewing her coated caramels.

"I'm sorry for the interruptions," said Annabelle. "Yes, the book is coming along well."

"Oh good," said Eddie. "Can you come over for dinner on Friday night?"

"Yes, actually."

"Great! I need to give you directions."

"That's not necessary," she said. "Just an address."

"Why do you need an address?" chirped Sarah.

"That's a computer term," said Annabelle.

"OK, you have a map?" he asked.

"Yes I do."

"Really? You have a street map of Somerville?"

"Yes. I do."

"Why? Oh, you mean you have an atlas of greater Boston and surrounding suburbs, something like that?"

"Yes."

Sarah had finished her caramels and was trying to make a whistle out of the box.

"OK, it's 4269 Liberty Street, Somerville. Right off the McGrath O'Brien Highway. What time?"

"Oh, seven?" she said.

"Good. Seven. I love you," he said, hanging up.

When Annabelle brought Sarah to Dennis's apartment on Friday evening, he scowled, stiffly holding the door open while Sarah slipped inside and turned on the television.

Dennis looked at Annabelle and whispered, "It sucks that I can't see her all the time. If you try to divorce me I'll get custody."

Annabelle had been too preoccupied about seeing Eddie to worry about Dennis. She looked down to make sure her coat was securely buttoned and her new pink-crystal necklace wasn't showing. Sarah had said it was pretty and Annabelle said she'd bought it at a thrift store. She hated lying to her daughter.

"Look," she said, "I supported Sarah for years with no help from you. I also supported you for a couple of years. You never supported me. I don't do drugs, Dennis, or drink the way you do. You're lucky I let you see her at all."

"You're in for the fight of your life," he shouted, slamming the door. Annabelle saw Sarah through the window, glued to the set, oblivious to the quarrel. Dennis came to the window and lowered the shade.

Annabelle drove slowly, even on Route 1. She had carefully plotted the course to Eddie's apartment in advance but now she wanted to turn back. At each exit she slowed down, and then sped up again.

1. *Dennis is telling Sarah terrible things about me right now.*
2. *I shouldn't have left Sarah with Dennis while he's in that state of mind.*
3. *I shouldn't be going to another man's apartment while I'm still legally married to Dennis.*
4. *I should turn back at the next exit.*
5. *I will turn back at the next exit.*
6. *I'll go to see Eddie, tell him about this, then go back to Gardenia and insist that Sarah come home with me right away.*

Annabelle arrived at Eddie's apartment in tears.

The building was like hers, the lower half of a house. Leaning against the porch was a huge papier-mâché puppet of St Francis of Assisi. *Another sign.*

She knocked at the door. Eddie answered it immediately and beckoned her in with an embrace, as though she were precious.

"I shouldn't be here. I should go back and get Sarah right away – Dennis is threatening me again and I don't know what to do. I'm afraid to have Sarah with him when he's in that state of mind."

Eddie smiled, kissed her cheek, and said, "Has he ever physically hurt Sarah?"

"No, but I'm afraid of what he might say to her about me."

"But this is his way of controlling you," said Eddie. "First thing next week you're getting a lawyer. Stop trying to do this divorce yourself – that only works in the most amicable situations – this is something you just can't handle yourself. The lawyer will take care of it all for you."

"But I can't afford a lawyer," said Annabelle, immediately regretting her words because Eddie said:

"I can give you all the money you need—"

"No you can't," she said, remembering her retirement account. "I have a few thousand dollars in an IRA... maybe I can use that?"

"I think you can borrow from it. But don't worry about money. Once you get a lawyer, everything will start coming together. OK? It will be your lawyer's job to take care of Dennis, you won't have to deal with him, the lawyer will do it for you and that will help you a lot. You also need to get an answering machine and let it answer all your calls so if Dennis calls just let him leave a message. If you're sure he won't hurt Sarah, then please don't go back there tonight, not just yet – if you do you'll be allowing him to control you again; you'll just continue playing his codependent games. Just stay here and have dinner and relax. I love you. You need a break. OK?"

He took her hand. "Come in and meet my bro," he said, leading her into the apartment.

Eddie's brother was standing in the kitchen, stirring a wok filled with Chinese vegetables. He reached out to shake Annabelle's hand, saying, "So you're Annabelle – we heard so much about you at Christmas. Ed is madly in love with you, you know. I'm preparing a stir-fry for dinner, I hope you like it. My name is Sam, by the way."

Sam took his hand back and continued stirring his dish. He was as tall as Eddie but a bit heavier, with bright-red hair and a ruddy face. Annabelle was amazed by how safe she felt to be standing between two huge men in a warm strange kitchen.

"Yes," continued Sam, "Ed and I have been room-mates here for three years now since he got divorced and I moved back from Minnesota. Lots of Swedes there. Do you have a soul, Annabelle?"

She smiled at him.

"Oh God, she smiled at me," bellowed Sam. "She is a goddess, Ed! Yes indeed. Ed said you have a great spirit. One must have a great spirit in order to sing. Do you sing?"

Annabelle said, "Yes, I love to sing—"

"That's wonderful, we'll have to hear you sometime, but not tonight, there's a film I want to watch and a book I'm reading. Some other time."

Sam reminded her of the Mad Hatter. She turned to Eddie, who was smiling, standing beside the dinner table: a small smooth door turned horizontal with three sturdy steel chairs surrounding it.

"Are you hungry?" asked Sam.

"Um…" said Annabelle.

"I love you," said Eddie.

"None of that! None of that right now," shouted Sam, "dinner's ready."

Annabelle was given a seat between Eddie and Sam. The table was tiny but both men were careful not to bump her knee. The kitchen was also tiny and utilitarian with various Japanese wood-block prints hanging on Sixties wallpaper: pastel stripes, wobbly rainbows.

Sam poured three large glasses of red wine from a gallon bottle, then sniffed, "Jug wine, ah yes. Yes indeed," he continued, leaning back between mouthfuls. "Is that the necklace Ed gave you?"

Annabelle glanced down at the pink beams darting around the kitchen, competing with the beeswax candlelight.

"It sparkles in the candlelight," said Sam. "It becomes you. Pardon me while I drool."

Annabelle looked at Eddie.

"Hi," he whispered.

"How do you like the meal?" asked Sam.

"Oh it's wonderful," said Annabelle.

"I cooked it," said Sam, "although Ed did prepare the rice. He doesn't cook much, I should warn you. And you should see the way he eats tofu – just slides the corner of the package off and slurps it down all at once—"

Eddie laughed.

"Are we embarrassing you, Annabelle?" asked Sam.

"No," she said.

"Good," said Sam, "because we come from a strange family where we say whatever we think whenever we think it. We get that from our mother. She taught us the virtue of the non sequitur. More rice?"

Annabelle shook her head.

"Drink your wine," ordered Sam, "it's good for you. One time Ed bought a five-pound tin of butterscotch pudding and that's all he ate for a week. You see, he just doesn't cook. But he did prepare the rice. And our father is trying to save the world, watch out for him. You have to be smart or forget it. You seem smart. Did anyone ever tell you that you resemble the Mona Lisa?"

Annabelle nodded, looking up between nervous mouthfuls.

"Uncanny resemblance, yes. More rice?" he repeated. "You must have more rice; Ed made it just for you. He never cooks when it's just the two of us – I should warn you about that, he's not the most domestic man you'll ever find. How tall are you?"

Annabelle paused, waiting for him to continue. Then she realized that he'd asked her a question.

"I'm five eleven," she said.

"And Ed's six seven so I'd say you'll have tall children. And you already know that you look like the Mona Lisa, remarkable likeness; thinner though, as our mother would say you're a slip of a girl, a little wisp. She'll ask you where your bosom is – you'll have to be strong you know, Eddie's not small—"

"Sam!" interrupted Eddie, looking beseechingly at Annabelle.

"Well you know that's what Joanne would say! That's our mother, Joanne. We call her mother but you can call her Joanne. I'm going to my room to read now. Save the dishes, I'll wash them in the morning; I always do."

With that Sam lumbered out of the room, waving a paperback copy of *The Catcher in the Rye*.

"That necklace does sparkle," said Eddie after Sam had gone to his room and closed the door.

For several moments they silently watched the tiny pink lights darting around the kitchen.

"What do you think of Sam?" asked Eddie.

"He's a real character."

"He likes you. He doesn't usually like people but he likes you."

"How do you know?"

"Because he talked to you. If he doesn't like someone he won't say a word to them."

Then they were silent again. "That was a lovely dinner," she said, finally.

"Sam keeps the heat at fifty-five in the winter," said Eddie. "It's warmer in my room next to the radiator. We could sit in there."

Annabelle nodded and Eddie led her to his bedroom.

The room had a futon curled up as a couch next to the radiator, a closet concealed by a madras drape, and a huge, round antique Queen Anne mahogany dining table with claw feet, covered with piles of neatly arranged books. That was it. No window curtains or pictures on the walls. But the table was amazing, belonging in a great hall of a mansion, or in a museum, not in a man's spartan bedroom. The windows were lined with white translucent sheets of plastic insulation. It was an intensely austere room, except for the outrageously ornate table.

"That's an incredible table," said Annabelle.

"Isn't that nice?" he said. "That's something that was in my family, my parents handed it down to me. It's all I got to keep in my divorce – she got the car, the TV, the stereo, the child. But at least I got to keep the table my parents gave me... and all the credit-card debt she ran up."

Eddie sat on the futon and Annabelle joined him. As they spoke they both looked straight ahead, at the radiator.

"Have you been reading the Tao?" he asked.

She nodded. "I've read a few pages. I like it so far."

"It's about creation and formlessness. I think of it when I work with my hands. It speaks of the master instead of a god. Are you afraid to be alone with me?"

Annabelle nodded. Eddie touched her hand and lifted it up. "You're very tense," he said.

She nodded again, shivering. "I'm worrying about Sarah."

Eddie went to the closet and carried back a patchwork quilt. "I know," he whispered, wrapping the quilt around her shoulders. "But it will be OK... My mother made this quilt. She makes lots of things – jewellery, dolls, clothes – she loves to make baby things."

Annabelle smiled. Eddie repeated, "You're tense."

"I'm sorry," she said.

"I could rub your back if you'd like. Would you be comfortable with that?"

Annabelle remembered the last massage she'd received, years earlier. It was during one of her separations from Dennis; one of his friends had been inviting her to poetry readings and to dinner and somehow they'd ended up alone together and he'd offered to give her a massage. She'd foolishly agreed and before she knew it his fingers were in her vagina and it was all she could do to get him out of her apartment that night. But now the wine swam in her head and she ached for Eddie.

1. *He doesn't seem promiscuous but anyone that good-looking easily could be.*
2. *Do not get physical. Think about* AIDS.
3. *If Dennis finds out that I've had physical involvement with another man he'll use it to fuel his custody battle.*

4. *If I make love to Eddie I'll find some subconscious way to punish myself for it.*

"I'd love it if you could rub my back a little," she heard herself say.
Eddie paused.
Finally he said, "It will be hard for me to touch you. It will be like reaching into a mirror and touching myself."
Annabelle smiled. "What do you mean?"
"You're my twin," he said, "that's how I feel."
They stood up. Eddie spread the futon across the floor. She lay on it, on her stomach.
"No," he said. "Lie on your back. I'll work on your feet first."
She turned over. He gently covered her body with the thick quilt. She saw that he was kneeling before her feet, his palms clasped together, pointing upwards, as though in prayer. She had never before received this kind of reverence. She stared at the ceiling.
First he slowly removed her black shoes and socks. Then he took her right foot in both hands and breathed on it. He paused a moment and she could hear him rubbing his hands together, making them warm.
When he touched her foot again, she could feel that he'd applied oil to his hands; the oil glided like silk across her sole, around her ankle, under her toes. He spent many minutes on the one foot, exploring every wrinkle, each crevice and bone.
He grasped her ankle with one hand and said, "Let your foot go." She let her foot hang loose and he patted its sole hard, stimulating the arch with oiled slaps. It tingled.
"God that feels good," she meant to exclaim, but murmured instead.
Then he gave the left foot the same attention as the right.
"Now I'll do your head," he said, and crawled around her, until he was sitting above her, cradling her neck.
He had wiped his hands on a towel and applied new oil, massaging her cheekbones, her temples, the rim of her nose, her chin, then her skull, following the lines, rocking her neck until she relaxed in his hands and they both heard a small crack and laughed.

"I don't think I've ever felt this good before," she whispered.

"You've never been loved before," he said. "Now I'll do your back."

She turned over, too content to fear him. For a long time he kneaded her shoulders and ribs. He didn't pull up her blouse. He skipped her hips and massaged the back of her lower thighs through her leggings, then her knees and calves, carefully avoiding every private place.

When he was through, he stood up, sat against the wall by her head, and stared into space.

"What's wrong?" she asked, her tissues spread limp across his futon.

"You don't have any muscles," he replied.

She didn't know what to say.

She finally said, "I'm sorry."

"I just never felt any muscles," he said. "It surprised me."

1. *I disappointed him.*
2. *Am I just completely inadequate?*

"I could develop some muscles," she said.

"Oh, you will."

"Um. Do you still... want to be with me?"

"Of course! I love you! I was just surprised!" He laughed.

"That was a wonderful massage. Thank you."

Eddie nodded. They were both silent for several minutes.

"Would you like to lie down with me?" she asked, surprised by her own question.

"I don't know," said Eddie, "that scares me."

"Why?" she asked, thinking she should be the one to express fear.

"I'm afraid of lying next to you. I'm afraid of what could happen."

"We could just touch a little bit," she said.

He crawled to the futon and lay beside her under the heavy quilt. They hugged. She reached for his mouth and kissed it, gently, slowly, not using her tongue. She backed away and placed a finger on his lips, encircling his mouth.

"You teach me what to do," he said.

"I don't think I'm a very good teacher," she whispered while he leant towards her, lightly kissing her, circling her lips with his fingers, as she'd done to him.

She placed her hand on his stomach. He placed his hand on her stomach.

"You show me the way," he said. "You're the master in my bed."

She caressed him. He returned her caresses as though he were a mirror, reflecting her tenderness. Never before had she been so aroused by touching and being touched. She made no attempt to feel his bare skin. He did not try to remove her clothes.

After several hours, she placed her hand between his legs and slowly squeezed his crotch. He did the same to her. They smiled at each other, fully dressed. She could feel his organ harden through his pants.

"I'm wet," he murmured.

"I feel like a teenager," she said, "and we're on the couch and we can't take off our clothes because we're afraid my mother will walk in."

"I never did this as a teenager," said Eddie, "I was too shy to date."

"I never did either," she said, "but it's what they call heavy petting."

"I think it's actually called Tantric prana," he said.

She moved closer, pressed her hips against his, stunned by the perfect sense of arousal, the waves coursing through her hardened clitoris and orifices; her mouth found Eddie's, they locked together at the lips until she shuddered and pulled away.

"You came!" he exclaimed.

She hid her face in the pillow they shared.

"I did," she said, "I'm so sorry. I couldn't help it."

"It was wonderful, why are you sorry?" he asked.

She placed her hand along his pants zipper, feeling his steady erection.

"I wanted to please you but I only pleased myself and I know I'm not being fair but I just can't do this yet. I can't let you inside me yet."

"Annabelle," he whispered, "I'm still wet. Taoists hold their wetness. You don't know how long it's been since I've been able to maintain an erection. For the past few years I've felt impotent. But I've been hard and wet all night. I can't tell you how much I've enjoyed lying here with you. You are the most sensuous woman I've ever met."

"Really?" she said. "You mean you like the fact that I came?"

"Of course! What a silly question."

"Well... Dennis would always get turned off when I'd get excited. I thought that men didn't like it when a woman showed that she was enjoying it."

"No," explained Eddie, "it works the opposite way! The man gets excited when the woman gets excited."

"But Dennis didn't like it if I'd get excited."

"Dennis didn't know what he had," sighed Eddie, rolling onto his back. "I don't think he likes women."

"He doesn't like anyone," she said.

"Including himself," said Eddie.

It was early morning, past midnight, and they'd just passed into the netherworld of illicit lovers.

And then, without warning, a rush of tears came as Annabelle bit her tongue. Eddie stared in her exhausted, watery eyes.

She finally sobbed, "He won't let me divorce him. He really won't ever let me. He refuses to cooperate and if I really do go to a lawyer it will cost a lot more than I could ever afford because he'll say terrible things about me and I'll have to defend myself. I know that will cost a lot – I just don't want to fight! It's been going on like this for years. It's just so awful; I never should have let it go on like this. I just don't know what to do. Every day I hate myself for having married him way back then. But you know, when you get married and you're saying 'I do' even if you're not sure, no one's there to warn you that you could be enslaving yourself for life! I'm sorry. I'm so upset. He says he'll get custody of Sarah. I know he wouldn't but if he says terrible things about me, then what? I've worked so hard for so long, I don't want to have to defend myself – I don't want anything to wreck my relationship with Sarah. I feel like Dennis has tried to steal her from me all her life. I love her so much."

Her nose was stuffy and she was embarrassed and confused.

Eddie reached for her hand.

"I'm not Dennis," he said, "but I know that no one can force you to stay married to him if you don't want to. You might not believe this but this really is a free country... even if we do have a Republican president right now. But it's all temporary." He paused. "I know that this is a hard time for you and maybe I shouldn't be wanting you now, maybe I should wait until you've had the time to deal with the divorce. I could go away for a while."

She stared at him and shivered under the quilt.

"But I don't want to do that," said Eddie.

"Do you still feel that you love me?"

He nodded.

"Can you promise me one thing?" she asked. "Can we make a promise to each other that if either of us ever wants to leave, for any reason whatsoever, then the other won't argue and fight about it?"

"I promise," he said. "That will be our first by-law."

"Do you still want to marry me?" she asked.

He smiled, nodded, and said, "Someday we'll be married. And you know what will happen then? We won't be thinking about this crazy stuff any more. We'll be spending the evenings paying bills and playing with our babies. And we'll have other problems then... like we'll have car trouble... flat tyres... all kinds of stuff... But all that will be fun too."

Annabelle closed her eyes, reflecting on the joys of mundane problems, imagining the possibility of future children.

He whispered, "You try to get some sleep now, my sweetie. I love you more than I can say and I know I'll love you more and more as I get to know you better."

He curled up beside her. Their arms and legs tangled together like a tenacious broad briar hedging a tremulous, timorous rose.

6

To: ABonney
From: EWRIGHT

FULL MOON WATERFALL LOVE

Lifting wings
Arching back
Leaping wet and heated
at last unbridled

Legs surrender
Seeking entrance
Taking in lover's womb
Life's stormy seed.

She read it over and over.

1. *Eddie is tired of waiting.*
2. *Eddie wants intercourse.*
3. *I have to consider the issue of* AIDS.

After reading the poem the fifth time, the telephone rang. It was an outside call but she picked it up, even though she'd been letting her office answering machine take all calls from outside lines.

"Hello Annabelle," said Dennis.

Her heart quickened. "Oh," she said, ready to tell him she had to go to a meeting.

"I'm sorry about what I said before."

"I have to go."

"I know you don't want to talk to me," he said, "but we have to talk about Sarah."

1. Should I tell Dennis about my meeting with the lawyer?
2. Should I tell him that my lawyer called him a creep and said he doesn't have a leg to stand on?
3. Should I tell him to expect a letter from my lawyer's office any day? Probably today?

"What is it?" she finally said.

"I'm just concerned for Sarah. This is such a crazy world. I know you don't think much of me as a father, but I have rights too. I want to protect her from things too."

"What are you getting at, Dennis?"

"She's getting older, Annie. We'll have to talk to her about AIDS soon. I mean the way things are going, there won't be any safe partners out there by the time she grows up – there aren't even any right now!"

"Dennis," interrupted Annabelle, "can we discuss this another time?"

"Haven't you been reading about it Annie? God – if we get divorced neither one of us will ever be able to have sex again! You just risk your life if you do that! At least we had good sex, Annie – you know that I'm safe—"

Annabelle held her breath. Was this a sign? A call from Dennis on just the topic she was worrying about.

1. Dennis is compulsively homophobic and although he smokes pot he hasn't shared a joint with anyone since reading the first story about herpes a long time ago.
2. I'm in love with Eddie who doesn't worry about anything. How do I know he doesn't have a wild sexual history? How do I know he didn't have a blood transfusion at a bad time?

3. *If this epidemic continues at its current rate, some experts predict that nearly half our country's population will be infected by the mid-1990s.*

"Dennis," she said, her heart pounding, "I don't want to talk about this – this is inappropriate. We haven't been lovers in ages – I don't want you! Stop it!"

"Please Annie! You know I just need time to get things together – you know how much I love you. I don't want to lose you! I worry about Sarah and this crazy world—"

Annabelle hung up. She waited a few moments, then started rereading a new chapter she'd written describing one of the MVI Access storage commands: "To store your file, press <CTRL>, then press…" *No.* "After you have completed the form, press <CTRL>, then…" *No.* She tapped her hands against the keyboard, saved her file, and stood up.

1. *Even if Eddie has* AIDS *I still love him. We could work around it.*
2. *But if he has* AIDS *we probably wouldn't have children.*
3. *We could still be lovers. We could find ways.*

For several minutes she stared across East Cambridge towards Charlestown, and then left for Eddie's office.

"Hello," he said, turning away from his monitor, his voice soft.

"I got your poem," she said.

"How'd you like it?" he asked, smiling broadly.

"What does it mean?" she asked, sitting in the swivel chair by his door.

He leant back and bellowed, "I want to make you pregnant!"

Annabelle glanced at his door, ajar, she cringed, her jaw agape: that was loud enough to be heard in other offices.

Does he say this to other women? Has he had numerous lovers?

She looked down at the industrial carpet. Finally Eddie whispered, "What's wrong?"

"I'm afraid."

"What are you afraid of?"

She clicked the door shut.

"AIDS," she whispered.

Eddie laughed and said, "Oh."

Annabelle shook her head, "I'm sorry, but it scares me. You read so much about it."

"Why are you worrying about that right now?" he asked. "Why now?"

"Well I've been worried about it for a while."

"But why are you bringing this up now? Because I sent you that poem?"

"Yes. And Dennis just called out of the blue and started talking about it. It scared me. I was worrying about it anyway and then he brought it up. It was a strange coincidence."

"Dennis really knows how to manipulate you, doesn't he," announced Eddie.

"Well it is a valid concern. I'm sorry."

"I don't have AIDS," said Eddie, "I've never been with a man. I've never used drugs or had a blood transfusion."

"But you could get it from a woman," she said.

Eddie continued smiling. He was staring out the window and nodding. "The only lovers I've ever had were Katie in college, my wife, then Jean and Fran after my divorce. Jean was a fifty-five-year-old physical therapist who had a great heart and a beautiful body for her age. She was just ending her thirty-year marriage. Fran was a forty-five-year-old psychiatrist yoga-health nut. They were all healthy."

Annabelle's mouth hung open even wider. "Your lovers were ten and twenty years older than you?"

"Older women are better. More mature. They've had time to form souls."

"I'm younger than you are."

"But you've got a great soul, not to mention a great spirit and an awesome body," he said, opening his wallet, handing her his blood donor card, turning it over in her palm. She looked at the list of dates on the back. He'd been giving blood every few months for the past three years.

"That's my most recent card," he said, "I've been giving blood since college. I'll need a new card pretty soon."

Annabelle stared at it.

"Does that help any?" he asked.

"What do you mean?" she said.

"You've never given blood?" he asked.

"No. I guess I ought to but I tend to be anaemic. And I had mono in junior high."

"Well," he explained, "every time you give blood they test you for all kinds of diseases, including AIDS. They even use experimental HIV tests so if you've got it they'll be the first to find it. It's really quite annoying, the questions they ask. When they first started asking, they wanted to know if I was gay or if I'd ever had sex with a man. Then they wanted to know if I'd ever been to Africa or Haiti or if I'd ever stuck my finger on a staple in a book store – stuff like that."

Annabelle handed him the card, "I guess that helps," she said, "I guess it helps."

"But you know," said Eddie, "in any relationship you take a risk. In the past I've gotten involved too quickly, like I did with Barbara and Jean and Fran. In college I was too young and I didn't know anything so that doesn't count, but later I should have waited. Because... when you make love too fast it tricks your body into a feeling of being in love and then sometimes you find that you're not really in love after all and you have to leave and the other person hates you for leaving because they thought you loved them."

Annabelle nodded.

"Does that make any sense?" asked Eddie.

"Yes," she whispered. "Do you still love me?"

Eddie laughed. "I'm crazy about you, you know that. But I don't think it's AIDS that you're worried about. I think you're afraid to get involved with anyone right now and that's OK. I'm scared too. I feel so much for you that it scares me. So I can wait to make love – we don't have to do it right away. We'll do it when you're ready; you're the master, you lead me, you tell me when—"

Bob Thomas, Eddie's boss, knocked on the glass office door.

"Ed, what's the scatter-graph status?" asked Bob, opening the door.

Annabelle stood up and started to leave.

"Don't leave on my account," said Bob. Annabelle paused.

"Want to see it?" said Eddie and they turned their heads towards Eddie's monitor while Annabelle slipped out the door.

1. *I've got to stop coming down to his office.*
2. *I've got to be more professional.*
3. AIDS *is probably not an issue here. Dennis is just trying to manipulate me. Still, it's good that Eddie and I talked about it.*
4. *I have to stop worrying all the time. That should be my number one priority.*

Arthur Ziminski was speaking, explaining. "Well the numbers were reserved by the chip as non-expressible values, don't you see? Their math library claimed that it could handle values between negative 420 million and positive eight billion. So we decided to use ten numbers reserved by the chip—"

"Oh please spare us the details, Arthur," interrupted Janette Fuller, making a rare appearance at the design meeting. "The point is, it blew up and we had a fourth-quarter first customer ship. Now we don't."

Arthur shook his head. "Don't say it," said Janette, glancing at her Rolex, leaving the room.

After she left, no one spoke for a minute. Her Opium scent lingered in the air.

Arthur sighed, heavily.

"Any other issues?" he said.

"I've got graph magnification working," said Eddie, enthusiastically.

"Anything else?" said Arthur.

"I'm wondering when we're going to see the doc," said Brian Anderson, turning towards Annabelle.

Annabelle looked at her day planner and said, "The outline I distributed lists the dates—" She stopped.

Bob Thomas was whispering in Eddie's ear and they were both stifling a laugh. Annabelle shuddered and continued, glaring at Eddie, "I'll distribute first review drafts on January 19th—"

"I don't think I got a copy of your outline," said Brian. "Do you have an extra copy?"

"Why were you laughing at me at the meeting?" said Annabelle, as she and Eddie walked towards East Cambridge at lunchtime.

"Oh that. It was just something Bob said."

"What did he say?" asked Annabelle.

"He said: 'She talks.'"

Annabelle stopped. "Why is that funny?"

"Bob didn't think you could talk. He's never heard you talk. You never say anything at meetings. You've developed a reputation for being very shy."

"I get my work done. Why is that a problem?"

"It's not a problem," said Eddie.

"Then why did he say that?" asked Annabelle, curt and defensive.

They had continued walking. "He has a crush on you," said Eddie.

"What?!"

"They all do. All the men at MVI want your body."

Annabelle was silent for several minutes.

"Where are we going?" she finally said.

"I'm getting you a present."

"What?"

"We're going to buy an answering machine for your apartment. You can set it to answer all your calls and you can pick up the phone or just let your caller leave a message. That way you'll never have to talk to anyone you don't want to talk to. Especially Dennis."

Annabelle let Eddie pick out the machine, but insisted on paying for it herself.

1. *Use the answering machine for all incoming calls.*
2. *Start speaking up in meetings.*
3. *Don't let anyone, even Eddie, run my life.*

7

Annabelle kept an ephemeris that listed the astrological position of planets and their aspects, and consulted it before making any important decisions. In early February, she realized that by the upcoming weekend all major aspects would be direct, an event that would last for only ten days and would not recur for another eight months.

"Dennis called and left a message on my machine," she told Eddie at lunchtime in her office. "He said he got the letter from my lawyer and he'd sign the 'fucking divorce papers' because he couldn't afford a lawyer." She shook her head.

Eddie nodded.

"So you won."

"That's what Dennis said. He said, 'You won.' I never wanted to have to do things this way." She paused, as if pondering her half-eaten bowl of cottage cheese. "Eddie, I need to tell you something. This weekend is significant. All major planetary influences will be direct for the first time in months."

Eddie stared at her, amused. "And… Why is that significant?"

"Those influences won't last long. It would be the best time to start new endeavours." She glanced out the window.

"Such as?"

"Well, if two people were to consummate a sexual relationship, this coming weekend would be the best time to do it. And if not then, they ought to wait until the fall."

Eddie put down his coffee cup. "Do you mean us?"

She nodded. "Well, timing is important. It would be the most auspicious time."

His laughter was like lightning, a sharp bolt of breath. He stopped when he saw she wasn't smiling.

"I'm sorry," he said, "I just wasn't expecting to make an appointment for it. I mean I thought it would be a little more spontaneous. But I'll take it when I can get it." He had lost her gaze.

"Oh sweetheart," he whispered. "You know I'll take it when I can…"

Sarah had been invited to spend the weekend with a friend, so Annabelle was free that evening. She and Eddie made plans to make love then.

To celebrate, Eddie took Annabelle to dinner at a Chinese restaurant in Cambridge.

Annabelle whispered, "I don't know if my diaphragm is still any good. It's been a long time since I used it."

Eddie smiled.

"I'll buy some condoms then," he said in his usual booming voice.

Annabelle looked at the other tables to see if anyone had heard him. "Shhhhh," she whispered, "if you get those then I should get some foam."

"No, you don't need foam."

"No, I keep reading that you need foam. It's very important."

"Well, it's up to you," he said, nibbling an egg roll.

All through dinner Annabelle pondered the insignificance of food on certain occasions. After dinner they walked down the street to a large pharmacy.

At the condom display, Eddie said, "Should I get ribbed or regular, lubricated or what?"

"Dennis never used them. I don't know," she whispered. "Get whatever makes you feel comfortable. I'm going to find the foam."

She was also thoroughly inexperienced at the procurement of foam, so she stood a while reading the labels, comparing prices, making sure the box she finally selected hadn't been tampered with.

When Eddie found her he held up a box of Trojans and grinned, announcing: "I'll get the jumbo economy pack."

She looked away, as though she didn't know him, and whispered, "I guess I'll get this kind of foam but could you pay for all this and I'll split the cost with you later? I'm just a little too embarrassed to wait in line to buy it."

Eddie took the foam from her hands and headed towards the cash register. Annabelle crept to a greeting-card display and pretended to read the assorted messages.

At last he came to her, cradling a brown paper bag. "We're all set," he said, opening the door.

They drove to Gardenia in silence.

Eddie surveyed the living room, pointing to the art prints hanging in scratched acrylic rectangles. "When we get married," he said, "I'm going to redo all of these. I'll give them some nice mats and real frames."

Annabelle silently sat on her twin bed.

She finally explained, "This would normally be the dining room but I needed it as a bedroom."

Eddie sat beside her and turned to kiss her clenched lips. She stood up and clasped her arms across her chest. He looked around.

"You have shrines everywhere," he said.

She started pacing along the edges of the woven rug in the middle of the room.

"I collect things," she said.

Eddie stared at her.

"I don't spend very much on my collections," she explained, "I get just about everything at yard sales or rummage sales. You'd be amazed at how many swans and Mona Lisa things you can find at yard sales, and owls and Cupids. Owls are sacred to Aphrodite. You can also find moon images and all that."

Eddie waved his right hand, beckoning her. "Sit with me."

Annabelle returned to the bed and sat by his side. He gently removed a small resin archaeological replica of the Venus of Willendorf from her sweaty hand.

"I love you," he said, "I want to make love to you. You said this would be the right time. What can I do to help you relax?"

"Would you like a beer?" she asked, jumping up.

Eddie nodded.

They drank several glasses of light Pilsner.

Silence sat between them.

After a while, Eddie kissed Annabelle's lips.

He unzipped her black dress, removed his shirt, and pressed his chest against hers. He sat up and stroked her small breasts.

"I love seeing you naked," he said, "I love you. I love you."

She touched his pants, felt his erection, and said, "Do you want to put on a condom now?"

"In a little while," he said.

"Well I think I should go use the foam," she said, jumping out of bed.

She grabbed the drugstore bag, pulled out the foam, and left for the bathroom. She spent several minutes washing the applicator and following the instructions. When she returned to bed, Eddie was lying back, staring at the ceiling.

"I'm ready," she said, waiting. Eddie kissed her mouth. She reached for his penis. It was limp.

"I lost it," he said, "I'm sorry."

She stroked him, trying to excite him. After several minutes of stroking he gently pushed away her hand.

"Nothing's happening," he said. "We can try later. I guess I couldn't wait for the foam."

"I'm sorry," she said.

He embraced her, kissing her. She felt moisture on her cheeks. She looked up at his wet eyes.

"I just wanted to please you," he said.

"I only wanted to make love because I thought you wanted to, I just wanted to please you!"

"Well, I'm sorry. I'm impotent."

Annabelle stared into his red eyes. "You're not impotent! I shouldn't have insisted on using the foam. I'm just terrified of getting pregnant right now. I mean Dennis hasn't even signed the papers yet so what would happen if I accidentally got pregnant?! It would be horrible!"

"Why?"

"Because I'd still be married to Dennis and pregnant with another man's baby! God! He'd use that against me and then I'd really be in trouble!"

"Annabelle, if you accidentally got pregnant it would be a beautiful blessing and we'd be happy as anything."

"Are you serious?"

"Stop being afraid of him."

"I think we were trying too hard," she said.

Eddie stroked her pink breasts, encircling each nipple.

Annabelle watched his massive fingers cover her chest. His enormous hands could break her neck with no effort at all. It was a strangely erotic feeling.

"It's like I cut my hair to give you the watch chain and you sold your watch to get me the hair combs," she said.

He leant on his elbow and smiled. "What?"

In the morning she felt something hard against her leg and reached down to discover Eddie's swollen penis. He was still sleeping. She quickly left for the bathroom, then returned to him and knelt by his side.

He opened his eyes. She began fondling him. "Good morning," she whispered.

He reached into the box of condoms beside the bed and rolled one on. She pulled his mouth to her lips, his chest to her breasts, spread her legs, and helped him inside. She squeezed. He pushed. She reached behind him, stroking the small of his back. A moment later he ejaculated.

"Thank you," he said, rolling on his side to avoid crushing her.

"You're welcome."

He sat and started dressing. He put on his turtleneck, stood up, and had a new erection.

"Hallelujah!" he shouted, watching it bob in the air. "I've been healed!"

He reached for Annabelle. "How can I please you?" he said. "Let me make you come. Teach me how."

"I'm fine," she said, "I just want some tea."

Eddie wandered around the apartment, touching her egg collection: painted eggs, wooden eggs, glass, hollow, alabaster, plastic.

Most of the pictures on the wall had swans in them: swans by themselves or with the moon or with the moon and irises or any combination. There was also a collection of Mona Lisa prints and everything had its own cheap acrylic frame.

He started studying her statue collection: wooden, glass, ceramic.

"It's like a museum here. You have so many shrines," he said, returning to the kitchen.

"You said that last night." She was pouring her second cup of tea. "Want some?"

For hours they watched cartoons on television.

They walked down Hesperus Avenue, to the playground by the ocean. Wind was blowing off the water; furious salty spray, harsh as February at sea. The sun was out but it wasn't warm. Annabelle kept looking around.

1. *Will Dennis or anyone he knows see us?*
2. *The lawyer said it was OK to be with Eddie so don't let fears of Dennis spoil this.*

The waves were high as elephants, wet mammoths jostling and frothing. She climbed the monkey bars and dangled, stretching her midriff. The swings had been taken down for the winter.

"Wait till you come up to my parents' farm this summer," said Eddie. "We've got a lake and cottages that only get rented out to the family. I can't wait to bring you up there. There are lots of kids for Sarah to play with."

Annabelle felt disconnected from the vacant children and tranquil scenes he described. She climbed the sliding board and sat at the top, staring at the lapping waves, the green tea water. It was another life, someone else's life.

On the way back to the apartment, Annabelle stopped at a convenience store to buy some sour cream while Eddie waited in the cold, his nose pressed against the plate glass, his breath steaming the window.

"I almost bought some orange toffee," she said, returning to him, carrying a small bag, "but I can get it for half the price in Gloucester."

Eddie sighed, "I missed you."

She smiled. "I didn't go anywhere!"

"I missed you," he repeated.

He watched while she cut onions and peppers for vegetable stew and mixed up a bowl of corn bread.

"Can I help you cook?" he asked.

"No," she said, humming, preheating the oven, her face flushed, pink.

"I'd like to help," he said.

"You can set the table," she said, handing him some unadorned stainless-steel flatware, simple brown ceramic plates, and plain green glasses.

"You never eat meat?" he asked while they ate.

"No. I don't believe in exploiting animals. Is that all right with you?"

"I love this food," he said. "Rabbit food. Makes me feel so light."

"This is heavier than what I usually cook."

"That's why you're so skinny."

"I'm not skinny! I'm fat," she said, cleaning her plate.

Eddie laughed and lifted her to her feet and to her bed while dirty dishes remained on the table and pans sat in the sink. "Could you be on top?" he whispered.

She gazed through the door at the kitchen while leaning against his chest. "I'd like to do the dishes," she said, "I don't like it when the kitchen's dirty."

"I want to clean your kitchen," he whispered, "I want to be intimate with your kitchen."

He removed her checkered flannel shirt. She studied his fingers and hands, speckled with dark hair. *Killer hands.*

"Oh, you're so beautiful," he sighed.

"I am?"

He kissed her until she pulled away. Eventually she guided him inside her and rode him like a cautious traveller with one eye on the road.

On Sunday morning Eddie washed the dishes, pots and pans, scrubbed the sink, and fixed the leaky kitchen faucet with his pocketknife.

He paused while working, and then turned to face Annabelle.

"But I don't understand why you're not a lesbian," he said.

She raised her eyebrows. "What do you mean?"

"I just thought that women who were sexually abused as children ended up hating men. I mean the character in your novel was abused that way so I assumed that you were. I don't understand it, that's all, it's just a preconceived notion of mine; I guess it's wrong."

He turned back to the sink and didn't speak.

"Well," said Annabelle slowly, whispering, "I do have some lesbian friends, Eddie, and none of them hate men. But regarding your concern, I guess I just separated it from sex."

He turned to face her, a blush spreading along his cheeks, towards his neck. "I'm sorry," he muttered, "I'm not sure why I said that. I guess I was a little afraid to make love to you. I was afraid of hurting you. I don't want to step on any landmines, you know?"

She nodded.

"What did you separate from sex?" he whispered finally, sitting beside her.

"The abuse… The rape…" She clasped her arms across her chest and pressed the back of her head against her chair as if to brace her body from the tremors of some invisible disaster. "Rape isn't really about sex at all. It's about domination and cruelty. I think he meant it as punishment. I have to keep telling myself that he simply had the instincts of a baboon… and it was his way of punishing me… controlling me…"

Eddie nodded. "Is it something you want to talk about?"

She shook her head while continuing to clench herself, to hold herself together. It always surprised her the way her body reacted whenever the issue came up.

"I mean," he said, "is it something you still need help with?"

She forced a smile. "Are you asking whether I need psychiatric help?" Her teeth chattered.

"No, I just wondered where you were with it. I just wanted to make sure I wouldn't step on any landmines. I don't want to do anything that might remind you of anything." He was looking at the floor.

"Eddie. Over the years I saw about… mmmm… one, two, three, four…" – she paused to consider – "…about four different therapists about it. They were all less than helpful. The first one was this horrible psychiatrist at my college, during my breakdown. When I finally told him about it he just rolled his eyes. He mocked me, actually. I guess it seemed too incredible to believe. So it was just insult to injury." She spoke slowly, her hands still clasped together. "So... I ended up finding support through a group called Take Back the Night. And... I met other survivors through them. What I finally learnt, after years... after years of struggling with the grief... What I finally learnt is that the only people who can possibly understand are the ones who've lived through it. And I learnt that in order to heal you have to grieve."

Eddie looked at her again and she forced another smile, attempting to hide her embarrassment.

"It's about grief, that's all. It's different from depression. It's just grief. And I feel all this grief for a good reason. So... I try to respect that." She drew a deep breath. "But sometimes memories come up all of a sudden and I just want to spend the day crying but I can't because of Sarah. But, you know, Sarah saved my life. My life would have had no meaning if she hadn't been born."

"I wish I could help," whispered Eddie. "It makes me feel helpless."

Annabelle sighed. "Well. I've found ways to heal. Natural remedies. Homeopathy. I buy them at the health-food store."

Eddie's brow wrinkled.

"Um," she continued, "homeopathy really does help. It helps the residual physical and emotional trauma. I've learnt to work through a lot of stuff by using things like remedies and good nutrition... I eat a lot of cottage cheese and black walnuts because they have high levels of tryptophan, which is an amino acid that helps the brain recover from trauma..." Annabelle paused and laughed again in embarrassment. "It's like I'm giving you the technical writer's guide to psycho-sexual healing..."

"That's OK," said Eddie, smiling sympathetically.

She paused again, reflecting, her speech halting and stiff. "But really, the hardest thing for me is getting past other people's judgements and preconceived notions; like, you know, all the Hollywood stereotypes. There's this pervasive attitude that if you've survived this kind of stuff then you just can't become a normal human being. And so, consequently, if you admit to having been abused, then people might think you've got multiple personalities, which I don't, or they might think you go around abusing other people, which I don't, or they might think that you subconsciously wish to be abused." She stopped.

"Which you don't?" he whispered.

She shook her head and her eyes glistened.

"That's the hardest thing," she said. "It's hard to say that I don't have that subconscious wish. Because I did marry Dennis, right?"

The room was silent for a long minute.

Finally she continued. "And that is precisely what Dennis lords over me, you know? He knows my secrets and he tries to use them against me as if they were in some way my fault. But our society is like that generally, Eddie. It's a society that blames the victims. Even talking about it now, just talking about it casually makes me feel like a victim again, somehow." She stared straight ahead, motionless.

"Annabelle, I just never want to hurt you," said Eddie finally, "but I just want to know how to avoid accidentally hurting you."

Her face stiffened from forcing another smile. She fingered the kitchen tabletop. "I know you would never try to hurt me…"

Finally she took another deep breath, "But if you want to avoid any kind of strange landmine, just promise you'll never write on me. Like not even if you're just kidding around. OK?" She abruptly stood up to turn the gas on under the teakettle.

"What?" Eddie frowned.

"Just promise that you'll never write on me. He used to mark me up."

"Exactly what do you mean?" Eddie's frown deepened.

"Well… he would write on different parts of me for different reasons." She held up the index and middle fingers on her right hand. "When I was three or four, I was still sucking these two fingers until one day he said that if I didn't stop doing that a horrible monster would come in my room that night and paint my nose red and my nose would be red for ever. But I kept sucking my fingers anyway. So the next morning when I looked in the mirror I saw that my nose was completely red – just totally, flaming, bright red." She shook her head and stared into space, "God, I still remember that and it's still so vivid. I couldn't wash it off, either. I really panicked. I was absolutely terrified. He had painted my nose with red nail polish while I was asleep. And when he finally admitted what he'd done, he just kept laughing about it. I never sucked my fingers again."

"That's horrible," whispered Eddie.

"That's nothing," she whispered, with a long, trembling sigh. "He used to write on my private parts with a magic marker as punishment and I just couldn't wash it off. In some ways the memory of that is as bad as the really violent stuff… So, do you see why I felt compelled to become a writer? You know – the pen is mightier than the sword. I suppose I've learnt to fight fire with fire."

She paused again. "My mother was helpless. A few years ago, when she was living with me, I asked her about it. She said that the first time I was hospitalized for haemorrhaging, when I was two and a half, the doctors had told her they thought I'd been abused. She said she asked my father about it and he told her, 'She has a level head. She'll survive.' Apparently the nurses wouldn't let her in the room while I was being examined and then came out in the hall and one was crying, saying, 'I can't believe someone could have done that to that baby.'"

"Why didn't the doctors do anything about it?" said Eddie, shaking his head.

"I don't know. That's a good question. My father was very, very powerful and very, very wealthy… Well, he still *is* wealthy, I suppose, but I haven't had any contact with him since I was nineteen… when he divorced my mom. He was systematic about that. Before he left, he lied to her about his assets, which he had hidden – then he sold our house and bought a cheap condominium for her to live in; *he* never lived there. So that's all she got out of the divorce, just that condominium, where she continued to deteriorate. And the reason I know he hid his assets is that a few years ago, I sorted through my mom's papers and found a letter from her lawyer, saying he'd received a letter from my father's *second* ex-wife! Apparently my father had left my mom for another woman, and when he divorced *her*, she tried to get revenge by writing to my mom's lawyer about my father's hidden assets! And of course, my mom, being who she was, never did anything about it; she obviously never responded to it. So once again, my father got away with everything."

Annabelle got up, then quickly sat down, and continued speaking, as if unable to stop: "But when I was growing up, he was chief engineer of ICA – they were Fortune 500 then – that kind of job title would equate to CTO these days…" Tears had welled in her eyes. "Anyway… When my mother told me that he was the reason I'd been hospitalized for haemorrhaging – both times – I asked her if she ever told anyone. And she said she did tell a priest in confession."

Eddie's frown continued to deepen, contorting his handsome features. "Why didn't the priest do anything?"

Another long dark sigh escaped from Annabelle, like the song of a small angry bird. "She said the priest told her she shouldn't have anything to do with him. But that's about it. She said she couldn't leave him because she needed him to support us."

Eddie's face reddened. "Are you saying a priest actually knew that your father had done these things but didn't tell anyone?"

Annabelle nodded, spilling tears, turning her head away from Eddie so that he couldn't see.

Eddie shook his head. "I don't see how that could happen," he whispered.

Annabelle focused on the stovetop and teapot, and forced herself to regain composure. "You don't know much about the Church of Rome," she whispered. "It has a long history of perpetrating abuse. Look at the Inquisition – the holocaust of women. So they were perfectly capable of overlooking someone else's infractions – especially someone with a lot of cash to donate each Sunday."

Eddie stared at her. "You think a priest really knew this had happened?" He was shocked.

"Sure," insisted Annabelle, trying to appear matter-of-fact. "You were raised as a Unitarian, Eddie. So it would seem that you just don't know about it. But I knew some very unhappy altar boys when I was little, and I can only imagine why they were so miserable. There are some wicked priests out there. It's so sad. It's a tragedy… when the people who are supposed to be protecting little children – like fathers and priests – go around destroying them."

"I wasn't that religious," said Eddie, "but I never heard of that kind of stuff happening at any UU Church. How can the Catholic Church go on operating if that stuff is going on?"

"Well, it's just sad," mused Annabelle finally, attempting to appear totally rational. "I actually do think Jesus was enlightened and there are lots of really good Catholic people out there who want to do the right thing – you know, they want to follow Jesus's vision... of peace. And in South America a lot of the priests there are living saints... but good and bad exist together. Obviously, though, if the Catholic Church recognized the rights of women – if they did some affirmative action and allowed only women to be pope for the next two millennia – then maybe they could begin to get kosher. Someday the Church will be called to account, but it probably won't be in our lifetime."

"It's just so hard to believe," whispered Eddie. Then he paused, and said, "I guess that just makes it harder for you."

"His wealth made him above reproach; I think that was part of it. Back then ICA was one of the biggest electronics companies in the country. One of the biggest companies in the world, really. I grew up in a... mansion... this monstrously large house across the street from a golf course."

She sighed once again, in tired resignation. "I know that by today's standards nobody would ever imagine that a man could get away with all that. But excuses must have been made and it must have been easier for the doctors to accept the excuses than to deal with the obvious. It was the early Sixties and things like that weren't supposed to happen and if they did then people were careful not to notice them. The other part of it is that... a lot of people were really afraid of him. In high school, kids told me rumours; they would hear their parents talk about him and then they told me what they heard. I rarely saw him by then, actually. He was basically living at his office. I didn't know what to think, except that the rumours were probably true... He collected lots of swastikas... and guns... that sort of thing." She shuddered. "I used to hide the bullets whenever I'd find them in his closet drawers."

"What else did your mother have to say?" Eddie was frowning; a livid blush spread across his cheeks.

"She was fighting dementia by the time we discussed it. But it was strange how she was so lucid regarding all the details. Then she started crying and I started crying and she hugged me and said, 'Just pray to forget about it. That's what I did.' She did forget; that's for sure. She not only forgot about my father, she also lost all ability to remember anything. So even though I'd really, really like to, I just refuse to forget it… you know? But I don't dwell on it, either. That wouldn't get me anywhere."

"Didn't you say you had a sister? Where does she fit in with all this?"

"Lenore." Annabelle sighed. "She's nine years older than me. I used to try to talk to her about it but she always insisted she couldn't remember her childhood. She ran off to get married when I was ten, and became an ultra-conservative Republican Christian fundamentalist… I can't talk to her about anything now. We don't even send each other Christmas cards any more."

The teakettle whistled and Annabelle prepared two cups.

"I'm sorry," whispered Eddie.

She poured the boiling water. "But getting back to your original question… I really don't hate men, Eddie. I had a wonderful math teacher named Mr Zuchowski in seventh grade and he really took the time to be nice to me. He got the other kids to stop picking on me and he taught me to love algebra. In high school I had a sweet English teacher named Mr Jackson who used to play chess with me at lunchtime. He was the dad I would have picked. And in college there was one professor, Dr Allen, who tried his best to listen when I was totally incoherent. They are all my real fathers."

She brought the teacups to the table.

Suddenly Annabelle noticed tears streaming from Eddie's eyes. She took his hand.

1. *This is quite amazing.*
2. *He really does seem to care.*
3. *He really does seem to care.*

"You exceeded my wildest expectations," he whispered.

Annabelle shook her head. "How did I do that?"

"You're just so gentle. You were so gentle with me," he murmured, looking away.

8

Annabelle stared at her reflection in Brian Anderson's round reading glasses. Brian had been sitting at his desk for ten minutes, shaking his head and waving around her chapter on averaging methods while she stood next to him, waiting for his overdue response.

He said, "The problem with this is..."

He paused and shook his head again.

She looked away, noticing that his left shoe was untied.

"The problem with this is... I just don't know if you've got it right. Did you try out these formulas?"

"On what?" she asked.

"On data."

"Such as?"

"Anything. Just on anything."

"Well, sure, I tried them out," said Annabelle, sighing, "I imported some values for a series of companies and applied the formulas."

"Where did you get the formulas?"

"From Frank."

"Didn't Frank review this?"

"Yes, but he said I should get your feedback."

"Why does he want my feedback?"

Annabelle smiled. "He didn't say."

Brian frowned, exasperated.

"Just leave the fucking thing with me," he said, "and I'll look it over later."

Annabelle watched while he placed the chapter on a pile of papers and turned his attention to his monitor.

To: EWRIGHT
From: ABonney

Dennis called and left a message on my machine asking if Sarah can stay with him this weekend. He said his mother is having a big party for one of his brothers and he wants to take Sarah to it. He hasn't been acting out lately, you know? No weird phone calls or anything. He hasn't signed the papers yet but at least he's behaving better. So I called and told him it was OK and that I would drop Sarah off at his mother's house early on Saturday afternoon. That way I won't have to see him at all. So I'm free from 2 p.m. Saturday until Sunday evening! (He'll drop her off on Sunday. I won't let him in.) Do you have any ideas?

On a work-related note, can you explain the mystery surrounding the MVI averaging methods? Frank Marks gave me a set of formulas to document but said I should be sure to have Brian Anderson sign off on them before publishing them. So when I asked for Brian's feedback, he was annoyed about it and has yet to review it. What's going on?

To: ABonney
From: EWRIGHT

Let's go on the trip to Brattleboro we've been talking about! There's an excellent health-food restaurant there and we'll get a motel room and have fun!

Re: work note: Yes. The averaging method calculations were written by Bradford Pickett, an eccentric consultant who no longer works for MVI. (Rumour has it he's now working as a stripper at the Big Violet Banana on Route 16.) Anyway, all of MVI's functions rest on those averaging formulas, but no one, with the possible exception of Bradford, understands them. Nor can anyone verify said accuracy. Let it go. Just pass the ball, stay in line, and keep the peace.

Love,
Eddie

They arrived in southern Vermont at twilight and parked in downtown Brattleboro behind the library.

"These Victorian houses are gorgeous," murmured Annabelle as they walked down a hill towards the main street.

"When we buy a house it will be a small Victorian, OK?" asked Eddie.

They turned the corner by a fabric store at the base of the hill.

"In my first marriage we bought a great big old house that needed so many repairs even I couldn't keep up with it," he explained, waiting for a response.

"Dennis is never going to sign those papers," sighed Annabelle, "we'll never be able to buy a house or anything else."

"Dennis is doing that to control you," said Eddie. "Maybe you need to contest it – if it costs more I'll help you pay—"

"But he keeps promising to sign them."

They arrived at the door of the Shared Earth restaurant and were seated in the middle of a large room. Annabelle clutched her arms across her chest and looked around.

"What's wrong?" said Eddie.

"Well, we're sitting in the middle of the room."

"So?"

"Nothing."

They were both silent. A woman with multiple earrings and tattoos came to take their order.

"I'll have the spinach pizza and some seltzer water," said Annabelle.

"I'll have that too," said Eddie. "And do you serve wine here?"

"Just organic wine," said the waitress. "Would you like to try the Green Mountain Blush?"

Eddie nodded and soon the bottle arrived; he filled two large glasses.

"Oh, this is nice and sweet," said Annabelle, taking several long sips. She finished it while they waited for their food and Eddie refilled her glass.

"Look at the menu special," she said, pointing to a blackboard by the kitchen, "there's a dish called the golden bowl. The golden bowl is broken and the spirit has flown for ever. Oh that bell sure does toll…" she slowly whispered.

"What's that?" said Eddie.

She smiled, "I'm thinking about a Poe poem. It's about death."

"What made you think of it?" he asked.

She started to laugh. "The dinner special. Just reminded me of that, that's all. You ever heard 'Annabelle Lee'?"

"No," said Eddie as the food arrived.

Annabelle slowly cut her pizza with her knife then sat for a long while with a large mound of spinach and cheese dangling from her fork.

She finally said, "Well, it's about this maiden and her lover. She lived by the sea. It's about death too."

Eddie stared at her. "Are you OK?"

"It's about time. It's about death," she softly sang.

Eddie smiled. "You liked the wine?"

"Oh yes," she said, taking another long sip. "I was named after her you know."

"Who?" he asked, between bites.

"'Annabelle Lee'. The poem."

"Oh." He nodded.

"Poe was a genius you know. He developed the theory of the collective unconscious before Jung did, in his little short story 'Shadow – A Parable'. He described the split personality before Freud did in his short story 'William Wilson'. He predicted computers in his essay 'Maelzel's Chess Player'. He developed the modern detective story before Arthur Conan Doyle did. He even described the Big Bang theory in 'Eureka', sort of. He was really something. You know what his friends called him?"

"No."

"Eddie!" she exclaimed, laughing uncontrollably, clutching her arms, trying not to choke. She looked at the people sitting to her right and hoped they weren't looking back. They weren't.

"Too bad he had such a hard life," said Annabelle, seriously, suddenly.

Eddie leant back in his chair, smiling. "He had a hard life? I don't know much about him."

"Oh it was terrible," she sighed. "His mother died when he was three. He was there in the house when she died, he may have actually seen her die... Then he was taken away with these other people and his whole life just changed, as though he'd never had a mother. Can you imagine that? That alone… And there was so much else…" Her eyes welled with tears that dripped heavily on the plate. She looked up at Eddie.

"I'm sorry," said Eddie, still smiling.

"Yes," she said. "It makes me very sad."

She finished only half her pizza.

While walking back to the car, Annabelle stumbled, then French kissed Eddie at a stoplight. He picked her up and carried her for half a block, ignoring the confused stares from the people they passed.

They slowly drove along Route 30, looking for a motel in town, ending up at the Green Mountaineer Motor Lodge. Annabelle waited in the car while Eddie checked in.

In the room, Annabelle unpacked jasmine incense, a red candle, and two purple balloons.

While Eddie was in the bathroom she enthusiastically blew up the balloons and tossed them at him as soon as he appeared.

"I've never been in a motel room with a woman before," he said, plopping on the bed, batting a balloon back to her.

"Not even with Barbara?" she asked.

"No, the only time I've ever stayed in a motel was with my parents on a trip we took to the Grand Canyon. When I was a teenager."

"Dennis and I went on a weekend hotel special once but he left me alone in the room while he went out to play hockey. He was on a team then."

"He left you alone in a hotel so he could play hockey?!" exclaimed Eddie.

"Well I had paid for the room and he was on a team," she said.

She had been attempting to light the candle she'd unpacked. Her hands were slow and unsteady. Finally she was successful. Then she used the long candle flame to light a stick of incense.

"That blush made your face red," said Eddie.

"It made me blush," she giggled, pouncing on him, poking his massive bare ribs.

"Stop it! They're going to throw us out of here!"

She stood up and he pulled her down again, kissing her, laughing. She turned around.

"I want to use this position," she said.

"What position?" he asked.

She rubbed his hand against her.

"From behind," she said.

"What do you mean?"

She reached behind her back, found his erection and guided it inside her, pushing against him.

"You're drunk," he whispered.

She kept pushing. He pushed back.

"Wait, I need a condom," he said, pulling out.

She stood up and leant over the bed.

"Let's stand up," she said.

She positioned him behind her and he entered her again. She stretched her legs, lifted her back, her face on the mattress, her hips high around him. He came fast, stopped, and said nothing.

She turned to face him.

"When did you learn how to do that?" he said, laughing, out of breath.

"I made it up," she whispered.

"You're a wild woman when you're drunk."

"I'm sorry," she whispered.

"Oh sweetie." He paused.

"You never made love in that position before?" she asked.

"No," he said, shaking his head.

"Did you like it?" she asked.

"I don't know. Yes. But I couldn't see your face."

"I liked it because you came in so deep. I had an orgasm all through my spine."

Eddie nodded, murmuring, "Shakti. Kundalini. You never did this before?"

Annabelle paused. "Well I did. Dennis did it that way one night out of the blue a long time ago. Sarah was just a baby then. Well, she was about three. One night he woke me up and did it. It was the first time I ever enjoyed intercourse."

"Well at least you enjoyed it with him sometimes."

"I got pregnant that time," she whispered, her voice fading.

A truck engine hummed in the parking lot. The red candle burned. The short stick of incense was reaching its end, a tiny hot dot straddling the air in a molded glass ashtray.

"What happened to the baby?" Eddie finally asked.

Annabelle tugged at the oak veneer nightstand drawer and pulled out the motel Bible.

"Listen to this," she said, opening to the Song of Solomon. "'I sleep, but my heart waketh: it is the voice of my beloved that knocketh, saying, Open to me, my sister, my love, my dove, my undefiled: for my head is filled with dew and my locks with the drops of the night.' Now that's pure erotica and I don't know why the Church refuses to acknowledge that."

Eddie was silent. Annabelle looked up from the book.

"After I told him I was pregnant he said it was over, you know, that he couldn't handle it. So he left for a few weeks. Then later I left him and we kept leaving each other for years afterwards. Before he came back I had a miscarriage. I guess that's why he came back. Then I realized I would never have another baby."

She placed the Bible back in the drawer. Eddie pulled her onto his lap.

"We'll have a baby," he whispered.

"Since then I've felt like I've got a baby ghost inside me. Some parts of me are just dead," she said, closing her lips. "My head is just spinning."

"Let me tuck you in," he whispered.

"How's your head?" asked Eddie in the morning.

Annabelle lay still, breathing traces of the previous evening's incense in morning motel air.

"There was a diesel truck parked outside the window all night, running its engine," said Eddie.

"I didn't hear it," said Annabelle.

"Thank you for teaching me the new position."

"I'm sorry I drank so much," she said, "I hadn't realized how much wine I had. Wine goes to my head very quickly."

"Can we try the new position again?" he asked.

She nodded.

This time she was shy.

He came hard, and then waited a moment, his penis still inside her.

"Uh oh," he murmured.

"What?" she said, starting to turn around.

"Don't move," he said, placing his hand closer to his penis, rustling around.

"What are you doing?" she asked.

"The condom broke. I'm trying to retrieve what's left of it."

"What?!" said Annabelle, counting the number of days since the beginning of her last period and squirming like a wild bird beneath him. "It's been twelve days since my last period, Eddie! I might have just gotten pregnant! Oh Jesus Eddie! Dennis hasn't signed the papers!"

"Calm down," said Eddie, fishing the last piece of latex from her labia.

"OK," he finally said. She turned around, sat down, limbs shaking.

"I'm pregnant," she repeated.

"You probably won't get pregnant. It doesn't usually happen this easily. Lots of couples try for years, you know."

"You usually ovulate about twelve days after the beginning of your last period and it's been twelve days! This is unbelievable! This is the twelfth day! I must be! I get pregnant so easily! I must be pregnant now. I don't know what to do!"

Eddie laughed, "It would be wonderful! We'll have a cute little happy baby."

"How can you say that? I'm not even divorced yet!"

"Well it might speed up the divorce," mused Eddie. "If you give birth to another man's baby he'll probably get the idea that the marriage is unsalvageable."

Annabelle shook her head. "Did you ever read *Anna Karenina*?"

"No," he said, "but I guess I should have. Could you give me a reading list?" He had started making the bed.

"You don't need to make the bed, this is a motel; the housekeeping staff will come in and take all the sheets and blankets off and wash them." She had become irritable and snappy. "You don't need to be sarcastic either."

"I love you," whispered Eddie, packing the candles.

He insisted on bringing the balloons with them. He stuck one under his sweatshirt and waddled around while packing the car. Annabelle didn't laugh. The bright balloons bopped up and down on their silent drive back to Gardenia.

"I'd like to come and meet Sarah," said Eddie, finally.

"If I'm pregnant then Dennis can say I'm morally corrupted."

"Oh he's a paragon of virtue himself. You'll be divorced before you start to show so it's really not a problem."

"Don't you think I'd have a hard time explaining it to Sarah?"

"Oh she'd be thrilled. She'd love to have a little baby to play with. Kids don't think about months and stuff. She'd just be happy to live in a real family for once."

"So you think I'm pregnant?"

"I suppose that you could be. I'm not sure what the mathematical odds are, but yeah, it's possible."

A late winter snow had started with flakes heavy as crocheted wool.

"What should I do?" whispered Annabelle.

"Relax," he said calmly. "Call your lawyer tomorrow and ask her what to do."

"Tell her I'm pregnant?!"

"No, tell her that Dennis keeps stalling and see if she can expedite the process."

The telephone rang. Eddie had left her apartment ten minutes earlier and Annabelle was sitting in silence.

"Hello," she said, not letting the answering machine take the call because she was waiting for Dennis to drop off Sarah and it might be Sarah calling.

"Where were you?" Sarah shouted, instead of "Hello".

"Hi Sarah, what do you mean? Are you OK?"

"I called you last night, I called you this morning," moaned Sarah. "You have to come and get me. Where were you?"

Annabelle felt her skin begin to crawl.

"What's wrong? Where are you?"

"I'm at Grandmom's. Just come and get me, OK?"

Annabelle sped to Dennis's mother's house. As soon as she parked, Dennis's sister Ellen led Sarah to the car.

Annabelle rolled down her window. "Hi, what's wrong?"

"Hi," said Ellen. "We didn't think Dennis should drive her home. Bye Sarah, we'll see you soon, OK?"

Sarah nodded and got in the car. Ellen waved and went back in the house.

Annabelle drove slowly.

"Something's wrong with Daddy," Sarah finally said.

"Really?" said Annabelle, negotiating her way around the Bell Circle rotary. The snow had turned to intermittent rain and big spots of wet drops splashed hard on the roof.

"What happened?" asked Annabelle.

"Well Grandmom had a birthday party for Uncle Gary but all during the party Daddy just kept walking around and around in circles in the living room, talking to himself. It was really strange. Everybody went home because they were upset about how Daddy was acting. Is Daddy crazy?"

Annabelle had barely enough strength to keep her foot on the accelerator. Other cars kept passing them.

"Well, I don't know."

"He doesn't want to get divorced," said Sarah, "but I don't know why. He doesn't love you."

Annabelle almost stopped the car.

"He doesn't love me either," continued Sarah, "Before the party he kept telling me that you're a bad mother and you don't love me. If he loved me he wouldn't say bad things about you."

Sarah was crying. Annabelle squeezed her hand, struggling to keep her left hand steady on the steering wheel.

"Your father has a hard time when things don't go his way," said Annabelle.

"Everybody does, Mom," snapped Sarah, "but Daddy's just a big baby."

Sarah bounced around the living room floor. Annabelle was sitting with her. They'd just eaten canned vegetable soup for dinner.

"You never watch TV, Mom!" said Sarah, smiling, repeatedly glancing over her shoulder at Annabelle.

They watched a show where people sent in videotapes of candid experiences. A bride spilling wine on her dress. A toddler singing the national anthem. Annabelle imagined a video of Dennis the previous evening, delirious at a party, talking to himself, his loved ones backing away, making excuses to leave, then a video of herself and Eddie, the condom breaking, the irony of life.

Shortly after Sarah fell asleep, the telephone rang. Annabelle paused, letting the answering machine pick up the call.

"Hello," said the voice, "this is Derek. I'd like to talk to you. My number is—"

Dennis's older brother. Annabelle picked up the receiver.

"Hello?" she said.

"Annie," said Derek, "how are you?"

"What's up?" she said, struggling to maintain her composure.

"Has anyone told you what happened this weekend?"

"Well Sarah said that Dennis was talking to himself during Gary's party."

"Yeah, quite a show. Our mother is pretty upset about it."

Annabelle was silent.

"Did you know that our mother has cancer?" asked Derek.

"No," said Annabelle, stunned by his words. She could feel a fever rising from her stomach.

"She didn't want everyone to know. She refuses to tell Dennis and won't let anyone else tell him either. She figures that he has so many problems as it is. She's very upset about your divorce."

"I'm sorry about your mom."

"It's pretty hard for her to see Dennis this way. She has lung cancer and doesn't have much time left. She's been in a lot of pain."

Annabelle shook her head.

"You see Annie, the idea is this. We just need to keep everything happy and calm for her, do you understand? We had the party for Gary as an excuse to get the whole family together. It's pretty clear to everyone that Dennis is in desperate need of psychiatric help, don't you think so?"

1. *Why is he calling?*
2. *What is he getting at?*

"Derek, I'm sorry," whispered Annabelle, "but I can't focus on Dennis's problems right now. We are in the process of a divorce."

"Our mother has cancer! She is going to die!"

"I'm sorry."

"Look, I have an idea. Dennis doesn't want the divorce and he keeps saying that he'll do anything to get you back. If you would be willing to reconcile he might get himself to a mental hospital. He's not in any condition to agree to a divorce. His mind isn't sound."

"Derek," she said, her voice rising, "this is just another one of his attempts to manipulate me!"

"This isn't about you, Annabelle! And I'm not suggesting that you never get divorced. I just want you to tell him that you're willing to consider reconciliation so that he'll see a psychiatrist. Once he gets some treatment and things calm down, then you can continue the divorce process."

Evaluation of Derek's Idea:

1. *It would be extremely difficult to divorce someone in a mental hospital.*
2. *I've already paid hundreds of dollars of Dennis's debts for parking tickets and defaulted loans and all manners of things.*
3. *This would delay the divorce by months or longer.*

She imagined her belly growing. Her baby born. A speeding train. Russian swans.

"No," she said, finally.

"Then I'll get a lawyer for him, and we'll have ourselves a good fight," hissed Derek.

"OK," whispered Annabelle.

Derek hung up.

Annabelle stood, needing to urinate. She went to the bathroom and waited and waited. Finally a stream began while she bit her hand. She returned to the kitchen and called Eddie.

"Eddie, Dennis was acting out this weekend and now his family is convinced he's crazy. His brother called and told me their mother is dying of cancer and they want me to reconcile with him so that he'll see a psychiatrist. And I'm probably pregnant. I told his brother I wouldn't so he threatened to get a lawyer for Dennis and force me to stop the divorce!"

"Is this a soap opera or what?" chuckled Eddie.

"I'm serious!" said Annabelle, beginning to cry. "They're not going to let me divorce him!"

Eddie whistled and said, "Sounds like bullying runs in the family."

"There's no hope," sobbed Annabelle.

"There is hope," laughed Eddie. "Nobody can be forced to stay married to someone! This is a free country!"

"I feel terrible about his mother," murmured Annabelle.

"I hear you. But it's not your problem."

"You say it's not, they say it is."

"It's not. It sounds like Dennis has an elaborate network of people who have always been codependent to his immature behaviour. It's time to end all of that."

"What should I do?" she asked, slouching against the chair.

"Call your lawyer tomorrow morning and tell her what Dennis's brother suggested. She'll know what to do."

They both paused for a long time.

"You need to get some sleep," said Eddie.

"I can't."

"OK, bring the phone over to your bed and lie down while you're talking to me."

She did.

"OK," he said, "are you lying down?"

"Yes."

"Good. I'm going to tell you a bedtime story."

Annabelle smiled in spite of herself.

"Get comfortable. Did you ever hear the story of the three sillies?"

"No."

"Are you comfortable yet? Are you still lying down?"

"Yes," she said.

"OK," he began. "Once upon a time there was a man who was dating this woman and he was over at her parents' house having a meal and they ran out of wine and they told the daughter to go downstairs to get some more wine and so she did."

The story continued for twenty minutes, Eddie's melodious voice becoming progressively softer until he whispered, "And so the man returned to the house and married the daughter and they lived happily ever after. Are you sleepy now?"

She was asleep.

"Good night," he sighed.

In the morning Annabelle called her lawyer, Eileen O'Malley, and described the situation with Dennis.

"Well of all the nerve!" exclaimed Eileen. "His brother is harassing you!"

"What should I do?"

"I think he's just trying to get his family to pity him. I think you should meet with him and carefully explain to him that you are proceeding with the divorce. You could read him some of the affidavit you wrote – explain that if he does contest it you'll present all the instances of abuse you documented. I really think he'll concede. But if he doesn't, we'll go ahead and file on the grounds of cruel and abusive treatment."

"What if his brother gets a lawyer for him?"

"That would be good, he should have a lawyer. Maybe then he'll take this whole thing seriously."

"So you think I should meet with him?"

"Yes, but for your sake do it in a public place so he doesn't attempt to harm you. I don't trust this guy."

"I feel terrible about his mother," said Annabelle.

"I'm sure you do. That's too bad but it's not your problem."

Annabelle called Dennis and arranged to meet him at noon at the doughnut shop around the corner from his mother's house.

Dennis was already sitting at a booth, sipping a cup of coffee when she arrived.

"I've missed you so much," he said before she sat down. He was smiling his little boy smile, the one that had always melted her and beckoned her back. He reserved it for special occasions, such as this.

She ordered a cup of tea.

"Your brother Derek called me the other night," she said.

Dennis raised his eyebrows.

"Did you know that your mother is dying?" she asked.

He squinted at her.

"What are you talking about?" he said.

"Your mother told your brothers and sisters not to tell you that. She has lung cancer."

"What are you talking about? Derek called you? Are you telling me that my brother Derek called you?"

"He told me a lot. He told me how you were behaving at Gary's birthday party. Did you know they were having the party to try to get your family together before your mother dies?"

"I don't believe this," said Dennis, shaking his head.

"Did you know that you've been behaving like a spoiled brat?" she asked.

Dennis nodded. "I just want to get back together, Annie. I'll do anything you ask."

"First, don't call me Annie. Do you want to know what else Derek told me?"

"I guess you're going to tell me."

Annabelle spoke very slowly, carefully enunciating each consonant: "Your family wants to admit you to a mental hospital. They think you need intense psychiatric help. Derek called to ask me to pretend to reconcile with you so that you would seek help. He wanted me to tell you that I would reconcile with you as long as you checked into a mental hospital. How do you like that?"

"This is crazy," said Dennis, nervously looking around the doughnut shop. "I don't believe this."

"They're doing this for your mother, Dennis. They want her last days to be happy and peaceful, not filled with the problems of a codependent son."

"What did you tell Derek?"

"What do you think? I told him no."

"Annabelle, are you sure? Are you sure you won't reconsider? Don't you have any love for me any more?" His little-boy face was pathetic.

Annabelle shook her head.

"I'm sorry," she said, "I have absolutely no love left for you."

"None at all?"

"Nope. None at all."

"Is there someone else?"

"That's none of your business."

"There's someone else."

"That's none of your business."

Dennis sighed. "All right," he said, "I'll sign the papers. I guess there's no use fighting any more."

"You've been saying you'll sign the papers for six months now."

"I really will this time."

"They need to be notarized," she said.

"OK."

She pulled a copy of the divorce agreement out of her briefcase.

"There's a notary public in this plaza." She pointed out the window. "See that building there? They have a notary public. You can walk over and sign it right now."

"You've planned all this."

"That's why I wanted to meet here. I checked the notary listing and there's a Mrs Paulson who does administrative work there. I called and asked if she would be there today and she said she's not leaving the office until five. So she's there right now and you can just go over and sign it."

"You've set this all up," he said, scowling. "I'll sign it but I'm not going over there."

"If you don't sign it right now, Dennis, I'll file on the grounds of cruel and abusive treatment and I'll do that this afternoon."

Dennis stared at her.

"You really do want a divorce, don't you," he said.

Annabelle's stomach churned. She thought of the baby inside her. "I am infuriated!" she shouted.

Dennis looked around the doughnut shop and rested his chin in the palm of his left hand.

"You set this all up," he repeated.

"I've always taken care of everything for you," she seethed. "Why should our divorce be any different?"

Dennis stood up. "OK, I'm going. Mrs Paulson, right there?" he said, pointing to the realty building.

"It costs five dollars. Do you have five dollars?"

Dennis nodded.

"I'll wait here for you," she said.

"OK," he said, "anything for you. Anything you want."

She turned around and watched through the plate glass as Dennis meandered towards the realty building and went inside. Twenty minutes later he returned, the papers signed and notarized. He handed them to Annabelle, and then walked with her to her car.

"So are you going to check yourself into a mental hospital?" she asked.

"My brother was crazy for suggesting that," he said, "I'm just very concerned about my mother. I can't believe I've been acting like that. I knew she was sick. I didn't know she had cancer. I wish someone had told me earlier. I don't know what I can do to make it up to her."

"Buy her some roses," said Annabelle, getting into her car. "Try to act normal so that she doesn't have to worry about you. That's the best thing you can do for her."

Once again, Dennis smiled; a strange, endearing mask. "I guess I'll see you in court," he said.

"The court will set a date in about a month and we'll appear soon after that."

"I don't think I should see Sarah for a little while," he whispered.

"That's OK," said Annabelle.

Dennis nodded and went back in the doughnut shop.

Annabelle drove off with the signed agreement in her briefcase and Dennis's image in her mind. She was inexplicably sad for him. She hadn't been his wife, she'd been his mother, and soon he'd be losing his other one.

9

Ellen's voice was smooth, but Annabelle couldn't read the underlying emotion. With Dennis as a brother, how can she be so normal? All of Dennis's siblings are successful. What happened to Dennis?

While Ellen spoke, Annabelle remembered holidays with her in-laws: Thanksgiving and Christmas dinners, occasional weddings, little more.

"So all in all," said Ellen, "I just wanted to tell you that Derek feels bad about what he said to you. He was just trying to help Mom. I just wanted to call and let you know that Dennis has gone back to his apartment and he's not acting out any more. I guess you told him that our mom has cancer?"

"I told him what Derek told me," said Annabelle.

"I guess one of us should have told him about it earlier but Mom made us swear we wouldn't. We only found out a month ago ourselves," she paused, her voice breaking. "But anyway, Dennis has made a miraculous recovery and things are looking up. So I just wanted to tell you."

"I'm glad you called," said Annabelle, softly.

"I think Dennis is relieved now that he's signed the papers and this thing is in motion," continued Ellen, sighing. "Everyone knew you two would get divorced someday. We all knew you guys weren't happy together. I hope things work out for you."

"Thank you," said Annabelle. "I'm really sorry that everyone got so upset about all this. I hope your mom gets better; she's a sweet person. I was very sorry to hear she's so sick... I was thinking about sending her a card. Do you think that would be OK?"

Ellen paused. "No," she finally said. "That might not be a good idea right now."

Annabelle swallowed hard and the conversation ended politely. *Dennis has always been the problem child; the one his mother worries about.*

1. *Did I somehow cause his mother's cancer?*
2. *Other people get divorced without harming their in-laws. How could I have so much power?*
3. *I am not responsible for her cancer.*
4. *I am only responsible for myself and for Sarah. And for this baby inside me.*
5. *No more soft drinks or beer or wine.*
6. *I just need to relax and accept this life. If I am pregnant, I need to relax. If I'm not pregnant, I still need to relax.*

The laser printer for the documentation department was situated in a hallway on the eighth floor. Annabelle stood beside it, waiting for the glossary she'd just written to appear. The pages came at even intervals. Frank Marks walked by. It was Friday afternoon and even the marketing people were casually dressed.

"Have you talked to Tam about portfolio report yet?" asked Frank.

Annabelle shook her head. "I just got the new spec this morning. I'll go down and talk to him this afternoon."

"Always looking for an excuse to visit the seventh floor, aren't you?" said Frank, winking.

Annabelle's mouth dropped. Eddie walked towards them.

"Hey, just the guy we've been waiting for!" bellowed Frank.

"Frank Marks!" bellowed Eddie.

"Ed Wright!" shouted Frank. They sounded like a couple of game-show hosts.

Frank nudged Annabelle and said, "This must be cosmic. I remember running into Ed by the printer once and he had such a... such a blissed-out look on his face. The guy defines the term 'nirvana'. Ed, if you weren't a programmer you'd be a yogi. Are you working on the eighth floor now?"

Eddie laughed. "I just visit a lot."

Frank turned to Annabelle and said, "What did the Buddhist priest say to the senior sales rep?"

Annabelle stiffly shrugged.

"Never mind!" bellowed Frank. "Get it? That's a Zen joke. I guess you had to be there." He headed down the hall.

Eddie followed Annabelle into her office.

"He keeps referring to our romance," said Annabelle, closing her door. "Is it that obvious?"

Eddie nodded. "Danny's with Barbara this weekend and I'd like to come meet Sarah."

Annabelle paused, and then nodded. "Well, if I am pregnant, then I suppose that Sarah needs to meet you soon."

"We're having a guest for dinner tonight," Annabelle told Sarah. It was early Saturday morning and Sarah was taking a break from cartoons to eat some oatmeal.

"Who? Kathryn?" Annabelle and Kathryn used to work together. They used to talk on the phone for hours.

1. *I've been neglecting all my women friends since Eddie came along.*
2. *I haven't returned any calls.*
3. *I ought to at least call Kathryn and Diane. I wonder if they'll still want to talk to me.*

"No," said Annabelle. "This is someone I work with now. His name is Eddie."

"He's a boy?" asked Sarah, laughing.

"Yes, he's real nice and I sort of owe him dinner because he's been helping me out with a lot of my work. He said he can do some work on our car too."

"OK," said Sarah, returning to the television.

When Eddie appeared that evening, Sarah came to the door with Annabelle.

"Hi Sarah!" he said.

"Hi," she whispered. Annabelle watched Sarah assess Eddie's immense proportions and long hair.

"Hey, I've got a riddle for you," he said.

"What?" said Sarah.

"Chilli pepper."

"Chilli pepper?"

"Chilli pepper."

"Chilli pepper what?"

"That's the riddle."

"That's not a riddle!"

"I've got a game for you."

"What?"

"Designated winner."

Annabelle led Eddie into the house. "Nice place you have here," he said, looking around, winking at Annabelle.

"What's designated winner?" asked Sarah, her eyes glued to his giant frame.

"Well, someone picks who's going to win. Someone has to pick who's going to win it."

"You mean I can pick who wins?" Sarah started to smile.

"Yeah."

"OK, I win," said Sarah.

"Here's the question," said Eddie as he and Sarah sat down at the kitchen table. Annabelle began cutting carrots and zucchini for dinner.

"If I had a dozen cookies how many of them could I eat? But wait, before you answer, what does Mom say?" He looked at Annabelle who looked up.

"What?" she said.

"If you had a dozen cookies, how many could you eat?"

"I really shouldn't eat any," said Annabelle, "but I guess I could eat a dozen."

"Now I'll answer the question," said Eddie. "I could eat two so they wouldn't spoil my dinner. OK Sarah, now it's your turn."

"Thirty," she said.

"That's right!" bellowed Eddie, laughing. "You're the designated winner. You can give me any answer and you win!"

Sarah beamed. "Can we play it again?"

"No, I brought a board game. Have you ever played Scrabble?"

"Yes of course," said Sarah, impatiently.

"OK, is Mom going to play?"

"Can I excuse myself from this one?" asked Annabelle. "I want to get dinner ready."

"OK," said Eddie, taking the game out of the box.

Eddie and Sarah played for forty-five minutes while Annabelle completed the vegetable cheese casserole. Sarah won with a thirty word score. After dinner Sarah asked Eddie if he'd like to read the books she'd written, so they read her stories together.

As soon as he left Annabelle said, "What did you think of him?"

"He's OK," said Sarah. "He's really big. He's funny."

1. *Sarah didn't make any remarks about his long hair.*
2. *Sarah liked him a lot.*
3. *He was so nice to her.*

Eddie came for dinner the next Thursday night and the Monday after that. The following Wednesday he was to come again. Annabelle's period was overdue. The divorce papers had been filed and Dennis hadn't called.

On Wednesday evening, Annabelle immediately began working on dinner. "Eddie's coming over tonight."

"I don't want him to come over any more," said Sarah, pouting, fishing her homework out of her backpack.

Annabelle looked up from the biscuit batter she was mixing. "Why not?"

"I can't tell you."

"What do you mean? Don't you like him?"

"I can't tell you."

"If you can't tell me can you write it down so I can read it?"

Sarah looked around the kitchen for a pencil and piece of paper. Finally she handed her a note: "WILL YOU MARRY HIM".

Annabelle smiled. "I'm not sure if we should be thinking about that right now. I think he's very nice though."

"I just don't want you to ever get married again," said Sarah.

"Don't worry about that, Sarah. He's just funny and it's fun to have him over."

"Are you sure you won't marry him?"

"Please stop worrying about that."

"You were already married," insisted Sarah, "and it didn't work out."

When Eddie arrived, Sarah remained aloof for several minutes, but soon he was describing a handshake game and Sarah was playing along.

1. *Sarah seems happier since the papers have been filed.*
2. *When I point out babies in the grocery store she always says how cute they are.*

By Friday, Annabelle's period still hadn't started.

"So let's buy a kit," said Eddie during lunch in Annabelle's office. "I'll go to the drugstore across the street right now."

"No! Someone might see you."

"Oh come on. Who cares?"

"Everyone at MVI would be talking about it if someone saw you! I'll stop at a drug store tonight."

That evening she took Sarah to a pharmacy and attempted to purchase a home pregnancy kit. But each time she neared the counter Sarah turned the corner around her and Annabelle hid the kit. After two attempts, she gave up and bought tampons instead.

When Eddie called that night Annabelle told him of her failed attempts.

"I'll buy one this weekend," he said, "and I'll bring it in on Monday. Can you wait that long?"

"I can wait. I know I am."

"How do you feel?"

"I feel good." She felt an intense excitement coupled with longing. "How do you like the name Lawrence for a boy?"

"Nope."

"Gwendolyn for a girl?"

"Too yuppie. Too preppie."

"What names do you like?"

"For a girl I like Lorelei."

"Oh no," she said. "Do you know who Lorelei was?"
"No. I bet you do."
"She tempted sailors from their ships into their graves. What names do you like for a boy?"
"Shanti. We'll call him Shanti Jesus Buddha."
"I think we'll call him Larry," she said.

On Saturday night Eddie called to say he'd bought the kit. He always called at ten and Annabelle always waited to hear his voice on the answering machine before picking up the receiver.

"Eddie, I had this terrible headache all day. Then after dinner I went to the bathroom and I'd started bleeding. I guess I'm not pregnant." She sobbed, amazed that the sorrow outweighed the relief.

"Oh," he said, "I'm sorry. I told Sam you were pregnant and we were getting married as soon as you got divorced."

"You told Sam?!"

"He said he was happy for me. But I think he was a little upset."

"Oh you shouldn't have told Sam! Will he tell your mother?"

"Well, he'll tell mother but he'll make her promise that she won't tell anyone he told her so she'll act like she never knew. And then she'll probably tell everyone else in the family. That's how my family works."

"Oh no."

"Well, I'll tell him you're not pregnant now. I guess he'll be relieved, I don't think he wants me to move out."

To: EWRIGHT
From: ABonney

Thank you for bringing the lunch today. I liked the seaweed.
   Can you forgive my sadness? I know this isn't the right time to have a baby but my dream is alive again. I love babies so much.
   I would very much like a hug.

To: ABonney
From: EWRIGHT

I'll be up in a minute for a hug.
   P.S. I wrote you a poem. Here it is –

It really is funny
How much I missed you
When you told me you were leaving

To go to the market
To buy sour cream.

You stood in line,
Behind the man buying lotto tickets
Or was it cigarettes?

Kakenya, do you remember
Before?
Before this time
The ringing bell
The call to arms
The proud flags and our last day...
Bag in hand, smiling
You return, talking of toffee.
Yes, Kakenya,
I missed you.

SHANTI,
Gen

Annabelle had never before seen Ken Neece at an MVI Access status meeting, but there he was, tapping his tapered fingers on the conference room table while Arthur Ziminski polled his team for details about their progress.

After Ted Aaron described a potential solution to the floating-point rounding problem he'd been having, Ken finally spoke.

"What I want to know," said Ken, "is how does MVI Access look on the LAN? What kind of problems have you guys been having? Any?"

Annabelle looked around the room. Of all twenty employees, every face was blank. Eddie was staring at the ceiling.

"The LAN," said Arthur.

"Yes," said Ken.

Arthur paused.

"You have been developing for our LAN, haven't you?" asked Ken.

"Well no," said Arthur. "Should we?"

"Should you?! You have been testing on the LAN? Porting to the LAN?"

"No."

"What kind of fucking idiots are you?! We've been promising to have MVI Access running on the LAN for first customer ship! We have ten clients who've signed up for just that reason!"

"Nobody told us that," said Arthur.

"Brian Anderson told you."

"No, he didn't."

"He fucking did. He fucking did."

Arthur shrugged his shoulders. "Sorry."

Ken jumped up. For a moment Annabelle feared he would strike Arthur. Then Ken left the room, slamming the door. For several long moments, white noise permeated the office space. Eyes were wide and averted.

Finally Arthur said, "I'd like to add one action item. Someone should start testing MVI Access on the LAN."

A smile appeared on his face while the room exploded in raucous laughter.

To: EWRIGHT
From: ABonney

Thank you for the beautiful poem. Makes me realize how irrelevant most of what we do here is...

People from Texxtpoint sure seem to enjoy storming out of meetings. It will be interesting to see what Brian Anderson has to say when he gets back. Do you have any idea how to configure MVI Access for the LAN?

I see that Danny's visiting you at the office this afternoon, so I won't stop by. I want to meet him, although it seems awkward to meet him while here at work. Maybe I should meet him without Sarah first? Please tell me the best way to approach this.

Sarah has been invited to go with a friend to her grandparents' farm in Maine for the weekend. She's very excited about it and it means that I have the weekend free. Do you want to spend it with me?

I love you,
Annabelle

To: ABonney
From: EWRIGHT

The LAN is our new buzzword down here. Tam is frantically trying to get the LAN team to give us some clue how to get MVI Access up and running on it. I'll let you know when we have a workable version.

Let's wait a bit before meeting Danny.

This weekend! Can I take you to Vermont to meet my parents? (I just called and asked if they'll be around and they're dying to meet you.)

To: EWRIGHT
From: ABonney

Yes.

10

Eddie described the new data-sorting program he'd written. Annabelle was silent while they drove, nodding her head every so often, which he didn't see because he was driving.

They stopped for tea at a fast-food restaurant halfway up Route 93 and when Annabelle returned from the restroom, she found Eddie sitting in a booth with two striped drinking straws proudly protruding, like tusks, from his nostrils. For the first time that day, she smiled.

"What's wrong?" he said, removing the straws. "You've been so sad."

She paused. *Why does he like to behave like a child? Well... he really just wants to cheer me up.* "I've just been wondering about something," she said. "You know I could have been pregnant. It could have been an early miscarriage."

"It could have been," agreed Eddie.

"Do you think it means I'll never have another baby? I mean if it was the second miscarriage in a row it could mean that."

"I'm sorry you're still sad about it," he said, "but we'll have a baby someday when the time is right. And won't it be nice, having a baby in a real family? We'll buy a house and have the baby's room all set up—"

"But maybe I can't have another baby."

"I think you think too much," he whispered, tapping the ends of the straws together.

Further north, Eddie said, "I'm so happy that you're going to meet my parents. I guess I should tell you something though."

He paused.

"What?" said Annabelle, watching the clouds skim the mountains like boats through a notch.

"My brother Andy is going through a divorce right now. He has a son named Ben, who's about the same age as Sarah... a few years older I guess... Anyway, apparently Andy's wife, Karen, was having an affair. So out of the blue one day, about two months ago, Andy came home and found that Karen and Ben had vanished, without a trace. Andy asked mother for help so she hired a private investigator, who found them in Texas. Karen had gone to Texas to live with her lover, and she took Ben along with her. So now the court has ordered them back to Connecticut, where they live... well, where Andy lives... to establish custody and all that. Andy and Karen aren't even legally divorced yet."

Silence.

"So your family is working on its own soap opera," said Annabelle finally.

"You might say that, but it does have repercussions. For us."

"How so?"

"Mother might equate you with Karen, that's all."

"Oh no. I can't meet her now. What have you told her about me? Why didn't you tell me this before?"

"You're not Karen, you're nothing like Karen. But it is a coincidence, you know, that you have Sarah and she has Ben and they're about the same age. Don't worry about it but you need to know because mother will probably mention it."

Annabelle resumed her rumination, but instead of worrying about miscarriages and her upcoming divorce, she began obsessing over what Eddie's mother would think of her.

They arrived at the huge family homestead at sundown. As they drove up the winding road to the house, they passed a lake. Eddie explained that his parent's house was on three hundred acres of land, including four acres of lakefront. The austere beauty of the cold land astonished Annabelle.

Eddie's mother answered the door, giving Annabelle a long, sombre look.

"Eddie," said his mother, "I'm all to pieces about what that Karen did."

She doesn't waste any time, thought Annabelle.

"Oh come on," said Eddie, "this was bound to happen."

Eddie's mother glowered at Annabelle.

"Mother," said Eddie, "I want you to meet my sweet friend, Annabelle Bonney. Annabelle, this is my mother, Joanne Wright."

Annabelle smiled and said, "Hello! It's so nice to meet you!"

"Are you divorced yet?" asked Joanne, still glowering.

Joanne was a tall, buxom woman with short white hair and deep wrinkles, engraved like armour, around her wide mouth.

"I'm working on it," said Annabelle.

Joanne shook her head and Eddie hugged her.

"Well, you look happy," Joanne said to Eddie, with irritated resignation.

"She's the best!" he bellowed, grabbing Annabelle's arm, pulling her into the living room.

"You have such a beautiful home," said Annabelle.

Joanne turned to Eddie. "You know," she said, "I gave so many of my mother's things to Karen and now they're lost. She probably sold them. She has no morals, that girl. She has absolutely no morals. She just took up and left with Ben! I'm just all to pieces, see," she repeated, her voice breaking, her eyes red.

Annabelle wanted to comfort her but Joanne continued to glare. Eddie appeared perfectly comfortable, as usual.

"Well Eddie's pretty happy with you," Joanne said to Annabelle, issuing a dubious judgement. "And you have a little girl?"

"Yes, Sarah. Would you like to see her picture?"

"Why are you getting divorced?" asked Joanne.

Annabelle looked at Eddie.

He smiled and said, "Annabelle and her husband were separated off and on for years. He's been abusive to her. It was never a real marriage."

"But if you've been separated off and on before, then why are you getting divorced now? Is it because of Eddie?"

Annabelle felt a fire rise in her cheeks. Eddie was right about his mother. She hadn't even offered her a snack or shown her where the bathroom was after such a long trip. She'd started the interrogation process immediately.

"I don't know," said Annabelle. "Before, whenever Dennis and I would break up he'd always insist that he'd change and that we should give it one more try. I'd always say no but eventually I'd give it another try. Maybe it's because of Eddie – because now I'm strong enough to say enough is enough."

"Well," said Joanne to Eddie, "just don't get married again. You were already married and it didn't work out. Are you hungry?"

Annabelle held her stomach, her appetite gone.

Joanne went to the kitchen; Eddie and Annabelle followed her and sat at an old oak table. The ancient floors creaked beneath them while a grandfather clock ticked from the hallway.

"Mother's not usually like this," said Eddie to Annabelle, taking a big bite from a large oatmeal cookie.

"Like what?" snapped Joanne.

"Angry," said Eddie.

"Well why shouldn't I be angry?" she retorted. "That Karen just did the worst thing she could have done. When she and Andy got married your father and I told her over and over that she must never leave him – his first wife did that, Annabelle. He never recovered; he was all broken up about it—"

"But first she gave him the clap," interjected Eddie. "Come on, mother. Andy likes what Andy likes."

"He was all broken up about it," continued Joanne, ignoring Eddie, "and then he met Karen and well, she came along and she promised us she would never leave Andy. So not only does she leave him, she steals Ben and runs off with a Texan lover—"

"What a tramp," said Eddie, chewing another cookie.

"As I was saying, when she married Andy she swore up and down that she'd never leave him. She promised us that she'd be good to him. Well, we know what her promises mean."

The ticking clock echoed through the kitchen.

"I'm sorry about it," said Eddie, "I wish I could help."

"Well there's nothing you can do," said Joanne. "She only married him for our money, but she's not getting any more of that, I'll tell you!" She paused. "You two can sleep in the front room," she continued. "It has twin beds."

Annabelle stared at her cookie, and then glanced around the room again, suddenly realizing that these were wealthy people. Not just well off, but honest-to-goodness, dyed-in-the-wool New England bluebloods.

She looked at Eddie, the man she loved, who'd told her how he once lived for a week on a five-pound tin of butterscotch pudding, in order to save money.

He'd told her that his father would rather dust worms off his prunes than waste a half-full box. She had thought of his parents as struggling farmers, but here they were with what looked like an original Beirstadt hanging in the kitchen. Already she had stepped on at least three antique Persian carpets. And this house was nestled in the most enchanting land she had ever seen.

Now Eddie's dining-room table made sense. It came from his family. He was an oversized prince, parading as a pauper. She was a fool. Tears filled her eyes. His mother had just ordered him not to marry her. And now she had to spend the weekend with them.

After puttering around the kitchen and straightening things up, Joanne broke the silence by saying, "I'm going to bed now. Good night."

"Dad's asleep?" asked Eddie.

"Yes," said Joanne, leaving the room, slowly padding up the staircase.

In the guest bedroom, Eddie shoved the two twin beds together. The house was more like a northern plantation than a farm. The bedroom was furnished with handmade quilts and woven rugs, a cherry bookcase, and a marble fireplace.

"So what should I call you now?" whispered Annabelle, her arms locked across her chest.

"Look," said Eddie, "a king-size bed! This will be fun." He smiled, patting the quilt, beckoning her to sit beside him.

She didn't move.

"What exactly is wrong?" he finally asked.

"You know," she said, looking away.

"I'm sorry but I don't. Why are you angry?"

"Who are you? I don't even know who you are."

"What do you mean?" he frowned. "What are you talking about? Of course you know who I am."

"Look. I can recognize excessive wealth. It's like a social disease. My father owned a Picasso. He probably still owns it. But I'm not part of that. You know I'm poor – I scrape by every week. Your parents will think I'm after they're money. They'll never accept me."

"My parents aren't expecting you to be wealthy, Annabelle. They don't really know anything about you except that I love you. That's all that matters."

"No it's not. Your mother just told you not to get married again. In front of me! She hates me!" Annabelle tried to whisper, which made her voice squeak.

"Come on," laughed Eddie, pulling down one of the quilts. "You met Sam. It's not like you had no warning. Joanne's just like that, she says whatever she's thinking. She'll love you once she gets to know you."

"Why didn't you tell me that your parents are rich?"

"Who cares about that? I did tell you about the farm. I told you about the lake."

"I thought it was a farm, Eddie, you know with chickens and cows. I didn't think you meant an estate."

"Well they call it a farm, OK? And it doesn't matter at all that they have money – it's their money, not mine. I earn every penny of my money."

He was starting to look angry. Annabelle had never seen him look angry before. She felt strangely aroused.

"Did they ever give you any money? Did they help you through college?" she asked, her irritation growing.

"Yes, they paid my tuition. They've given me money when I needed it. But I don't need it any more."

"I've been on my own since I was nineteen," she whispered. "Nobody has ever supported me."

"I'm sorry you had it so rough. My parents are generous people. I don't want to have to defend them."

"Your mother hates me," she finally said, tears streaming down her cheeks.

"I'll support you," whispered Eddie. "I'll be your mother. I'll be your father."

1. *I am so confused.*
2. *I am infuriated.*
3. *I am so confused.*

He held his arms out. She stumbled to the bed and sat beside him.

The guest room was next to Joanne's room. Annabelle was keenly aware that they might be overheard.

Eddie unzipped Annabelle's black dress, tugging it over her head. He pulled off her boots, pantyhose and panties.

"Do what I say," he whispered. "Lie back."

She lay on her back. He removed his sweatshirt and jeans.

"Be quiet," he whispered. The lamp was off. She could barely see him.

"Are you my going to take care of me?" she whispered.

"Yes," he said, searching for her groin.

"Are you going to punish me?" she whispered.

"Yes," he said, pushing inside her, startling her, exciting her.

Her body was made of panic and tension, lust in the mind, her lover whispering forbidden things in the guest room next to his wealthy sleeping mother.

The old bed squeaked with every sturdy thrust. They shook the house.

Annabelle woke with the sun, confused by the room, forgetting where she was. That night she had dreamt of fire in a house, fire engines coming to the door, a strange longhair dog.

Eddie was wrapped around her.

"Eddie," she whispered. "Wake up."

He opened his eyes and smiled.

"Can we get up and eat something?" she whispered.

He nodded and she jumped out of bed.

Eddie brought her to the kitchen and lit the stove under the teakettle. Then he showed her the breakfast room: a veranda lit by huge plate-glass windows with views of the meadow, the lawn, the rolling mountains and the lake. Adjoining the veranda was a greenhouse filled with potted herbs, tomato seedlings, rubber trees and gardenias.

"This is unbelievable," whispered Annabelle, clutching her sweater, gazing at the lake.

"There's Dad," said Eddie, pointing to a figure appearing on the driveway winding through the meadow.

The meadow was still covered by snow and a thin old man was spryly jogging up the hill, on the ploughed asphalt. When he reached the top he turned and started his descent.

"Dad jogs every day," said Eddie, "up and down the driveway."

"I can't believe this view," said Annabelle.

"My parents built this addition about six years ago. They really love this room. Mom uses her greenhouse all the time. Wait until you see her garden this summer. She grows potatoes, tomatoes, carrots, asparagus and sugar-snap peas. There's absolutely nothing on earth better than fresh-picked sugar-snap peas. Except your body. Your body is better than anything."

Annabelle shook her head. The refrigerator door slammed shut and Joanne shuffled into the room, carrying a cup of coffee.

"Look at this day!" she exclaimed. "Isn't this just marvellous?" She was wearing a fuzzy blue bathrobe and matching blue slippers.

The sun was rising, brightening the snow. The mountains, meadow and lake competed for light.

"How'd you sleep?" said Joanne to Eddie.

"Oh mother," he said, "I never had a better night!"

"It sounded like it," she laughed, her eyes twinkling.

Annabelle blushed. Joanne turned to her. "Isn't it beautiful up here? It does wonders for the constitution. I just love the country. We lived in Weston when the boys were young, see, but it's too close to the city. Although I miss the minds down there in Boston. All the people around here are lunkheads, see. You trade brains for beauty. I love the morning."

Joanne was a different person now, alive and happy. Her diction reminded Annabelle of someone. Jimmy Cagney, that was it, see.

The front door slammed and soon a tall, trim, elderly man strode into the room.

"Edward," he said. "Good to see you."

Eddie stood still while his father patted his shoulders in a distant embrace.

"This must be Annabelle," he said. His voice was deep, his long limbs stiff.

"Yes," said Annabelle. She stood up and held out her hand. He shook it and smiled.

"Don," said Joanne, "did you bring up the paper?"

"Yes Joanne," he said, "Edward, did you receive the papers I sent you on the national science conference?"

"Where is it?" said Joanne.

"Yes Dad," said Eddie, "but I don't think I can go this year."

"It's on the kitchen counter," said Don to Joanne.

"He's been forgetting things lately," Joanne said to Annabelle. "I have to keep reminding him."

"Why can't you go?" said Don to Eddie.

"I have deadlines at work, Dad."

"I see," said Don.

"Your father lives for those stupid science conferences," said Joanne, "He doesn't understand the real world. He just likes to leave me to go to those stupid things."

Don turned to Annabelle. "How do you like the view?" he asked, ignoring Joanne.

Annabelle smiled and nodded. Eddie's parents were an odd pair, one so formal, one so candid, both so proud.

Eddie and his father sat down together to discuss Don's latest theory on the sociological implications of technology in inner-city schools while Joanne showed Annabelle her greenhouse, describing each plant.

"Well I'm so happy you came up to see us," said Joanne, "Eddie just won't stop talking about you. I've never seen him like this before. I'm happy for you. This one doesn't need much water – it gets root rot. This is grape ivy, you can give it too much sun; it likes partial shade. His first wife abused him – you should have heard her – she used to call him stupid and she screamed at him, that was all, see. This is a form of pothos; always wash your hands after touching it because it can burn your tongue."

Annabelle remained silent, nodding when appropriate.

"I've been so upset about that Karen girl," continued Joanne, "it was just such a shock to all of us. I really think divorce is terrible for kids. You shouldn't do that to kids. I would have divorced Don but I stayed with him for the kids."

Annabelle stared out a window at the snow glistening on the meadow, the icy lake with its patches of blue.

"Don't you think you should stay with your husband for your child's sake?" said Joanne.

Joanne was voicing Annabelle's guilt, the thing she couldn't escape, the burning house, the dying dog.

"I've thought about that and thought about it," said Annabelle, "but when we were together we just fought all the time and I can't believe it's healthy for Sarah to be around that."

"Well," said Joanne, "it takes two to tango."

Annabelle grimaced, remembering details. She couldn't explain the incessant fighting, the hatred she felt for herself while with Dennis, the insane worst they brought out in each other.

"I've tried to work things out," mumbled Annabelle.

"Well, Annabelle," said Joanne, "sometimes you just can't have your cake and eat it too. But you know what's best for yourself, I guess. However," she sighed, "in my day people didn't get divorced like they do now."

The room was utterly silent while Annabelle considered some kind of response. Then she heard Eddie's booming footsteps coming down the hall. He burst in the greenhouse and said, "Can we borrow your snowshoes, Mom? I want to show Annabelle the falls."

"Of course," said Joanne, "you might get a glimpse of the foxes up there."

Joanne led them to a large closet off the hallway and removed two sets of snowshoes.

"You need better boots than those," she said, pointing to Annabelle's vinyl shoes.

"Can she borrow some of yours?" asked Eddie.

"I don't know," said Joanne, "she has awfully little feet."

Annabelle laughed, shocked by the comment. She wore a size-ten shoe, sometimes size eleven.

"I wear size twelve," said Joanne, handing him a pair of leather boots, "but these are a little small for me, see. Tie them tightly and they might do. Annabelle, you must have trouble finding shoes with those little feet!"

Annabelle obediently laced the boots. No one had ever before called her feet small.

They put on their jackets and Eddie laced her into the snowshoes, helping her step across the red-slate foyer and out the front door while Joanne padded back to the kitchen.

The snow was blinding at first but soon they were walking up a trail in the forest, Annabelle stumbling along in the snowshoes.

"How do you like this?" asked Eddie.

"This is such a beautiful place," she whispered. "Are there any deer around here?"

"Millions of deer and fox and woodchuck and moose and bear."

"Bear?" said Annabelle, stopping short, almost falling out of the boots.

"They're still asleep," said Eddie.

"Are you sure?"

"They're all asleep. And they're more afraid of us than we are of them. One time my father was climbing that mountain over there and he stood at a ledge and starting pissing – then he looked up and realized he was pissing on a bear!"

"What happened?—"

"The bear ran away. Come on."

Annabelle gingerly followed him along the trail until they heard water running. "We're getting close to the falls," he said.

At the falls Annabelle stopped in awe at the sight of blue water flowing deep and clear off the icy banks and ledges. This land was exquisite.

"Salmon spawn in this brook so it's closed for fishing," said Eddie.

Annabelle shivered. "We need to get you a warmer jacket," he said. "Women's clothes are too flimsy."

He wrapped his arms around her, pulling her face up to look at him.

"What are you thinking about?" he asked.

"I was remembering last night," she said. Her legs and groin were still tight, aching from orgasms in the squeaking bed.

"What were you thinking?"

"I was thinking that at best, sex is silly. I can enjoy it but as soon as it's over I feel so embarrassed."

"That's right," he laughed, leaning over to toss a twig in the brook. "Sex is something you can't understand with your rational mind. It's your primal, reptilian mind that likes it."

Annabelle nodded, blushing. "It used to be considered sacred," she said. "In ancient times... there were these prolific, enduring... peaceful cultures who worshipped God in female form. They worshipped God as mother and creator. Then these patriarchal, warrior bands overthrew them and imposed their hierarchical practices – of domination – along with their violent gods – and sex stopped being sacred and became cruel."

She was staring off into space. Eddie waited for her to continue.

"This was in Old Europe," she said finally. "There are some new books out that document all of it. I should lend them to you. You should definitely read some of Riane Eisler's research."

She sighed.

"Sex is still sacred," said Eddie finally, "in the Tao, in Tantra. It's still sacred... Did I please you last night?"

She sighed again. "Yes, but it embarrassed me. When you said you would take care of me... and all that... and you told me what to do... I got very aroused and I really shouldn't have."

"Why not?" he asked. "We were playing. You can't judge sex."

"But it makes me wonder if my mind is sick, because I even allowed myself to say something like that. But on the other hand, as an abuse survivor, maybe it's sort of healing for me, in a way, because I got to feel like I was in control and I could have stopped it if I'd wanted to. But I don't want to do anything immoral. Does that make sense?"

"Imagine that you're an animal then," he said. "Suppose that you're a cat in heat. You would just show me your backside and that would be that. And that's OK, that's nature."

"Do you ever have fantasies?" she asked.

He nodded, backing away from the falls. "Come on," he said, "I have a special place I want to show you."

She followed him up the trail for a few hundred feet; then he started walking among the trees. He pulled her hand, leading her through the woods.

All of a sudden they came to a remote clearing where only faint patches of snow remained. The rest of the forest floor was covered with pine needles and logs. All around stood massive firs, protecting the earth. The place smelt like incense: musk and aloes. It was warm there, sheltered from the wind.

Annabelle was clammy from traipsing among the tree limbs. Eddie leant down and unlaced her snowshoes; then he unlaced his. She tiptoed in the large boots on top of the pine needles.

"This is where Danny and I like to camp," said Eddie. "Isn't this something? It's so sheltered it's almost like a house."

He sat on a fallen log and stretched his huge arms and legs.

"What do you fantasize about?" he asked.

"Oh I don't know," she said, inhaling the rich, earthy pine smell.

"I fantasize about you. I fantasize about pleasing you."

She smiled.

"Can you describe your fantasies to me?" he asked.

"No."

"Annabelle, I would do anything for you. I would do anything I could to let you live your fantasies."

"My fantasies are terrible," she said, surprised by her honesty and sadness.

"Are they sexual?" he asked.

"They're just wrong."

"Can you stop judging yourself?" he asked.

"No."

"You can't love yourself and judge yourself at the same time. I want to know everything about you," he said, standing up, stroking her arms. "Just tell me what you want. I'll do my best."

"You'll think I'm awful."

"No I won't."

"Yes you will."

"I promise that I won't. I adore you."

She thought about her conversation with Joanne and her guilt over leaving Dennis. Her brain was all guilt: here she was, sharing her body with a man who chose to please her. She wanted to escape responsibility for that passion. She was a house burning up.

"I want you to rape me," she whispered, shocked by the statement. It hadn't come out right. She had meant to say, "I want you to take me," or even, "I want you to force me," but it was too late; she had said it and meant it.

For a long minute Eddie stared into her eyes. Then he bowed before her and kissed her hand.

"I don't think a man should ever rape a woman, for any reason, ever," he said. "I don't think any creature should ever rape any other creature, ever."

She nodded. "You are absolutely right," she whispered.

"But it's your fantasy?" he asked.

She nodded again, turning away. "Only with you. You are the only person I would ever say that to or want that from. I know it must seem absurd that I could ever fantasize about that, given what I've been through... But I love you so much that I want you... to own me. And when we make love you're always so sweet. I don't want to have this fantasy. I think it's because when I *was* raped – it was so indescribably painful and horrible... It scared me to death... So I just want to erase those memories by superseding them somehow... Do you understand? When he raped me, it felt like he owned me, and I had no choice about it. That's what it was like... it was like not existing... like not having a self... I know there's no way I can ever erase those memories, but I still want to. Does that make any sense?

"I think I understand," he whispered.

He took off his jacket, laying it lengthwise on the pine-needle lace; then he knelt on it, his head resting on her lap.

Time passed. Annabelle inhaled the pine and studied the koan: master and slave, slave and master, the same thing, the wet Tao.

Eddie suddenly stood up and unzipped her trousers, wrenching them to her knees. He pulled her down on his jacket and held her arms over her head. With his left hand he clasped her wrists together. With his right hand he forced himself inside her and thrust like a bear and kept thrusting, biting her lips. She opened so completely that he barely had time to come out and come on the forest floor, anointing the earth on that twelfth day of spring.

11

Afterwards they sat up and Annabelle laughed: awkwardly, nervously.

"I feel really embarrassed now," she said.

Eddie smiled, resting his head in her lap again. She watched shafts of white light pour through the pine.

"How do you feel?" she asked after a while.

"Well it was hard," he said, slowly combing her hair with his huge fingers, removing pine needles, small twigs, and bits of dry leaves.

"Why was it hard?"

"No one ever asked me to do that before. It violated the code of honour."

She stopped smiling. "I'm sorry," she said.

"I didn't want to hurt you. I'm a very big guy. It must have been painful. I feel sorry about that."

"It didn't hurt," she said, suddenly realizing how much her groin hurt.

He touched her mouth. "Your lip is bleeding a little bit," he said. She covered her lower lip with her tongue, tasting the bruise.

He stood up, extending his hand to her, giving her a long look. "Well you look like you've just been attacked in the woods."

"What should we tell your parents?" she asked.

"We'll tell them you fell down coming back from the falls."

Joanne was standing in the foyer straightening out the coat closet when Annabelle and Eddie arrived at the house.

"Did you see the foxes?" said Joanne, her head still in the closet.

"No, Mom," said Eddie, unlacing the snowshoes he'd been wearing.

"Wait until the summer, Annabelle, there are hundreds of jack-in-the-pulpits up on the banks of the falls," said Joanne, emerging from the closet, her arms laden with sweaters and hats.

She paused, then exclaimed, "What happened to you?"

Eddie and Annabelle looked at each other.

"We were frolicking in the pine grove," Eddie finally said.

Annabelle turned to him and grimaced.

"A frolic," retorted Joanne, "in my boots. You look like you were in a fight, Annabelle."

Eddie had started untying Annabelle's laces.

"Don't you and Dad ever frolic?" laughed Eddie.

"Don?" snorted Joanne. "Frolic? Bah."

Annabelle stood motionless. *How could Eddie have said that?*

"Annabelle," said Joanne, "I've been waiting for you to come back. Eddie tells me that you love yard sales and there's a big one advertised down the road. I want to take you."

Annabelle didn't want to be alone with Joanne again, especially after what Eddie had just said to her; especially after the rush of emotions following her fantasy in the woods, so she turned to Eddie, hoping her pained expression would beseech him to create an excuse for her not to go.

"That sounds great!" said Eddie. "I promised Dad I'd help him with his computer. Are you going right now?"

"Don't take off your coat, Annabelle, I'll be ready in a second," said Joanne.

"Ummm," said Annabelle, "I'd like to wash up for a minute first."

"Why of course," said Joanne, "I'll wait for you in my car."

"Well Eddie's quite taken with you," said Joanne, buckling herself into her blue Mercedes. "In my day girls didn't have sex with a man unless they were married. I don't know why they'd want to anyway. I never liked it at all."

"I'm sorry?" said Annabelle, helpless as to how to respond.

"Sex!" exclaimed Joanne, navigating her way down the winding driveway. "I don't know how any girl could enjoy something like that. Don always wanted to poke me. I hated that! All that sticky stuff oozing down my legs afterwards. That was awful, running to the bathroom and washing all that stuff off. He still wants to poke me, can you imagine that? You'd think an old man like that would just forget about all that stuff. If he's going to forget about anything I'd like him to forget about all that! But he has this fierceness to him. You wouldn't know it by looking at him. Is Eddie like that?"

Annabelle shook her head, unable to speak.

"Well I think Eddie should cut his hair, don't you?" Joanne finally said.

"He likes having long hair," said Annabelle, eager to change the subject.

"He looks foolish. He doesn't look professional. If he'd cut his hair he'd look like a million bucks. OK, here we go," she said, abruptly turning onto a dirt road. "The newspaper said it was down here – there it is."

They stopped at a rickety clapboard house and got out, walking around together for a few minutes until Annabelle discovered a stack of record albums to inspect. Joanne soon found her, nudged her ribs, and said, "Just a lot of junk, if you ask me. I thought I'd get this scarf. They want seventy-five cents for it. Can you imagine that? I'll offer fifty cents, see." She ambled over to a man with a change belt.

Annabelle stared as Joanne loudly argued with the man about the value of the scarf. Eddie somehow resembled this blunt, proud woman, so determined to find a bargain.

Later that afternoon, Eddie said, "Dad wants to meet with us in his office." His voice was unusually low and serious, imitating his father.

There were no curtains on the numerous windows in Don's office.

Annabelle and Eddie sat on a brown leather sofa, facing two of the windows. Don sat at one of his desks by a corner window. Above his head hung a rock, the size of a soccer ball, dangling from a thin wire. The rock twirled slowly as they spoke and Annabelle couldn't help staring at it from time to time.

Finally Eddie said, "That's Dad's rock."

"My sword of Damocles," smiled Don. "One of many. Getting back to the topic at hand, Edward, now that you know about my ideas for involving children in this process, do either of you have any ideas? You both have children at such important ages for this work." He spoke so slowly and paused so often that Annabelle kept thinking he had finished speaking mid-sentence or had lost his train of thought.

Eddie turned to Don and said, "Well I've done some of that with computer science. I went down to Danny's school and taught a three-day course on computer imaging."

Then the room was silent again.

"What do you think, Annabelle?" said Don, finally.

"I think the work you're doing is very valuable," she said. "And I guess I only have two comments. Um. First, I think you might want to consider going to a few classrooms yourself and talking with the children, to see what they think. Um. Also, before they can learn and get involved they have to be cared for. They need food and shelter and all those things. Ketchup is not a vegetable after all. A lot of the children you're most concerned about – and I'm most concerned about – are deprived of the most basic necessities, especially with the GOP in charge, so before they can learn anything new and get involved in saving the world, they have to be cared for as individuals. At Sarah's school we have fundraisers to help shelters and such. The kids help raise the money, and when children get involved in helping others, they start developing social consciences."

Annabelle spoke longer than she'd intended. Don wrote all the while she spoke. Then he didn't respond, but sat and stared in space.

The room was silent again.

Finally Don pulled a white index card out of his white shirt pocket. "Joanne and I would like to take you two out to dinner this evening," he said, glancing at the card, "I very much appreciate your taking the time to discuss these important matters with me."

He stood up and Eddie tapped Annabelle's hand, beckoning her out of the office. They returned to the guest room and started dressing for dinner.

"What do you think of my parents?" laughed Eddie.

"They're quite a pair. Your mother told me that your father always wants to poke her!"

"She loves to talk about sex and how much she hates it. My father loves to talk about saving the world. We call him Don Quixote."

"I think he's sweet," said Annabelle.

"He'd give all his money to the poor if mother would let him. But if he tried it she'd have him committed. But... you have to watch yourself with him you know: he's very critical."

"What do you mean? Did I say something wrong?"

"I don't think so," said Eddie, "but if ever you do, I'll hear about it. He keeps files on all us brothers. And our spouses and our children. And our girlfriends."

"Are you serious?" said Annabelle, frowning.

Eddie smiled. "Everything you said today will go in your file. He probably made a new file for you the first time I told him about you."

"Well," said Annabelle, unsure about whether Eddie was being serious, "at least he seems to be doing good humanitarian work," she sighed. "I wonder what he'd make of my father? I'll never forget the time, when I was about twelve, I was looking through the bookshelves in my parents' bedroom and I found my father's copy of *Mein Kampf*." She lowered her voice. "It had annotations in the margin, like 'good point' and 'makes sense to me'. He used to say that Hitler was a genius... as if that made it all right..."

She stared into space.

Eddie frowned and reached for her hand.

They left the following morning, as mist rose around the lake. Once on the highway, Eddie began reminiscing.

"I remember one time my mother was having wine with another man in the middle of the afternoon – he was the father of one of Andy's friends. When Dad found out he ran around with an axe, yelling that he would chop down our house."

"What did your mother do?"

"She told him to stop being an old fool. Then there was the time they had a fight and she served him a tuna sandwich made with canned cat food."

"My father would have murdered my mother for doing something like that; literally killed her."

"But do you see how they fulfil each other's needs?" said Eddie. "She's always been his challenge. He needs that."

Annabelle paused. "Well, in a way you're fortunate to have parents like them. They seem so concerned about all their children.

Not like my parents, although my mother can't help it if she isn't. But it always hurts that she doesn't remember my birthday."

"I want to meet her."

Annabelle smiled. "You want to stop at the nursing home on the way home?"

"No, I'll cook dinner. Can you bring her over to my apartment for dinner, maybe in a couple of weeks? Next weekend I want you and Sarah to come over and meet Danny."

The doorbell rang at nine-thirty at night while Annabelle was in the kitchen waiting for Eddie to call. Sarah was asleep in her room.

Annabelle turned off the lights, crept to the window, and peered out. Dennis was standing at the door, hands tucked in his jacket pockets, his car parked across the street.

She froze.

He rang the doorbell again. She remained motionless. Minutes went by. Finally he knocked, and then pounded. At ten the phone rang. She hurried through the darkness, into the kitchen, and picked up the receiver.

"Eddie," she whispered.

"What's wrong?"

"Dennis is outside. He's been out there for a half-hour, ringing the doorbell and banging on the door. I don't know what to do."

"Call the police," said Eddie.

"I'd hate to do that," she whispered.

"He preys on your insecurities. You can't let him harass you like this."

"He must be drunk."

"Sweetheart, you can call the police. It wouldn't hurt anything to do that."

"It's just that whenever I think things are under control he pops out of nowhere and starts acting out again."

"And all that is going to end," insisted Eddie, "You're not a victim any more. I really want you to call the police. You need to stop worrying about persecution, let him know you won't be bullied."

Annabelle paused. It had been quiet for several minutes.

"I think he left," she finally said.

"I'll wait if you want to go check."

She put down the phone and looked out the living-room window. His car was gone. She crept back to the kitchen.

"He's gone. I hate this. I feel like I've been living with a false sense of security. He'll never stop bothering me."

"I think you should call the police if he ever tries that again."

"I hate this."

"Maybe it's time for him to become aware of me," said Eddie.

"What do you mean?"

"I think he'll stop bothering you if he sees you with me. I'm twice his size. I could kill him with one hand."

Eddie's first glimmer of fierceness: a strange comfort.

Dennis called Annabelle at her office the next day. She picked up the receiver.

"I'm sorry about last night—" he started.

"If you ever do that again," she shouted, "I'll call the police!"

She hung up. He didn't call back.

Eddie came to dinner that night. The early April evening was unusually warm, like the promise of safety after a cold, restless night. Sarah went to sleep early, and then Annabelle and Eddie sat outside on the porch swing, defiantly kissing, their arms locked around each other.

The street was quiet, with little traffic. In less than an hour Annabelle spotted Dennis's car at the top of the hill, creeping along. Dennis glanced at Annabelle and Eddie on the porch, then sped up and was soon out of sight.

"I wonder how long he's been stalking the house," said Annabelle, after he left.

"Don't worry about that. He won't be back."

She remembered the paralegal work she'd done years earlier and all the cases of ex-husbands abusing their ex-wives. Once, while doing intake work, a man had called saying he was seeking custody of his grandchildren. When Annabelle asked about the children's parents, the man, who was the fraternal grandfather, said their mother was dead and their father, his son, was in jail.

"He offed her," said the man.

Annabelle had asked the man to repeat the statement several times, unable to understand the meaning, until the man impatiently retorted, "He killed her. Offed her. OK?"

The legal office decided not to take the case.
Annabelle shivered and leant against Eddie.

1. *Dennis would never try to kill me.*
2. *Women who get killed always think that.*

The porch swing creaked. Eddie stroked her hair.

Eddie was agitated at lunch at work the next day.

"Why is it so hard to get free?" he said. "You have to protect yourself from Dennis and I have to pay through the nose for my freedom."

What do you mean?" said Annabelle, taking a bite of her cottage-cheese fruit salad.

"I had to buy my freedom from Barbara... but every day I'm thankful that I no longer have to look at her. That bitch."

Annabelle's eyes widened. "I didn't know you were capable of this much anger."

"I've been controlling my anger all my life. Men aren't allowed to have feelings or to be sad. Our culture doesn't accept it."

"Why are you suddenly angry?"

"I always have to control my anger at Barbara. Even though she continues to wreak havoc on my life." He paused. "I've just been thinking about this coming weekend when you'll meet Danny. There are some things I need to tell you about him."

Annabelle frowned.

"He has some socialization problems," continued Eddie. "He's extremely bright. He's brilliant. But he has a lot of trouble relating to other children. That's one of the reasons I enjoy being with Sarah so much, she's a kid. She acts like a kid, she has an imagination. She plays. I wish Danny could do that. I don't think Danny has an imagination."

Annabelle smiled, "Eddie. Everyone has an imagination."

Eddie had stopped eating and was staring out the window.

"Well exactly what kinds of socialization problems does he have?"

"He can be somewhat violent. I wish I could reach him. It's very complicated." Eddie sighed. "During our divorce, Barbara became a born-again Christian. She apparently feeds him stories about how I left them... I never, ever wanted to leave Danny. But I had to leave Barbara. I had to."

Eddie remained perfectly calm, half-smiling.

Annabelle frowned. "What do you mean by violent?"

"Oh, Danny? Well, he'll sometimes clobber other kids for no reason... I guess he has his reasons, but they don't make sense sometimes. Part of the problem is that he's so big. Even though he's only ten, he's the size of a fifteen year old, maybe bigger. Not only does he have my genes, but for reasons I cannot begin to fathom, his skinny, anorexic mother insists on feeding him red meat every single day. And I can't help feeling sorry for him because he's only ten and people expect him to behave like he's five years older than he is because of his size."

Annabelle closed her eyes, envisioning a child monster.

1. *Wait. I've seen this child in Eddie's office. He doesn't look so big or so bad.*
2. *But he's always been sitting down whenever I've gotten a glimpse of him...*

"Have you brought him to counseling?" she asked, thinking Danny might benefit from Nux Vomica, a homeopathic remedy for irritable, fault-finding meat-eaters.

"Oh, Barbara adores psychiatry and has had Danny in therapy since he was three. Now Danny thinks that everyone has to relate to him with the same sensitivity that his therapist shows him. But real life can't be like that, you know?"

Annabelle stared out the window. "Why didn't you tell me this before?"

"I just thought I should warn you," said Eddie, "because Barbara has been very critical of my former girlfriends. I did consider fighting for custody. But then... what good would that have done? It would have shredded Danny to pieces. I care too much about him to do that. I even care too much about Barbara to do that. Even though leaving Danny was the hardest thing I've ever done, fighting over him would have been the worst thing I could have done. Children are the last battleground in divorce, you know. But I, for one, refuse to fight."

Sarah paused on Eddie's porch, pointing to the huge papier-mâché mask of St Francis of Assisi. "What's that?" asked Sarah.

"That's a mask of St Francis of Assisi. He was the patron saint of animals."

"What's he doing on Eddie's porch?" asked Sarah.

"I think he belongs to Eddie's brother," said Annabelle, ringing the doorbell. "It's a Bread and Puppet thing."

"What's Bread and Puppet?"

"It's social theatre."

Eddie appeared at the door. He reached out to hug Annabelle but she backed away. He nodded.

"Hi!" he boomed. "Come on in!"

Sarah cautiously stepped up into the apartment and Annabelle followed her. Eddie waved them into the living room where a large boy sat, his face covered by a copy of *Scientific American*.

"This is my son Danny," said Eddie, nudging Danny who stood up and put down the magazine.

"Hi," said Sarah in a dour voice.

Danny sauntered over and stood in front of Sarah. "Ayyyhhh!" he shouted in Sarah's face.

"Argghhh!" screamed Sarah, running behind Annabelle. Then she peeked out and Danny shouted in her face again.

Annabelle gave Eddie a concerned expression.

Eddie laughed and said, "Are you guys hungry? I made a pizza and we've been waiting for you to start eating."

They all sat around the tiny kitchen table. Eddie served everyone a piece of plain cheese pizza.

"Where's Sam?" asked Annabelle.

"He has a concert," said Eddie. "What should we do today?"

"What's the capital of Oklahoma?" said Sarah to Danny. "I bet you don't know."

"Oklahoma City," said Danny, confidently.

"OK," she said, "What's the capital of Wyoming?"

"Cheyenne," said Danny. "What's the capital of Argentina?"

Sarah paused.

"Buenos Aires," said Danny. "I bet I can sing something you can't."

"What's that?" said Eddie.

Danny took a sip of apple juice, cleared his throat, and began singing in Latin, in a clear alto voice. Sarah put down her pizza and stared at him.

When Danny was finished he smiled and said, "That was from *Huc me sydereo descendere jussit Olympo.*" His voice was low and smooth, like a classical radio disk jockey.

Nobody said anything.

"It's Renaissance music," explained Danny.

"That was very nice," Eddie said at last and Annabelle nodded emphatically.

"Yeah," said Sarah, "that was good. I bet I can sing something you can't."

"What?" challenged Danny.

Sarah raised the index and middle fingers on both hands and waved them from side to side, chirping, "Little bunny foo foo hopping through the forest, picking up the field mice and boppin' 'em on the head—" She made a fist with her right hand and tapped it with the palm of her left hand.

"That's an absolutely ridiculous song!" interrupted Danny.

"Don't interrupt," said Eddie. "Keep going, Sarah."

Sarah continued and Eddie joined in, "Down came a fairy and she said..." Sarah and Eddie shook their index fingers at each other. "Little bunny foo foo don't you go hopping through the forest, picking up the field mice and boppin' 'em on the head!"

Annabelle, Eddie and Sarah all laughed. "Where did you learn that?" said Annabelle to Sarah.

"From TV," said Sarah.

"That's an old camp song," said Eddie. Danny was scowling.

"Don't you think it's funny?" asked Eddie.

"No, it's very stupid," said Danny.

"I bet you can't sing it," smirked Sarah.

"Of course I can," said Danny.

"Go ahead," she said.

Danny sang the song, waving his index and middle fingers; then Sarah and Eddie joined in until Danny laughed.

They spent the afternoon playing basketball at a park by the Mystic River. At dusk Eddie heated up two cans of tomato soup.

"Are you going to stay overnight?" Danny said to Annabelle.

"No," said Annabelle, shaking her head. Sarah looked incredulous.

"That's too bad," said Danny.

"Why would we stay overnight?" said Sarah, spilling a spoonful of soup on her sweater and looking down to see where it had landed.

"My father's other girlfriends used to stay overnight," said Danny.

"My mother is not your father's girlfriend," Sarah carefully explained.

"Oh no?" said Danny, raising his right eyebrow.

"No!" insisted Sarah, looking at Eddie. "He helps us with our car. They're just friends."

Annabelle and Eddie looked at each other.

"She's your girlfriend, isn't she?" asked Danny, pointing at Annabelle.

Eddie took Annabelle's hand. "She's my best friend," he said.

Danny and Sarah looked at each other.

"I told you so," said Danny.

Eddie called a little later than usual that evening.

"Sarah interrogated me about our relationship all the way home," said Annabelle.

"I think the kids had a great day!" said Eddie.

"Once again she informed me that I must never get married again because I already did that and it didn't work. But she doesn't seem to be upset about you being my boyfriend. She had a good time too."

"Didn't they?" said Eddie. "They ended up playing very well together. I think Danny enjoyed being with Sarah more than he enjoyed being with me. That really surprised me because usually he's so antisocial. They have him in controlled play settings at school but today he was actually spontaneous. And then he was disappointed that you wouldn't be staying overnight. That never happened before!"

"So we met with his approval?"

Eddie paused. "Why are you angry?" he asked eventually.

Annabelle shook her head in exasperation.

"What's wrong?" said Eddie to the silent telephone.

"If we hadn't met with his approval what would you have done? Cut us off like you did all your other girlfriends?"

"Annabelle, if Sarah hadn't liked me, wouldn't you have been disappointed?"

Annabelle remained silent, realizing she would have ended their relationship if Sarah hadn't liked Eddie.

"We're trying to do a lot," said Eddie finally, interrupting Annabelle's thoughts. "We're trying to get two only children together with as little friction as possible. I love you. And I love Danny and Sarah and I've just been so happy about everyone getting along. I'm looking forward to meeting your mom next weekend. Danny won't be there and neither will Sam. Will you be more relaxed then?"

"I'm sorry," sighed Annabelle. "It's just that there have been so many changes in my life recently – and I've come to feel as if I'm being inspected by Sam and Joanne and Don and Danny... And I wonder if our relationship depends on their approval."

"I'm sorry you feel that way. What can I do to help?"

To: EWRIGHT
From: ABonney

Thank you for bringing lunch today. Our relationship is complex. I do love you. And I am happy that everything went well when we met Danny.

I just drafted some new poems. Here they are:

(Currently Untitled)

Did you ever notice
That my daughter and your son
Wear the eyes of their other parents,
The ones that came before us
And now hide in the bushes
Of our cerebrums?
Did you ever catch those eyes
And look away
From the stranger

On the path we walked once
Long ago, into that dark forest
Where trees had grabby arms
And wouldn't let go
And pounded on our doors
At midnight?

Why do neither of our children
Have our eyes? Where did they go?
X and X and
X and Y, his green,
Not brown like yours,
Hers blue, not hazel
Like mine.

Last night the moon was full
Of negotiations. We plan
To meet again.
A long time ago now
You asked me to teach you
About poems. On the telephone last night
My voice had iron in it.

This morning is so early it's black
Except for the light bulbs I've lit.
I need to make eyes with you
So we can see ourselves
Looking back. I need to understand
This baby mania, this passion casserole
They call parenthood.

   Danger

Don't you see the danger
I'm in? Wanting
To grow now and blossom and bloom
With sprouts and new leaves and pulp and earth?
Once I saw a tree trunk

With the body of a woman,
It's torso reclining, watching
The night.
Last night I dreamt four men
Were forcing a dead Christmas tree
Through my door
And I kept begging: "Take it out!"
And they kept screaming: "No, it's yours!"
Don't you see the danger
I'm in
Now that the pine cone matters?
Now do you see
How hopelessly I want to
Forebear and bear
New fruit?

To: ABonney
From: EWRIGHT

A new poem for you, Annabelle:

How could you have known
You were the dream
I had several years ago
Of my perfect love?

Dreams can't dream.

When was the last time
You saw the angels
Walk across the sky?

A star lights up
Shows you the way

Though a forest silent
With trees

So patiently
Calling out.

It's the telephone.
It's for you.
It's God.

While Annabelle drove, Sarah spoke non-stop to her Grandma Mary.

It had been an effort to get Mary into the car. Annabelle signed her out of the nursing home and slowly walked with her, opened each door and waited and waited. She realized she hadn't been visiting nearly as often since she'd been with Eddie; now her visits were limited to quick trips in and out of the building on Sundays instead of the extended visits she used to make during which Mary would become increasingly confused.

When they arrived at Eddie's house, Sarah explained the huge mask on Eddie's porch.

"That's St Francis of Assisi," said Sarah, "he belongs to Eddie's brother."

"Oh that's nice," said Mary, "his brother."

Eddie opened the door and led them all in. "What's that smell?" said Sarah.

"Baked potatoes and chicken!"

"I'm not eating any chicken," said Sarah.

"You can watch television until lunch is ready," he said.

Annabelle introduced Mary to Eddie. He had pulled his long hair back in a tight ponytail in deference to her. Mary was extremely quiet, nodding her head and smiling for no apparent reason.

Sarah and Annabelle never ate meat and although Annabelle cut Mary's chicken into bite-size pieces, Mary didn't eat any either.

After devouring her potato, Sarah ran back to the living room to watch more television while Annabelle, Eddie and Mary remained at the kitchen table.

Mary fingered her paper napkin and folded it carefully. She held it up to Annabelle and solemnly announced, "I want you to have this."

Annabelle smiled and took the napkin. "Thank you," she said.

Mary continued working on her potato, which she had slowly consumed with her spoon and now there were only tiny bits of white pulp attached to the brown skin that she didn't try to eat.

"Well it's very nice that you could come here for lunch today," said Eddie, smiling, his arm around Annabelle.

Mary looked at him, then stiffly raised her right arm and held it out straight, high in front of her. "Heil Hitler!" she exclaimed.

Annabelle and Eddie looked at each other. "What's that?" said Eddie, still smiling.

"She will do anything you say," said Mary.

Annabelle grimaced and said, "What are you talking about Mom?!"

Mary returned to her potato and continued humming.

Annabelle helped Eddie wash the dishes while Mary sat at the table, still scraping the potato skin around the plate.

"She never said anything like that before," Annabelle whispered.

"Maybe I remind her of your father," said Eddie. "He was a big guy, right? Maybe that's symbolic of how your father treated her... Maybe seeing you with me brought back some image of when she was with him."

Just when those memories had faded far enough to seem like distant nightmares, something happens to jolt me awake and it all comes back and it never goes away.

There are just too many variables to figure all this out... All the paraphernalia my father left behind when he left Mom – his army jacket, which Mom gave to Dennis while we were dating – it has that mysterious spearhead insignia that Dennis kept obsessively researching, claiming it was the symbol of the OSS... That kid in high school, whose dad was openly involved in organized crime, telling me that my father had sponsored his father to join our country club...

At least my father took all his guns with him when he left, along with all his money.

But after all this time, why did Mom say that?

Annabelle shuddered, staring at her mother, a strange and tender woman who had prayed to forget.

12

"What if he doesn't show up?" said Annabelle.

"He'll show up," said Eddie. "He'll be in contempt if he doesn't."

"Well what if he shows up but says he doesn't want the divorce?"

"What if you were to stop worrying about it?" said Eddie.

"I was like this the night before we got married," Annabelle said. "I was absolutely convinced that he wouldn't show up, that he'd leave me standing at the altar."

"If only he had," whispered Eddie.

She was strangely calm in the morning. After taking Sarah to school, Annabelle drove to the courthouse, and found her way to the hearing room. She was supposed to appear at nine but discovered that half the room was to appear then and she would have to wait until her case was called. Her elderly lawyer, Eileen O'Malley, showed up at 8:50, and a few minutes later Dennis arrived.

Eileen sat next to Annabelle and quietly reiterated that the entire process should take no more than two minutes. The judge would ask if she and Dennis wanted the divorce; they would both say yes and then it would be over.

Dennis sat across the room from her, scowling. Annabelle pointed him out to Eileen, who said, "He's so morose. How did you stand it?"

Finally they were called.

Dennis said "Yes" when the judge asked if he wanted the divorce. The judge looked up because Dennis spat out the word.

Then it was over.

Dennis quickly left and didn't look back.

Outside the hearing room, Eileen shook Annabelle's hand.

"Well, congratulations, now it's finally over. Good luck. Let me know if anything else comes up. I have to get back to the office."

Annabelle sat on a hall bench and waited a few minutes before descending the courthouse stairs. Once outside, near her car, she found Dennis waiting for her. His eyes were red and wet.

"Well I guess that's it," he said.

Annabelle nodded.

"My life is over," he said.

Annabelle looked away.

"Your life is just beginning, Dennis. Now you're free. You never wanted to be married anyway."

Her clammy hands clutched her briefcase, which dangled before her. Her car sat in the beating sun. She reached for her keys, and then paused.

"I guess you're right, Annie. I never really wanted to marry you. But we made a great kid, didn't we?"

"We did. Are you going to start seeing her again?"

"I think I'm gonna move on. I'm moving to Canada. I don't know."

"Why don't you go back to school for your art? You could become a graphic artist."

"No. Life just sucks, I don't care."

"Well I've got to go," she said.

"I hope you have a good life," he said.

"You too."

"I guess we should have done this a long time ago."

"That would have saved a lot of stress on both of us, wouldn't it," she agreed.

"Listen." He paused. "I really don't want there to be hard feelings between us. It's best for Sarah if we can get along. We're divorced now, can we just go get a cup of coffee and talk about things?"

Annabelle stared at the street. Finally she nodded and they got into her car.

They sat on wrought-iron patio chairs in a small Italian bakery. Annabelle watched the revolving pastry case filled with whipped-cream cakes and felt her stomach turn along with the desserts.

Neither spoke. Finally she said, "I really think you should go back to school for art. I've always admired your paintings."

Dennis stared into space.

"Well, what are you going to do now?" she said.

He started to cry.

"I guess we should go now," she said, gulping her tea. It was hot. It burnt her throat.

Dennis followed her to her car. Neither spoke. She dropped him off at his apartment, then drove home, called Eddie, and described all that had happened.

Eddie said, "Uh oh."

"What's wrong?"

"You shouldn't have done that."

"I know. But he looked so forlorn. It always takes him a long time to adjust to changes."

"You need to just stay away from him, Annabelle. If you give him an inch he'll take it for all it's worth."

"Well I won't see him any more," she said.

"I love you," he said.

Her response stuck in her scalded throat.

That afternoon Annabelle scrubbed the bathtub and kitchen floor, intent on getting her house in order.

1. *Now I am divorced.*
2. *What now?*

The whole thing had seemed too easy, so uncharacteristic of their chaotic marriage.

She picked up Sarah after school.

"You didn't tell me I didn't have to go to after-school today," Sarah happily said. "Are you and Daddy divorced now?"

Annabelle nodded.

Sarah sat in the kitchen while Annabelle kneaded a loaf a rye bread.

"Do we have to do anything else?" asked Sarah, half-heartedly reading her social-studies book.

"About what?" said Annabelle.

"About the divorce? Is that all you have to do?"

"Yup. That's it," said Annabelle, shaping the loaf into a large glass pan.

Sarah closed her book. "Can I go ride my bike?"

Annabelle nodded. Soon after Sarah had gone outside, the front door screen slammed and she ran back into the house, carrying a bouquet of roses.

"Daddy's outside," she said, frowning. "He told me to give you these. He told me that we'll never see him again."

Annabelle washed and dried her hands, told Sarah to stay in the kitchen, and walked out on the porch.

"Thank you for the flowers, Dennis," she said, "but I don't want them."

"I wanted to give them to you before I die," he said.

"You're going to die?"

"Yes, I'm going to kill myself now," he said, getting in his car. He started the engine and drove away.

Annabelle went back in the apartment and sat at her kitchen table.

"What's going on?" said Sarah.

"Can you go watch television for a little while?" asked Annabelle.

"Can't I ride my bike?"

"No, don't go outside right now. I have to think."

As soon as Sarah was sitting in the living room with the TV switched on Annabelle called Eddie, and described what had happened.

"Well, you better call the police," he said.

"I hate this. I knew it seemed too easy. I knew he'd do something like this."

"Or call someone in his family. Call his sister, the one you like. If someone threatens suicide, you really have to try to stop them."

"I know," she whispered.

"This is hard. Do you want me to come over?"

"No," she said, hanging up.

She called Dennis's sister Ellen.

"Oh Jesus," shouted Ellen. "When did this happen?"

"A few minutes ago."

"Have you called the police?"

"Not yet."

"I'll call them. Did he say where he was going?"

"No."

"Well, I'm going to call the police now."

While the dinner noodles boiled, the doorbell rang. Two patrol officers, a young woman and a middle-aged man, stood outside. Annabelle invited them in.

The woman had short dark hair and a walkie-talkie. She asked Annabelle to explain exactly what had happened.

"We've alerted the cruisers in town to look for him. We'd like to wait here and see if he gets in touch with you."

Annabelle served Sarah some spinach noodles with butter. The telephone rang.

Annabelle moved the phone to the living room.

"Hi Annie," breathed Dennis. "What are you doing?"

She could hear the alcohol in his voice.

"Where are you?" she asked.

"When we went out today I knew you still loved me. I know you do, Annie. Just give it up, OK?"

"Dennis, where are you?" Annabelle looked at the female officer who then signalled to the other officer waiting in the patrol car.

"We're trying to trace it," whispered the woman.

Annabelle held her hand over the mouthpiece and nodded.

"Just keep him on," said the woman.

"I want to fuck you so hard," said Dennis, "I just want to fuck you so hard. I know you want me, just admit it."

Annabelle looked at the phone.

1. Here I am, trying to save his life, and all he can do is be offensive.
2. Now there are police in my house with a blinking blue light outside and the door wide open while Sarah is sitting there eating dinner alone with her eyes wide open.
3. Now the neighbours really will talk about me. Good old Dennis.

"Are you there?" he shouted.

"Where are you, Dennis?"

The walkie-talkie made a sudden, high-pitched, static sound.

"Are there cops there Annie?" he said, his voice quick.

"Why would there be?—"

He hung up the phone.

Annabelle looked at the policewoman who stood up and went outside to the cruiser. Moments later she returned, saying, "We'll just have to wait for him to call back."

Annabelle asked her to sit down. They began talking about the town, the loveliness of Gardenia, and boy, can't men be jerks.

"Can you guess why I wanted the divorce?" said Annabelle.

She felt that nauseating excitement, just like old times. Dennis always liked to fight in loud, dramatic ways. Soon he called back and the process began again.

Dennis described his sexual desires in ever greater graphic detail while Annabelle held the phone away from her ear, tuning in only long enough to hear him shout, "Are you listening to me?" And she would say "Yes" and he would resume the verbal rape. She found herself meditating on her guilt: was this punishment somehow deserved, after what she'd asked from Eddie in the pine grove?

Three times Dennis hung up, and then called back. After another hour, the policeman outside yelled, "We found him! He's at the booth in back of the Pawn's Pride."

The officer inside explained that Dennis would be taken to a psychiatric hospital in Waltham and thanked Annabelle for her assistance. Then they left.

Annabelle had helped Sarah get ready for bed throughout the deepening chaos. Now Sarah stood on her bed in her pyjamas, her chubby hands on her thin hips.

"So Daddy is crazy," said Sarah, "I know that he is, Mom."

"He had a bad day," explained Annabelle.

They lay down together and sang each other to sleep.

The telephone woke Annabelle in the morning. She answered it in a weary mental fog.

"Hello?" she said, expecting Eddie's voice.

"Hello," said Dennis.

Annabelle felt a sharp shock. *No.*

"Where are you?" she said.

"I'm at a phone booth."

"What? What?"

"Do you know what happened? They handcuffed me, and then they took me to a stupid, frigging mental hospital."

"They let you out?!"

"No one stopped me. You really do hate me, don't you," he seethed.

"You escaped!" she shouted, slamming down the phone.

She called Eddie.

"Come on over," he said, "I'll take the day off."

"What about Sarah? I don't know if I should send her to school today."

"I'd send her, but tell her teacher and the school office that her father is not allowed to pick her up. In your agreement he has to have permission from you to see her, right?"

"Yes he does," she sighed. "I have physical custody, so he has to ask first."

"Make sure they know that, and then come over here. We'll figure out what to do when you get here."

1. *I shouldn't keep asking for Eddie's advice.*
2. *I'm too tired to think for myself.*

After taking Sarah to school and talking to her teacher and the principal about Dennis, Annabelle stopped back at her apartment to call Daryl.

"I'm not coming in today." She described the events of the previous night.

"Can you stay at Ed's this weekend?" said Daryl.

"I don't think I should. I'd worry about Sarah saying we stayed at her mother's boyfriend's house. It would just complicate things right now. I might go to a motel."

"Stay here," said Daryl.

1. *Daryl is house-sitting for an MVI Vice President who's been transferred to Japan.*
2. *It would probably be easier to stay with Daryl than at a motel. It would be free, at least.*
3. *It would be best to get out of Gardenia for a few days.*

"Come on, it's a big house," said Daryl. "It wouldn't be a problem. It's not even mine."

"OK," she finally said. "If you're sure we won't inconvenience you."

"Meet me at the office at five," he said. "You can follow me over."

After packing overnight clothes for herself and for Sarah, Annabelle started out the door. Then she paused, went back to the kitchen, and called Dennis's sister.

"I'm just going out the door," said Ellen. "He called me from a bus station. I'm going to pick him up."

"So they just let him out? Just like that?"

"Yeah, they said he was intoxicated but didn't appear to be suicidal. They couldn't hold him in the psychiatric unit for that. But he shouldn't have been driving so now he has other problems with the police. Maybe this time we'll be able to control him a little bit."

"Sarah and I are going to stay at a friend's house tonight. Can I call you tomorrow and find out how things are going?"

"Yeah," said Ellen, "he's got to get his act together this time. We have too much to worry about with Mom. We're going to get him to straighten out and fly right."

Eddie had taken the plastic sheets of insulation off the windows in his apartment. Annabelle lay with him on his futon as they stared through clear glass after sharing tea and bagels and lighting incense and candles.

"I probably don't need to be here," Annabelle said after a time. "I'm sorry you took the day off from work. Dennis's little escapades always set off chain reactions. We took sick days and his sister probably did too. And Sarah's school is watching for him and last night the entire police force in Gardenia got involved. He likes to share his problems."

"He likes to transfer them to anyone willing to go along," said Eddie, "I've never heard of anyone with so many codependent relationships before. Can we not talk about him for a while?"

They were both silent for a long time.

"Do you want to talk about getting married?" asked Annabelle. She looked at Eddie. He smiled, nodded.

"Do you want to set a date right now?" he asked.

"No, but I was just thinking about something. You know that

when I married Dennis I didn't take his name. I don't think women should symbolically lose their identity that way. When we get married you don't want me to take your name, do you?"

Eddie frowned. "Well, I was hoping you would," he finally said.

"Really? Why?"

"To become part of the family."

"Hhhhmmmm. I didn't think it would matter to you. I was also wondering whether you would wear a wedding ring. I've never seen you wear any jewellery. When we're married will you wear a ring?"

Eddie sighed. "I don't like rings. I didn't wear one when I was married to Barbara. She had this friend who did silversmith work, and she commissioned him to make me the ugliest ring I'd ever seen. It was all gnarled and twisted and after a few months it was all tarnished. Kind of symbolic of our marriage."

Annabelle laughed. "I'll get you a gold one and will you wear it?"

Eddie looked away. "Do I have to? I don't like jewellery."

"How about this. I'll take your name if you wear my ring."

Eddie took her hand in his and whispered, "I'll wear your ring with great honour and devotion whether or not you take my name."

1. Women don't really have names in this culture; a woman takes her father's name.
2. My father was absolutely heinous. I don't want his name.
3. What kind of feminist statement is it to keep your father's name?
4. I could change my name to something like Annabelle Marydaughter.
5. That sounds really stupid.

"OK," she whispered.

In early evening, Sarah raced around the empty corporate halls while she and Annabelle waited for Daryl to complete his weekly status report. On the way out, Sarah insisted on punching the elevator buttons, interrogating Daryl about his house and private life.

"Do you have kids?" she asked, following Daryl to the multi-level parking garage where senior employees parked.

"I have two," said Daryl. "But they're older than you."

"How old?"

"My daughter Kyra is twenty-four and my son Evan is twenty-eight."

"Wow," said Sarah. "They're not really kids. They won't be there?"

"No," said Daryl, reaching his car. "They don't live with me any more. Annabelle, I'll drive out to the Front Street exit and wait for you there; you follow me along Mem Drive. OK?"

They followed Daryl's red convertible through rush hour traffic to Newton.

"This is some house," said Annabelle, getting out of her car.

Daryl stood with her and looked at the house.

"Yeah," he said. "Too bad it isn't mine."

While Sarah wandered around the massive gardens, Annabelle asked Daryl if he would mind having Eddie come by for dinner.

"He said he'd pick up some Chinese food for us," said Annabelle.

"Sure, have him over," said Daryl, "but I'm going to meet a friend in Harvard Square. You can hang out in any room downstairs. I get lonely here sometimes." He smiled, watching Sarah attempt to climb an ornamental cherry tree.

Eddie arrived at seven that evening, just as Daryl was leaving.

"Mom didn't tell me you were coming over," complained Sarah, watching Eddie carefully carry the large bag of food.

"I got you something," said Eddie.

"What?"

He put the bag on the kitchen table and handed her a pocket pegboard game.

"Can we play this?" she said.

"That's why I got it for you," he said.

Annabelle served the tofu lo mein and egg rolls, startled by the elegant kitchen plates.

After eating dinner and playing her new game, Sarah wanted four bedtime songs before she would consider sleeping on the convertible sofa she and Annabelle would be sharing. Annabelle sang; Sarah called her back twice. Finally she was asleep.

Annabelle returned to the kitchen and sat at the table with Eddie. The high windows had no curtains or shades but there was great privacy, the entire area being enclosed by huge fences covered with flowering vines.

Eddie stood up, turned off the lights, and sat on the floor by the work island in the middle of the room. Annabelle joined him in the darkness, on the floor. They both stared through the windows at the huge full moon that was just starting to wane.

"Do you want to kiss me?" whispered Annabelle.

Eddie leant back against the butcher-block leg, the raw, smooth wood.

"I always want to kiss you," he said, "I want to eat you up."

Annabelle sighed. "Why is that? Why do you feel that way about me?"

Eddie laughed. "Why do you want to know? Why do you have to have reasons for everything?"

He leant over, kissed her, and slid down on his back. She slid on top of him.

"Rape me," he whispered, opening his mouth wide.

Annabelle laughed, "Right here on the floor?"

"Do me," he said.

Annabelle assessed the situation.

1. Sarah is a heavy sleeper; probably won't wake up until morning.
2. Even if she wakes up, she would probably just call for me; unlikely that she'd venture out of bed.
3. Even if she ventured out of bed and found her way to the kitchen, she wouldn't know how to turn on the lights, so we'd be shielded by darkness.
4. I guess it's OK.

Annabelle finally, obediently unzipped Eddie's blue jeans and tugged them to his ankles. Then she lifted her dress and pulled off her underwear.

"Daryl better not get back while we're doing this," she mumbled. "I hope Sarah doesn't wake up."

"I'm your slave," said Eddie.

She paused and then pulled his erection inside her and pushed down hard. He moaned so she did it again, holding his arms above his head, pressing her mouth against his neck, and kneading his skin with her lips.

She became aware of herself in triplicate. She was a detached observer, scanning the kitchen door, contemplating the absurdity of the moment, the lavish cooking utensils, the elaborate windows with the moon shining in and a huge man seemingly powerless beneath her. She was herself, in her body, sensing his hair mingling with hers, his scent and his murmurs. And she was he, embracing surrender, lowering her legs, wrapping her feet around his calves and pulling him deeper inside her in waves of fury.

Then she wasn't aware of herself at all; all at once she was lost in the pleasure of power, an entirely new door, a new way of opening.

13

For weeks there was no word from Dennis. The calmness of the situation made Annabelle nervous.

She turned her attention to a different conflict.

When Eddie visited Annabelle's apartment, he often brought Danny, who would explore the drawers and closets. Once he found her pack of Tarot cards and flung them high in the air.

"What are these?!" exclaimed Danny.

Before Annabelle could respond, Eddie was gathering the cards, saying, "This is not your property. I want you to apologize."

Danny ignored Eddie and Eddie did not pressure Danny. *It is the way they are.*

Annabelle shuddered. Earlier she had carefully arranged the cards in a star pattern, projecting her goals and wishes. *Eddie and Danny do not understand the significance of this for me, the significance of symbol language.*

Later at the office, Eddie warned her: "I need to ask a favour. Could you keep your Wicca things hidden better? If Barbara finds out that you have a pack of Tarot cards, she'll cause all kinds of problems for us."

"Are you serious?" said Annabelle.

"She's a Christian fundamentalist," said Eddie. "She has very strong objections to the occult."

"No, I meant were you serious about your request. You obviously were. You are such an intelligent person. I don't understand how you can ask for such a favour. Why don't you just stop Danny from going through my drawers?" *Is he saying that Barbara's spirituality is more valid than mine?* Her cheeks were flushed; her hands trembled.

"It really is in your best interest to keep this stuff out of Danny's reach," Eddie finally said. "Maybe we shouldn't visit your apartment so much."

"Eddie," said Annabelle, "this is a problem. This presents a real problem for our relationship."

"I don't think so," he said. "Don't get upset about it."

"Well, maybe we should address this."

"No. Forget I mentioned it. Just let it go."

They took sullen Danny and sceptical Sarah on day trips together, to the beach and to the zoo, where Danny would yank Sarah's hair, or scratch and gouge her arm, drawing blood.

1. *Thankfully Sarah is surprisingly forgiving of Danny.*
2. *But when Eddie admonishes Danny it sounds like he's apologizing to him.*
3. *Eddie thinks that allowing him to behave any way he wants is a way of showing his love.*
4. *Or does everyone simply believe that Danny cannot control his own behaviour?*
5. *Am I missing something?*

Comments about the relationship between Eddie and Danny often came to Annabelle's tongue, but stopped there. *He is Danny's father and even if his ex-wife won't allow him to have any authority with his son, it's not my place to interfere.*

Yet when he had time alone, Eddie returned to Annabelle's apartment, visiting at least three evenings a week, always leaving in the middle of the night, like a bandit, hidden from Sarah.

At the summer solstice, Eddie and Annabelle had a free day alone together, and spent the evening walking along the beach in Gardenia.

"What do you want for your birthday?" asked Annabelle.

"Nothing," he said. "Please don't get me anything."

"Come on. What do you want?"

"I really don't need anything. I'm perfectly happy."

"Can you come over for dinner? I'll cook you any meal you want."

"No." He paused. "I'm going to play chess with Mitchell that night. We haven't had a chance to get together in a while."

Annabelle looked away.

"You'd rather spend your birthday with Mitchell than with me?"

"Well I haven't really had a chance to keep up with other people lately. Hasn't that happened to you? Don't you have other friends you'd like to spend some time with?"

1. *Here it comes; he's bored.*
2. *He was only interested in me because I was unavailable.*
3. *Now that I'm free he doesn't want me any more.*
4. *Men are like that.*

Unwelcome tears menaced her eyes, which inadvertently glanced at Eddie's annoyed expression. He said nothing.

"Yes, I have lost touch with my other friends. We've been spending a lot of time together."

"I think it's important to have other friends," said Eddie.

"Do you still want to marry me?" she whispered.

Eddie threw back his head and laughed. "Why in the world do you want to get married again?"

They had walked back to Annabelle's apartment; she slowly closed the door behind them, then sat on her bed, her head in her hands.

"You seem depressed," he said, not sitting down. "Should I leave?"

"You don't want to get married now."

"I think we should wait a while before we make any decisions. Marriage is a big step and we both rushed into it the first time. We could live together first."

Annabelle shook her head. "I lived with Dennis before we got married and that didn't work."

"I didn't live with Barbara first and I wish I had. It would have given me a chance to see what a bitch she is."

Eddie, I thought I knew you. Where did you go?

"Why don't you want to marry me?"

He sat on the floor, stretching his legs.

"I'm just afraid," he said.

"What are you afraid of?"

"I'm afraid of being trapped again."

"You're afraid of being trapped by me?"

He nodded. "I told my parents that we wanted to get married. They said we should live together first."

Annabelle shook her head, "Eddie, I am almost thirty-four years old. If I'm going to have another baby I want to start trying soon and I want to get married before I get pregnant."

"Well I think my parents are right."

"I do not care what your parents think!" she shouted, amazed at her expression of anger. "I really can't understand why their opinion is so important to you. I've never consulted either of my parents before making any decision."

"It's not my problem that your parents never cared about you," he said.

1. *Mr Hyde. I finally convince myself that this guy is different from all the others and that this time the other shoe won't drop.*
2. *His shoe is bigger than any I've ever seen: size fifteen at least.*

"I only made love to you because we were going to get married," she whispered.

Eddie looked perplexed. "I can make love to anyone I want!" he exclaimed.

"Not to me."

"What do you mean? We've made love lots of times."

"Not any more."

"You won't make love to me because I don't want to get married?" She nodded.

"That's an ultimatum," he announced. "Nobody issues me an ultimatum."

Annabelle sighed. "I'm sorry I yelled at you. I want you to leave now."

Eddie stared at her. "I just think that my parents are right, I just think we should live together first."

"I can't do that. There have been cases where women have lost custody of their children because they were living with their lovers. You and I both know that Dennis would give me nothing but grief if we were to live together without first getting married."

"I don't care about Dennis! Dennis is not my problem! We can't centre our lives around his expectations!"

"I'm just saying that I'm not risking Sarah for your sake. And I want to have another baby while I still have time. Either we get married or we break up."

"I can't take an ultimatum!"

"When did you talk to your parents about this?"

"Last weekend when they came over to visit with me and Sam. I told them we wanted to get married but they insisted we shouldn't. My mom is still awfully upset about Karen and Andy and they made me realize that it is wise to wait. It is."

"I don't want to be part of your family anyway."

"Let's just give it time. I love you so much," he sighed.

Annabelle laughed. "You just love my body. I'm just a sex object to you."

"I love you."

"You told me that you wanted to marry me."

"We have to live together first."

Neither spoke until Annabelle walked to the front door and opened it.

"I do not want to see you any more."

Eddie nodded, stood up, and walked out the door.

She watched from the window as he got in his jeep. He sat there for an hour. He came back to the door. She opened it. They were both crying.

"I want to marry you," he said.

She shook her head.

"I don't want to marry you."

He shrugged. Neither moved.

"I want to marry you," he repeated.

She stared at him.

"Listen, I'm crazy about you. I never said I didn't want to marry you."

"Yes, you did."

"I said I wanted to live together first."

"That's the same thing."

"I still want to marry you."

"Even without living with me first?"

"Yes."

"Even if your parents disapprove?"

"Yes."

To: ABonney
From: EWRIGHT

I feel sick from fighting with you. Then when Sarah got dropped off from her play date in the middle of it we didn't have a chance to get through all the feelings. You didn't answer the phone when I called last night.

I'm so sorry.

My parents have their opinions and I have mine. Like you, I want to have a baby and if you feel a need to marry beforehand, then let's do it. My parents are caught in my brother's problems right now and so they equate you with Karen.

I wrote a letter to Andy last night. I got thinking about how rushed life can become. I've shared so many special moments with you and Sarah. So busy. Our children both so cute and young. So much to learn so quickly. Thought about Thich Nhat Hanh. Thought about Andy, in crisis. Our lives are all filled with all we can possibly handle. In my letter, I told Andy about what we say during massage...

"No place to go"

"Nothing to do"

"Just be here now"

Something really clicked in all this.

I reasoned as follows:

If we seek approval from others for our self worth we become their slaves. AND if we seek happiness from our achievements or the weather or any reason we become their slaves also. So if not NOW then when? What reason! This is the lesson of the Tao. Do you see it? We're still slaves to our minds. Reasons deciding whether we're happy or not.

So just be happy. Right now. FOR NO REASON.

In Peace and Love,

Eddie

To: EWRIGHT
From: ABonney

It's a little after 3 p.m. I just realized that my MVI Access user guide is in better shape than I thought it was.

So for a while today I looked through my old mail messages, starting with your Next machine message last November.

Rereading those messages reminded me of how beautiful you have been to me.

    I never meant to issue you an ultimatum but my biological clock is ticking. Do you understand?

    Annabelle

To: ABonney
From: EWRIGHT

Of Ferns and Clay

Over and Over
Over and Over
I feel you come
take shape
As your legs stiffen
I thrill
Our paths
Like hand signals
in spirit land
Our Sperm + Egg
dancing

From the glade's edge
I place a green fern
on your beautiful swollen belly
its leaves a symbol
of the coming birth

The mother and child
The clay and little fern

...Eddie

14

Over a plate of fettuccine at their favourite Italian restaurant, Annabelle told Sarah the plan.

"We're going away for the Fourth of July," she said, while Sarah slurped the saucy noodles.

"Where?" asked Sarah, inspecting the complementary sugar packets in a cut-glass bowl on the table.

"Northern Vermont."

"You mean we're really going somewhere?" beamed Sarah. "For more than one day?"

"Yes."

"Where will we stay?"

"Eddie's parents have cottages on a lake up there and we'll stay in one of the cottages."

"Eddie? I don't want to stay with Eddie!"

Annabelle lifted her palms and lowered them slowly, gesturing for Sarah to lower her voice.

"Why not?" said Annabelle.

"Is Danny going to be there?"

"No, Danny will be spending the holiday with his mom."

"I just want it to be me and you," insisted Sarah. "If Eddie goes then I'm not going!"

"Well, the cottage is free so we could either stay in Gardenia for the weekend and not do anything or we could go up to Eddie's parents' farm and stay in a cottage."

"Let me think about it," pouted Sarah.

Sarah silently watched while Annabelle and Eddie piled their weekend clothes, towels and bedding into Eddie's red jeep. Then they stuffed Sarah in the back seat, surrounded by pillows.

They arrived at seven in the evening, as the sun arched high in the west. Tall poplars surrounded the dirt path to the cottage.

Eddie ambled onto the creaky porch and felt around the rafters for the old iron key, then opened the ancient wooden door. Sarah raced out of the car and Annabelle followed.

"You can go first," said Annabelle to Sarah.

"Where is it?" said Sarah, bouncing up and down.

"Here," said Eddie, showing Sarah the door to the bathroom. "I hope the water's been turned on." He walked around the corner to the kitchen and turned on the faucet. "Good," he said, "the water's on."

While Annabelle assessed the living room, Eddie grabbed her, lifting her high in the air. "How do you like the cottage?"

She continued looking around. "It's old."

"It's very old. It was the original milk house when this place was a farm. Mother had it renovated a few years ago but she kept most of the original features."

They brought in their bags, then they left for the beach.

Sarah baulked when she saw at least a dozen children of various ages darting around on the sand.

"This is it," said Eddie. "How do you like it?"

"Does your family own the beach?" asked Sarah.

"Yeah, this is all family land."

"Is everyone here your family?" she asked.

"Yep," he said as they got closer.

They were greeted by a young woman carrying a large toddler.

"Eddie!" she exclaimed. "How are you!"

"Carol," said Eddie, "this is Annabelle and Sarah. Carol is married to my cousin Mark. And this is Ethan, he's gotten huge!"

"Hi," said Carol, "welcome to the lake." She looked at Sarah and said, "There are lots of kids here."

Sarah grimaced. "I can see that."

Carol reached down and took her hand, "Come on," she said. "You have to meet Julie and Beth. They've been dying to meet you. Three eight-year-old girls are here, can you believe that!"

"I turned nine two months ago," said Sarah, reluctantly walking with Carol and her large placid baby.

One by one Annabelle was introduced to Eddie's brothers, their wives, his cousins and his uncle. Then Joanne appeared.

"You made it," she said. "Where's Sarah?"

Eddie pointed her out as she stood talking with Julie. "Well, she looks just like her mother," said Joanne to Annabelle, who was soon immersed in family chatter juxtaposed with rolling mountains, wide water, and a red Vermont setting sun.

That night, after Sarah had fallen asleep, Annabelle crept downstairs to the front porch and snuggled beside Eddie as he slept. For a while she listened to the brook sing and the cicadas hum. Then she reached down and fondled him, his gentle sleeping organ, until it became hard in her hands. She rubbed and kissed it and it stayed hard and it throbbed. Then she crept back upstairs.

Early the next morning there was a loud knock on the back porch door. Annabelle woke to hear voices on the porch. She quickly put on a sundress and hurried downstairs.

"Hiii," said Julie's mother, Donna, "I hope we didn't wake you, Julie couldn't wait to see Sarah again."

Donna's short hair was fair, her face open, her eyes wide.

"No, it's OK," said Annabelle, "I'll go wake her up."

Sarah and Julie went off to play and Donna stayed to share some coffee.

"How do you like it up here?" asked Donna. A warm breeze lifted the poplar leaves outside the porch.

"It's just beautiful," said Annabelle.

"Yeah," said Donna. "It can be a little overwhelming at first."

"What?" said Eddie. "How can this place be overwhelming?"

"Oh Ed," said Donna, "you know what I mean. The politics of it all."

"What politics?" said Eddie. They looked at each other and laughed, sharing a private joke.

Annabelle squinted.

"Your mother," Donna finally said, "your intimidating mother!"

"My mother? Intimidating?" said Eddie, laughing again.

"Those Wright boys," said Donna. "Carl's just the same way. We all forgive Joanne though. She really has a heart of gold."

"The problem is that she thinks Annabelle must be just like Karen," said Eddie.

"Karen?" asked Donna. "Why Karen?"

"You know, because she left her husband, and Sarah is close to the same age as Ben. Guilt by resemblance."

"Well the resemblance stops there, obviously," said Donna. "Annabelle, if you were anything like Karen you'd be drinking whiskey right now instead of herbal tea and you'd have a long pink streak in your hair and multiple tattoos and body piercings. Karen really was a wild one. But I think that was why Joanne loved her so much. Joanne loves to shock people. Have you noticed that, Annabelle?"

Annabelle nodded and Donna laughed again.

"I'll never forget the first time she got me alone," said Donna. "She went on and on about how Don always wants to poke her! I mean what was I to say?"

"She said that to me too!" said Annabelle.

"And the first time I ever came to dinner at their house," continued Donna, "I was talking about NYU, where I went to school. And out of the blue, Joanne said, 'So, you ever been raped?' Don and Carl just ignored it. Carl asked me to pass the potatoes, and I said, 'Why no, Joanne, actually, I never was raped.' Then she started talking about her garden. Now Ed, wouldn't you find that intimidating?"

"That's just Joanne," said Eddie.

"That's right," said Donna. "So Annabelle, she's like that to all of us. You have to take it with a grain of salt."

Annabelle attempted to smile and stared into space. *What if Joanne ever asks me that? Then she'll have me cornered and I'll have no defences. A grain of salt. A pillar of tears. It's all about the salt in the tears: looking back... at the terror, the sorrow, ingrained in the salt...*

"Why are you so quiet today?" said Eddie after Donna left. "I guess you really don't like it here."

"Actually, I love the lake," she whispered. "This is the most beautiful place I've ever been."

"Sarah seems to be having a great time. What are you thinking about?"

"Do you know what I did last night?"
"What do you mean?"
"While you were sleeping. Did I wake you?"
"No," he said, confused.
"I came down and lay beside you while you were sleeping on the porch."

Eddie smiled. "That's nice."
"I fondled you."
"You did?"
"You got very hard."
"Why didn't you wake me up?"
"I don't know, I thought it would wake you up."
"I wish it had. That would be a wonderful way to wake up."
"You think it was OK? I didn't think you'd mind."
"Of course it's OK. Why do you ask?"
"I feel like I did something improper."
"By fondling me?"
"In your sleep. Without your permission. Sometimes sex scares me. Sometimes it brings things up."

Eddie got up, returned with another cup of instant coffee for himself, another cup of tea for her. They were still sitting around the back-porch table, covered by a red-and-white-checkered cloth, a remnant from someone's kitchen in the 1950s. Fly swatters hung on exposed beams; there were no flies.

"We need to go to town this morning for some food," he said. "Tonight we're having a potluck on the lake. Then there are fireworks and the kids make these newspaper boats which we set on fire and sail out into the lake. Then we have a big bonfire."

Annabelle remained silent.

"I'd like to make a new by-law," said Eddie.
"What's that?"
"You can fondle me any time you want. You can make love to me in my sleep."

She nodded. "I thought you'd feel that way, but I just felt strange afterwards."

"Can I fondle you in your sleep? Can I make love to you then?"
"I don't know about that," she whispered, the hot cup at her lips, steam in her eyes.

After lunch, Julie insisted that Sarah stay and swim with her. Donna offered to watch them at the beach, so Eddie led Annabelle to the falls.

Along the way, he pointed to the earth around the banks and said, "There they are, mother's beloved jack-in-the-pulpits." Annabelle knelt down to inspect one.

"Wow, you really have to be looking for them; they blend right in with the ferns."

Eddie knelt beside her. "I always thought they were very sexual looking. Like little vulvas popping out of the ground."

Annabelle looked at him.

"Want to see the pine grove?" he asked.

She followed him through the woods; this time there was a hint of a path, not just snowy limbs.

The grove hadn't changed much since early spring although now it was warmer, muskier. The smell of pine was stronger.

Eddie sat on the log where he'd sat months earlier.

"Remember this place? Remember what we did here?"

Annabelle nodded, looking around.

"Want to sit with me?" he said.

She wandered beside him and sat on the log. Occasionally small creatures made sounds in the woods around them.

"The bears must be up by now," said Annabelle.

"Oh yeah, but they can smell us. They don't like to come near humans."

"But sometimes I read about bear attacks in parks."

"Those are grizzlies. We only have shy old black bears. Don't worry about them."

"It's really beautiful here."

"You like it? Have you forgiven my parents yet?"

Annabelle looked away. "I honestly do think your parents are nice but I don't think they like me."

"Sure they do. Last night mother told me what a doll Sarah is. She's happy that she's fitting right in with Julie and Beth. Sarah and Julie are really hitting it off."

"I know. I hope she's not upset that we're gone right now."

"She'll be OK."

Eddie was wearing yellow nylon shorts and a plain blue shirt.

Annabelle still wore her flowered sundress. Their colours beamed in the brown and green grove.

Annabelle raised her left hand, lifting the elastic waist of Eddie's shorts, slowly sliding inside. With both hands she gently tugged at his organ until it protruded from under the elastic. She pulled her hair behind her ears, lowered her face, and kissed his penis, suckling it. A minute later she looked up. He touched her cheek.

"You don't have to do that," he said.

"Do you like it?" she asked.

"Do you like it?"

"It's interesting."

"I'm not convinced that most women really enjoy doing it," he said, "I think women think men like it and that's why they do it."

Annabelle said nothing.

"Is that why you did it or is it because you like it?" he asked.

"Well I thought you'd like it."

"But do you like it? You never did that before."

She paused. "Well you know I had braces a few years ago. Before I got them men were always telling me how sexy my mouth was. Dennis used to insist I do it and I didn't like that. But I want to please you. I just want to please you."

"I only want to do what pleases you," he said. "That's how true love works. If you're not enjoying it I can't enjoy it."

"You are so different from Dennis," she whispered. "It's not that I hate it, I'm sort of indifferent to it. Maybe I have some healing to do around it. I really just want to please you."

"But you don't especially enjoy it?" he asked.

"Well, no."

"Then please don't do it. I think it's demeaning for you to do something you don't really enjoy. Would you like me to taste you?"

Annabelle laughed. "Not exactly."

They were both silent.

"We don't have to have sex all the time," he said. "We can just make love by sitting together, holding hands."

They sat in silence for several minutes.

"But I just want to please you," Annabelle finally whispered. "I don't feel like I have any value to you unless I'm pleasing you."

Eddie frowned at her. "Do you remember when you accused me of using you as a sex object? I'm not trying to do that to you. Maybe you just think of yourself that way."

She frowned. "Maybe you're right," she whispered. "There's a part of me that feels useless unless I'm earning something. And with you... maybe I feel... maybe I always feel like I need to earn your love."

Eddie thought for a moment. "I could pay you," he finally said.

"What?"

"I could give you fifty dollars each time we make love. Would that make you feel better?"

She scowled. "Are you trying to hurt me?" she whispered.

"No," he said. "No, not at all. I'm honestly trying to help. I want to please you as much as you want to please me. If you want to feel that making love is something worthwhile to me, then I could pay you for it."

They stared at each other. Annabelle shook her head.

"You're missing my point," she said. "I just want to feel like I'm pleasing you. That's all. I just want to satisfy your fantasies so that I can validate my own sexual existence."

Eddie smiled. "OK," he whispered. "I have a new fantasy."

He stood up and slowly unbuttoned the top of her dress, gingerly lifting it over her head. He gently folded it and laid it across a log. Then he removed her bra and panties.

She trembled, although the grove was hot.

"This is all I want," he whispered. "I just want to stand here in awe of perfection."

He stared at her body.

"This gives me great pleasure," he whispered. "Thank you."

Annabelle nervously looked around.

"Nobody can see you," he whispered. "Nobody but me."

"Does this really please you?" she asked. "Even if you don't come?"

"This pleases me immensely. I'll be hot all day. That pleases me. The Tao teaches men to hold back, it increases virility."

Several more minutes passed. Annabelle reached for her dress. "We need to find Sarah and make some lunch," she said. "I hope she hasn't been looking for us."

"Did you stay at the beach all morning?" asked Annabelle after lunch. She was applying more sunscreen to Sarah's sturdy back while Sarah was attempting to vault into the water.

"No. Donna made us get out of the sun. Julie showed me the falls. It's really pretty up there."

Annabelle paused. *How close had Sarah come to observing me with Eddie this morning?*

"Did you see the pine grove?" asked Annabelle.

"No," said Sarah, "Julie told me about it but she's not allowed to go up that far without a grown-up."

Annabelle sighed. Then Eddie beckoned her into the cold water.

"Julie took Sarah up to the falls this morning while we were in the pine grove," Annabelle told Eddie that afternoon when Sarah was playing at Julie's cottage.

"Don't worry about that," he said, pulling her onto his lap. "The kids aren't allowed to come near the pine grove without an adult."

"Why not?"

"Bears."

"But you said it was safe!"

"It is; we just tell them that. We just don't want them wandering that far off."

They were back on the porch, back at the 1950s kitchen table. Annabelle heard a noise from the wooden footbridge across the brook and peered over.

"Look, what's that?" she said, pointing at a chubby creature poised in the ferns, loudly chewing the vegetation.

Eddie looked. "The woodchuck is back."

"Oh, he is so cute!" exclaimed Annabelle.

"Not to my mother. That little guy could destroy her garden in a matter of hours."

She watched the woodchuck for a while, then looked back at Eddie. He was crying.

"What's wrong?" she exclaimed.

He smiled. "Your breasts are so gorgeous in that dress, all tan at the top. I can see your bathing suit line." He fingered the dress bodice and spaghetti straps. "You like it here, don't you?"

She nodded. His eyes were red.

"This is my Shangri-La. It's Brigadoon. It comes out of the mist every summer and I spend a few weeks here. I've been coming here all my life. When I was a kid I didn't appreciate it so much because it was always there. I really took it for granted. Other kids got to go on trips to all kinds of different places but I always had to come up to the lake and visit my grandparents. Back then my grandparents rented out the cottages but after my grandfather died and grandmother was starting to get old my mother and her brother took it over and it became a place just for our family."

"How long has it been in your family?"

"My grandfather was a stockbroker in New York City. Just before the depression he got sick of it all and decided to become a farmer up north. So he cashed it all in and bought this place outright. Back then it was quite a fortune, now it's really something."

Tears spilt from his eyes again.

"What is wrong?" insisted Annabelle.

"Nothing! I'm just so happy that I can share this with you and Sarah. I've been lonely here. I hated bringing Barbara here. We always had our worst fights here. She and my mom used to scream at each other."

He paused.

"I'd like to bring Sarah up here every year. It's a wonderful place for kids; it's like a dream in the winter that comes true every summer. I'd like to bring you here with our babies."

Annabelle smiled.

"Will you marry me?" he said.

She paused, and then nodded.

They both cried.

"Soon," he said, "in October. Under the full moon. OK?"

Annabelle thought for a moment. "That's a good time. Everything will be direct again. Full moon in October. That would be sun in Libra, moon in Aries, a good time to form partnerships, lots of passion."

"Can we tell everyone tonight?" he asked, smiling.

Annabelle shook her head. "I need to talk with Sarah about it first."

"When will you talk to her?"

"Can we get my ring first?"
"Your ring?"
"Engagement ring."
Eddie paused. "I never gave one of those to Barbara."
"Dennis never gave me one either."
"Do you want a diamond?"
"No, I don't want to support diamond mining. I'd like a ruby or an emerald. A ruby could symbolize passion but emeralds are sacred to Aphrodite. My birthday is next week."
Eddie nodded. "Yes, your birthday is next week. OK, we'll do that first. We'll get you a nice ring."

The night went as Eddie had predicted. There was a potluck dinner with all kinds of pasta casseroles, hamburgers, steaks, salads, strange jellied-fruit moulds, ice cream, soda and beer. Someone lit fireworks across the lake and everyone stood watching, slapping the last of the black flies and the first mosquitoes. Joanne helped the children make paper boats out of Don's old copies of the *New York Times*. They set the boats on fire, launched them on the lake, watched them sink, built a bonfire, put the babies to bed, cleaned off the picnic tables, and stayed up late singing folk songs in broad shadows of huge flames.

"Didn't you just love the lake?" asked Sarah over and over as Annabelle straightened the apartment after their weekend away. Sarah spoke only of the lake and Julie and Eddie's marvellous family.
Annabelle kept agreeing, wondering how to broach the subject of Eddie's proposal.
"Could you ask Eddie to marry you?" Sarah suddenly asked.
Annabelle stopped working and looked at her. "I thought you said you didn't want me to get married again!"
"Well, didn't you just love the lake? If you marry him we could go there all the time."
"Well how would you feel about having Eddie as a stepfather?"
"If I have to have a stepfather, I think he's the nicest one I could get. He's more like a dad than Daddy was."

Sarah hadn't mentioned her father since the weekend after the divorce. Annabelle had told her Dennis would probably wait a while longer before seeing her again. He'd sent her two postcards, saying that he'd moved to a small studio in East Boston. Annabelle wasn't sure what he was doing for work but had tried not to let it concern her. He had mailed a fifty-dollar child-support cheque for the two months since the divorce and that was the extent of his communication.

She had wondered whether to renew counselling for Sarah, to help her work out her feelings about Dennis, but since things had remained calm she hadn't bothered. Now Sarah wanted her to marry Eddie and things suddenly seemed too easy.

"I won't ask him to marry me, Sarah. But what if he asks me? Should I say yes?"

"Yes! Say yes!"

"Well he should give me a ring if he wants to marry me. My birthday is Wednesday so maybe he'll give me a ring. Wouldn't that be nice?"

"Well if he doesn't, don't be too disappointed," cautioned Sarah. "And if he doesn't ask you to marry him by the end of next week, why don't you just go ahead and ask him?"

"I'll think about it," said Annabelle.

During his lunch hour on Annabelle's birthday, Eddie ventured into Harvard Square and purchased an antique emerald ring in a Victorian setting, slipping it on her finger in the office, with the door closed. Annabelle wore it to the afternoon planning meeting.

Brian Anderson was dominating the meeting again. Arthur Ziminski was explaining that a final version of the new user interface wouldn't be ready for another month, a week after the first draft of Annabelle's book was scheduled for preliminary release to beta clients.

"You'll have the book ready to go, won't you?" said Brian to Annabelle.

"How can we possibly do that?" asked Patty, Annabelle's editor. "If the UI won't be ready, she won't even be able to create screen shots." Patty had started attending the weekly MVI Access meetings when schedules began heating up.

"You don't really need screen shots," said Brian.

Annabelle and Patty looked at each other. "Well, we really do," said Patty, "the book is filled with references to screens. It won't make any sense at all if it doesn't have any screen shots."

"You have that snazzy desktop-publishing system, can't you just make them up on that?" insisted Brian.

"I could," said Annabelle, "but if the UI won't be ready, how will I know what they'll look like?"

"Arthur," said Brian, "everything's all specked out, right? You guys could just tell her what will be on the screens, couldn't you?"

"I suppose so," said Arthur, "assuming we don't need to change anything."

"OK," said Brian, "that's it, it's not a problem."

"Wait," said Annabelle, "what if they do need to change something? It will make the documentation look wrong."

"That doesn't matter," said Brian, "Nobody reads the doc anyway."

To: ABonney
From: EWRIGHT

Here are some happy birthday poems to you.

200 Mile Love

Our love is a multicoloured limo
speeding down the highway

our limo has those big fins
that were popular in the late fifties
a full bath
and some beer

our love plays with images
and fills a rear view mirror.

The Changeling

My father
called you
a changeling

A paratrooper
hitting the ground
roughed, standard issue
running

but to where?
There are no enemies left.

To: EWRIGHT
From: ABonney

Thank you for the poems but there are enemies left! Brian Anderson! "Nobody reads the doc anyway!" Could you believe that? What a nerve! Why do they bother paying me to write these books if nobody reads them?

Patty and I had a long talk after the meeting. We're both upset by this business of producing the book before the software's ready. It's like I'm being asked to write telepathically. It's a good thing I took so many creative-writing courses in college!

Patty noticed the ring and I told her we're engaged. Have you told anyone yet? I wonder how quickly word will spread.

Tonight I'll tell Sarah.

I love you,
Annabelle

To: ABonney
From: EWRIGHT

Go home and read the Tao. As you write a book that nobody will read, think of the Tao. You are writing the Tao of Software, the eternal Documentation, infinitely important, never to be removed from its shrink-wrapped case, never to be read by clients, never to be followed, only to exist.

I have told everyone on the seventh floor that we are to be married in October.

I love you,
Eddie

In the parking lot at Sarah's day camp, Annabelle waited until Sarah was sitting in the car with her seatbelt buckled. Then she held up her left hand.

"See what Eddie gave me?" she said.

Sarah looked at her hand. "What?" she said.

"The ring!" exclaimed Annabelle.

Sarah looked at it. "That ring?"

"Yes! Do you like it?"

"Does that mean that he asked you?" said Sarah, becoming excited.

"Yes! What do you think?"

"And you said you would? You said you would?"

"Yes!"

"You're going to marry him?"

"Yes!"

"You are?"

"Yes!"

Sarah became quiet. "When?" she whispered.

"In the fall. In October."

"Can we go back to the lake then? Will you get married up there?"

"Yes."

"Good," whispered Sarah. "That's very good."

15

Three weeks later they returned to the lake, this time for a week's vacation, and they brought Danny with them.

They left with the sunshine but drove into unrelenting rain. Each time Sarah started playing games and singing Christmas carols, Danny told her to shut up.

"Danny likes things to be quiet," explained Eddie. They rode the remaining two hundred miles in silence, except for the occasional sneeze and cough.

Once they arrived at the cottage, it continued to rain, so they all ventured up the hill to Eddie's parents' house

Joanne greeted Annabelle with a hug and a gift: a happy engagement card and an expensive vegetarian cookbook; Danny and Sarah headed to the study to watch public television.

"So you're planning an October wedding?" she said. "Where will it be?"

"We'd like to get married up here," said Eddie.

"Here?" said Joanne. "At the Congregational Church?"

"No, in the pine grove."

"The pine grove?! Bah. You can't get married there."

"Why not?" said Eddie.

"You can't expect people to hike up to a wedding!"

"Where would you suggest?" asked Eddie.

"The Congregational Church."

Eddie looked at Annabelle. "Is that OK?"

She nodded.

"Do you want a minister?" asked Joanne.

"No, we want you," said Eddie. Annabelle nodded again.

"What do you mean?" said Joanne, frowning.

"You're a justice of the peace, right? Could you perform the ceremony?"

Joanne laughed, glancing back and forth between them.

"I could do that," she said, "I haven't married anyone before. You really want me to?"

They both nodded.

"Well, all right," said Joanne, beaming.

Back at their cottage, Sarah and Danny went to their respective rooms, read from books they'd brought, and ate candy.

Annabelle cooked dinner in the tiny kitchen while Eddie followed her around, embracing her, accidentally tripping her. Finally she gave him a job peeling carrots on the back porch. He kept the door open between the kitchen and porch and together they listened to the rain while they worked.

"What is this?" said Danny at dinner.

Eddie had served Danny first, seating him at the chair furthest from the kitchen, furthest from Annabelle and Sarah. Eddie handed a bowl to Sarah, then brought two more bowls for himself and Annabelle.

"Well?" insisted Danny after everyone was seated.

"It's soup," said Eddie.

"Duhhh," said Sarah, sarcastically.

"I know it's soup," said Danny, impatiently. "What kind?"

"Miso."

"What's that?"

"Japanese."

"Why are we eating Japanese soup? I'd like a hamburger."

"We don't eat meat here," said Eddie.

"What?" scowled Danny.

"Annabelle and Sarah don't eat meat so we don't eat it here."

"We always used to eat meat."

"Just try it," said Sarah, halfway through her bowl.

Danny took a small sip.

"This is repugnant," said Danny, slamming down his spoon.

"No, Danny," said Eddie, "it's soup."

In the unrelenting rain, Annabelle bristled, awkward around Danny, and ruminating about possible topics of conversation with him.

On the fourth day of heavy precipitation, Annabelle and Eddie sat alone on the porch while Danny read upstairs and Sarah was at Carol's cottage.

"Your mother is very excited about the wedding," said Annabelle. "I'm surprised by how she's really getting into this, given that a few months ago she didn't want you to marry me."

"She only suggested that I live with you first because I screwed up so badly with Barbara. As she gets to know you she's learning that you're nothing like Barbara. I told her that we have lunch together every day at work and she realizes that we've spent a lot of time together already, probably more than most couples spend before getting married."

Why does he care so much about what his mother thinks?
Annabelle paused. "Well I'm glad she's excited about it."
He reached for her hand.

"Last week Dad called and told me that making wedding plans has helped take her mind off Karen and all of Andy's divorce problems. Mom never had a daughter; she's never had the chance to plan a wedding for anyone, even herself. She and Dad were married in a city hall during the war."

"It's so nice of her to be doing all this for us, I really appreciate it," said Annabelle, "And I understand that you really love them, but why is it so important for you to get their approval?"

"She'll do a wonderful job with the wedding," said Eddie.
Annabelle stared at him.

1. *Didn't he hear my question?*
2. *Was that his answer?*

On the fifth day of rain, Eddie dealt cards on the back porch table after lunch, to play a game of hearts while the weather slowed to drizzle with moments of clearing.

Danny took the game very seriously and was clearly winning, repeatedly losing his hearts to Sarah, who eventually surprised everyone by suddenly shooting the moon.

For a moment, Danny was silent and his face turned red. Then he flung his cards in the air while huge tears streamed from his eyes.

"Don't be a baby," said Sarah.

"I can't believe you're actually going to marry that woman," screamed Danny, pointing at Annabelle. "If you marry her I'll make you get divorced! You don't love me at all, Dad! You wouldn't be doing this to me if you loved me!"

Annabelle stood up, saying, "Come on, Sarah."

"Sore loser," shouted Sarah as Annabelle found her purse and umbrella and she and Sarah headed out the door. Danny was still crying, loudly, angrily criticizing Eddie's choice in women.

"If you marry her I'll come to the wedding and object!" shouted Danny as they turned the corner outside the cottage.

Annabelle clutched her purse although she wasn't sure why she'd brought it with her.

"Don't let him bother you," said Sarah as they walked in the drizzle down to the beach. Annabelle was wearing canvas sneakers that were getting soaked from the moist grass.

"I'm pretty upset," said Annabelle. They walked to the dock and stood together under the large yellow umbrella.

"The rain is going away," said Sarah, "maybe tomorrow we can swim."

I do not want to be the source of misery for anyone; for Eddie's son. Maybe this is all too much for him. Maybe this is too much for all of us. Maybe this won't work out.

"I'm not sure if Eddie and I should get married," Annabelle heard herself say.

"Oh Mom, that's exactly what Danny wants. You can't let him run your life."

Annabelle glanced at Sarah and smiled.

"I'm sorry," she said, "I really shouldn't be talking about this to you, Sarah. And maybe you shouldn't call Danny a sore loser or call him a baby."

"Why not?" asked Sarah. "Danny is just a baby, Mom. I've had a lot more adjustments to make than he has and I'm not falling apart."

Annabelle didn't say anything. She and Dennis had separated and reunited six times in the nine years they were married. Sarah had woefully moved from apartment to apartment, school to school, always trying to find new friends, and here she was now, hoping her mother's new life with Eddie would stop the earth from shifting under her feet. It seemed that it already had; Sarah was in love with the lake and all its occupants. Most of the time she even seemed to like Danny and sometimes they played well together.

Finally Sarah said, "I'm going to see if Carol needs any help with the kids, OK?"

Annabelle nodded and watched Sarah walk towards Carol's beach-front cottage. The drizzle had stopped. Annabelle folded her umbrella.

She looked up and whispered aloud: "I need a sign, dear Holy Mother. If this whole thing is actually going to work out... If I really should marry Eddie, I need some kind of sign. A rainbow. A rainbow for Iris, for temperance."

She stared at the sky as clouds lifted and patches of late-afternoon sunshine appeared across Barton Mountain. After watching for a few minutes, she headed back towards the cottage, and saw Eddie walking towards her in the field of wet grass.

"Where's Danny?" she asked.

"He went up to Mom and Dad's to watch TV. He really hates to lose, Annabelle. I'm sorry he acted like that."

"Can we go home tonight?"

"It's supposed to be sunny tomorrow. Let's just stay until Sunday. Donna and Carl are coming up tonight for the weekend. We'll be able to swim. We deserve at least two days of vacation."

"We'll see," mumbled Annabelle.

"Look at that," said Eddie, pointing to a tiny rainbow forming over Mount Pageant.

Annabelle was silent.

"Danny and I talked about why he's so upset about us getting married," continued Eddie. "We used to come up here with his mother. He was really young, but he still remembers that... and he wants me to remarry her. If you and I get married, then his fantasy is over. Danny doesn't hate you. He just doesn't want the fantasy to end."

Annabelle nodded, staring at the sky. The rainbow had faded.

"I can understand how it's really hard for him to be thrust into a relationship with Sarah and me. I can understand all that… but I'm worried about the way you try to pacify him, instead of addressing his anger. I think you need to help him work through the feelings."

"What would you like me to do?" asked Eddie.

"You're always trying to calm him down, Eddie. He keeps all this rage bubbling just below the surface. And you just let it bubble there; you don't do anything to diffuse it."

"So you're saying I'm not hard enough on him?"

"That's not it at all. But it's like you fear him." Her feet squirmed in their wet sneakers. "It's not just that you never admonish him, but except for today, you never even talk to him about his feelings. It's like that part of him doesn't exist to you."

"But I want him to want to see me," said Eddie. "If I criticize him he won't want to come over and see me."

Annabelle shook her head and sighed. *He's just not getting this.*

"We have a little time alone together right now," said Eddie. "Can't we just be together right now without talking about problems?"

Annabelle shook her head. "If we don't talk about it now, when will we talk about it? It seems that you never want to deal with things when they come up. You seem to ignore your problems."

"Yes," smiled Eddie, "and most problems go away if you ignore them."

Annabelle looked at the clearing sky and whispered, "I might go away." She said it so softly he didn't hear her; he was walking towards the lake.

"We're so happy that you and Eddie are getting married," said Donna the next day. The sun was finally hot and all the children were playing in the water. Donna and Annabelle sat on the beach, their bodies soaked with sunscreen.

Annabelle smiled and looked away.

Donna continued, "Ever since his divorce Eddie's been talking about finding the right woman and trying again. On his weekends with Danny he used to come visit us a lot but Danny and Julie never got along. So Julie is extremely pleased that Sarah will be her cousin."

Annabelle nodded. "I know Sarah's happy to have made friends with Julie."

"How have things been with Danny here?" asked Donna.

Annabelle told her about the game of hearts.

"That sounds like Danny," nodded Donna. "Poor Eddie; I know he's trying so hard. It's too bad. Actually, it sounds like Danny's week hasn't been too terrific either. I wouldn't take the things he says personally, I think he just wants to make his mother happy; he's so devoted to her."

Annabelle studied the sky; the heavy clouds moving in from the south. "Well... it does make me wonder whether we should get married. Danny really seems to hate me."

"Danny won't be living with you," said Donna, "Barbara will never give up custody; she and Danny are like two plants whose roots have grown together. And Eddie isn't about to fight for custody; he doesn't have it in him; he's such a sweetheart, he'd never fight with anyone. So in the final analysis, Danny can have all the objections he wants, but you can't let your kids control you. So what if this isn't exactly what he wants? Too bad, that's life. Life doesn't always go the way you want it to. Sooner or later even Danny will have to learn that."

16

Sarah answered the phone and spoke quietly into the receiver, instead of summoning Annabelle who listened from the living room, hanging damp laundry on a clothes-drying rack. Clearly it wasn't one of Sarah's friends calling. Annabelle walked to the kitchen. Sarah looked at her.

"It's Daddy," said Sarah, looking confused, holding the mouthpiece against her stomach.

"Oh," said Annabelle, waiting for Sarah to say more.

"He said he wants to see me this weekend. Can I?"

Annabelle nodded. "It's up to you."

"Uh huh," said Sarah into the phone, "I'll see you on Saturday. Bye." She hung up and looked at her mother.

"Daddy said that Grandmom is better. She's in remission or something."

"That's good!" said Annabelle.

Sarah scowled. "Why do you care?"

"It's good that your grandmother is getting better."

"She wants to see me," mused Sarah. "I'd like to go see her. I feel bad that I haven't seen her for so long. She must think I forgot about her and that I don't love her."

"She doesn't think that," insisted Annabelle. "It was your father's responsibility to arrange visits with her."

"It wasn't mine? Are you sure?"

"Yes."

"Are you positive?" asked Sarah.

"Yes."

"What if Daddy asks what I've been doing? Can I tell him about Eddie and the lake?"

"What do you mean?"

"Can I tell him that you're getting married?"

Annabelle paused.

"I'm afraid that if you tell him that he might try to stop us."

"Do you want me to lie to him?" Sarah scowled again.

"No, I don't want you to lie to him. Maybe you just shouldn't say anything about it."

"That's lying, Mom!"

"No it's not."

"Yes it is."

Annabelle sat on a kitchen chair, a wet towel dangling from her hands.

"I'll call my lawyer tomorrow and ask her what to do, OK?"

"She'll tell you what the right thing to do is?" asked Sarah.

"Yes, she'll advise me."

"Good," said Sarah. "I don't want to lie."

The next day Annabelle called her lawyer, who explained that she had every right to remarry.

"So I just shouldn't talk about it?" said Sarah that night.

Annabelle nodded.

"And that's OK? That's legal?" asked Sarah.

Annabelle nodded again.

"What if Daddy asks?"

"Why would he ask?"

"But what if he does?"

"Don't lie. I'm not asking you to lie."

"If he knows you're getting married he might go crazy again!"

Annabelle shrugged, attempting to appear unconcerned.

"I can't believe you're doing this to me!" shouted Sarah.

"Doing what?"

"Why didn't you just say that I can't see him?"

"Because it's up to you. When I divorced him I agreed that I would let him see you as long as you wanted to."

"I ought to see Grandma. I feel like a terrible person," moaned Sarah. "Grandma probably thinks I don't care about her."

"You are definitely not terrible, Sarah," insisted Annabelle. "You've just been stuck in the middle of your parent's problems. I'm really sorry about that." *Sometimes my words are so insignificant. Sarah, if you could read my mind you would know how terribly sorry I am.*

Sarah's disposition became darker and angrier as the weekend approached. By Sunday, Annabelle was nearly relieved when Dennis appeared at the door to take Sarah away.

She returned that evening appearing happy, then angry, then confused and tired.

"How was your Grandma?"

"She didn't look very good to me, but Daddy said she's getting better. She didn't talk very much. I didn't tell Daddy that you're getting married. He told me that it's hard for him to get up here so he said we'll probably only be able to visit only once a month or so. I told him that was fine. It's only two months until you marry Eddie. Then can I tell him?"

"I'll mail your father a letter the day before the wedding, so he'll get it right away."

"Will he go crazy again?"

"I don't know," said Annabelle, "but it's possible that this will be the best thing for him; he'll have to realize that the marriage we had is over for good… and maybe that will make it easier for him to move on."

"But it's like you two were never really married," said Sarah. "You seem more married to Eddie right now than you ever did to Daddy. Why did you marry Daddy?"

Annabelle smiled.

I could be honest and tell her that I was very self-destructive back then and marrying Dennis was the ultimate attack I could wage against myself.

"He was very good looking," sighed Annabelle, "and I was very young."

The weeks that followed were so eerily uneventful that Annabelle began obsessing about Dennis plotting some kind of revenge.

Nevertheless, she began contacting old friends with her news; with each phone call she was greeted with similar responses:

"Where have you been? I left messages on your machine."

"I've been wondering how you were."

"I was afraid we'd lost touch! Did you get my letter?"

Then she'd say she'd gotten divorced:

"It's about time!"

"I was wondering when that would happen."

"Good for you!"

And was getting remarried:

"Really? So soon?"

"That's awfully sudden."

"Wow."

Annabelle and Joanne began weekly telephone conversations, in which Joanne described each aspect of the ceremony in great detail.

"I'll take care of everything, see," said Joanne, "all you have to do is show up."

"I really appreciate this," said Annabelle. "Work is just crazy right now. Eddie and I are working on the same project and the deadline pressures are unreal."

"Well don't worry about anything up here. When you come up next month to get your licence you can pick out the flowers you want and pick out a cake. And bring up your dress so I can adjust it if it needs any alterations, see."

"I haven't bought the dress yet."

"Well you better hurry up."

To: ABonney
From: EWRIGHT

Mom called and said we won't be happy living in your apartment; we should buy a house right now. Then Dad got on the phone and said he'd lend us the money for a down payment. I know we're both kind of out of time right now but I think they're right. I also have an inheritance from my grandmother that's just sitting in the bank. How do you feel about this? We could just do it, just go out and buy a house.

To: EWRIGHT
From: ABonney

Really?
 Well, unfortunately, I don't have any savings, so I wouldn't be able to contribute towards the down payment if we were to buy a house. Also, I don't want to move out of Gardenia because I don't want to uproot Sarah. Is there any way we could afford a house in Gardenia so Sarah wouldn't have to change schools again or lose her friends?

To: ABonney
From: EWRIGHT

I just called a realtor in Gardenia and she said she has some nice houses in our price range. I know you're flat out right now but do you mind if I go up and look tomorrow? If I like one, can I make an offer?
 I love you.

To: EWRIGHT
From: ABonney

This whole house thing seems to be happening pretty quickly.
 I have to bring a bunch of files home to work on tonight; they've moved the printing schedule up another week! I don't know how I'll finish this book before the wedding. I'm sorry I can't meet you for lunch today.
 If you want to go and look tomorrow, that's fine. All I care about is whether the house has a fireplace and a china cabinet.
 There's one other thing (and you're going to think I'm paranoid for worrying about it): Gardenia is a very small town and Dennis still has friends there from all the partying he used to do. It's conceivable that someone in the real-estate office might know him, or, more likely, know someone who knows him. When you talk to the realtor, could you ask her to keep us confidential (if you have to give her information about me)? I think that's important.
 (Also, are you sure you feel OK about handling a down payment yourself? I still can't believe we might actually buy a house.)

Eddie tapped at Annabelle's office door after returning from his trip to Gardenia.

"Can you have lunch today?" he said, holding up a bag of groceries.

She turned off her monitor. "Did you see any houses you liked?"

He set the bag of food on her desk. "I bought one," he said.

She frowned. "You bought one?"

"I put in an offer. You said I could."

"Where is it? Is it in Gardenia?"

Eddie nodded. "It's not on the water or anything but it's very nice. It has a fireplace like you wanted. It has three bedrooms, one for me and you, one for Sarah, and one for Danny when he visits, until we have a baby."

"I can't believe this!"

"Are you upset?" asked Eddie, confused.

"I'm not upset but usually when someone looks for a house they spend… a while looking at everything available and weighing all the options. How many houses did you look at?"

"Four. I liked this one the best. It's in a very nice neighborhood. There are lots of kids around."

"What kind of house is it?"

"It's empty right now so we can move right in after we pass papers," he said, handing her the realtor's description of the property, which included a photograph.

She stared at the little house. "It looks nice."

"I made the offer and called my father. He can get the money to me tomorrow. If they accept the offer we can pass papers a few days before the wedding."

Annabelle held her breath.

"I think you'll really love it."

"Wait," she said suddenly, some worry occurring to her. "Did you tell the realtor to be confidential about us?"

Eddie nodded. "I told her that you don't want your ex-husband to know you're buying a house so she said mum's the word. OK?"

She covered her mouth with her hand. "Well, if you told her not to say anything about it, she may be more likely to say something about it…"

Eddie shook his head and whispered, "You're just terrified of becoming successful."

The meeting was running on and Brian Anderson was still pontificating. Eddie had arrived late and sat next to Annabelle. At one point, he leant against her chair and squeezed her arm. She swivelled away, ignoring him. At that point, Arthur Ziminski interrupted Brian, saying, "Ed, have you had a chance to look at the graphics doc yet?"

"Yes," laughed Eddie, "I love it. I just worship all of it."

Annabelle grimaced, looking out the window. The meeting went on.

Eddie organized the paperwork and finances necessary for the property purchase. He made arrangements for Annabelle and Sarah to see the house. The bank approved the loan quickly, with no complications.

Annabelle picked up the finalized divorce certificate from the court and obsessively kept the document with her, guarding it in her purse.

In mid-September they left for their last visit to Vermont before the wedding. They stayed with Eddie's parents and Joanne explained the final details of the ceremony.

"You really need to decide what kind of cake you want," insisted Joanne.

1. *A wedding cake is the least of my problems.*
2. *Why is Joanne so concerned about the cake?*

"I always liked rum cakes," said Annabelle.

"Oh." Joanne paused. "You mean those Italian cakes? I don't think you can get one of those up here. I mean gold or chocolate, that kind of thing."

Annabelle and Eddie agreed to invite only their closest few friends and family members, and with Joanne's additions, the list turned into fifty people.

"My friend Kathryn – the maid of honour – will be coming with her partner," said Annabelle. "My friend Diane and her husband will also come. I'd like to bring my mother, but the nursing home doctor won't allow her on overnight visits, and I don't think I should sign her out without his consent."

"Well that's for the best," said Joanne, "what would she do here anyway? So you have four coming, well that's enough. Eddie just has more family than you do, that's all. And I have a few friends across the lake. I have to invite them. That's all right, isn't it?"

Annabelle nodded.

1. *Why wouldn't it be all right?*
2. *Why wouldn't it?*

"How much did you pay for this?" asked Joanne when Annabelle modelled the wedding gown she'd bought at a vintage-clothing store.

"Ninety dollars."

"Well it's worth six hundred! Look at that lace, that's all handmade French lace and all that beading is all done by hand. But the bodice is much too big. You don't have any bosom, see. It just sags on you. Here, take it off, I'll sew it up right now."

While Joanne altered the bodice, and Sarah watched television, Eddie and Annabelle walked to the town hall to apply for the marriage licence.

"Do you think they'll want to see my divorce decree?" Annabelle asked, the divorce decree safely stored in her purse.

"No," he said.

"At the top it cites a statute which says that both parties have the right to remarry as though the other were dead."

"Are you afraid of something?" asked Eddie.

She nodded. They could see the town hall, down the street, next to the church where they would be married. Eddie pointed to the lake, across the street. The water reflected bits of leaves just turning gold and crimson. The scene couldn't have been more tranquil.

"The lake was formed by a glacier," he said. "Some people say that the ice at the bottom has never melted."

She stared at him, puzzled.

Then he began walking ahead of her towards the tiny town hall.

Back at the house, Joanne instructed Annabelle to try on the dress again.

"Oh that looks much better," said Joanne.

The bodice was too tight. Annabelle could barely breathe. She thanked Joanne for her work, then went to the guest bedroom and sobbed.

Eddie followed her and Annabelle whispered, "Joanne made the dress so tight that I can't wear it! She was trying to be nice and I just can't criticize the work she did but now I can't wear it!"

"Just tell her it's too small. She'll fix it."

"I can't. She'll be upset."

"No," said Eddie, "with mother you just have to tell her. Just tell her."

"No! I can't!"

Eddie left the room and returned a few minutes later. "She's letting it out again," he said, "but she says you'll have to wear a padded bra."

"I just couldn't breathe in it."

"It's not a problem now," he insisted.

"I just couldn't breathe," she repeated.

Dennis called in mid-September, three weeks before the wedding.

"Can I see Sarah on Sunday?"

"I'll ask her," said Annabelle. She covered the mouthpiece with her flat palm. "Do you want to see your father on Sunday?"

"I guess I should," said Sarah, slowly.

"OK," Annabelle said to Dennis.

"Tell her that we're going to visit my mother."

"OK," said Annabelle.

"You haven't even sent her a get-well card, have you?" hissed Dennis.

"Don't start," said Annabelle.

"You could have at least done that," he said, hanging up.

1. *I'd like to write to Dennis's mother, but Ellen told me not to.*
2. *If I wrote her a letter what would I say? "By the way, I'm getting married again"?*
3. *Sarah doesn't want to see Dennis. She's doing it out of guilt.*
4. *Sarah is really starting to take after me.*

After returning from the visit on Sunday, Sarah collapsed on Annabelle's bed. "Now I don't have to see him again until after you're married. I hate living this way, Mom."

"Do you still want me to marry Eddie?"

"Yes," she impatiently insisted.

Sarah was to be in charge of carrying the wedding rings. Joanne had explained her role to her over and over while they were in Vermont. Sarah wanted to be absolutely certain she understood exactly what she would have to do. She wanted to perform her job perfectly.

"Here are some pictures of him," said Annabelle to her friend Kathryn, handing her three photographs of Eddie, two by himself and one with Danny.

"He's incredibly good looking," exclaimed Kathryn. "Don't you think so?"

Annabelle smiled. "You mean Eddie?"

"Yeah! Look at him. You know, he looks like John Lennon."

Annabelle squinted. "Eddie?"

Kathryn pointed to a snapshot. "Yeah, he looks just like him."

Annabelle studied the picture.

"I guess he does; if he was shorter and thinner and if he had little round glasses, then he'd look a bit like him."

"Like his double," said Kathryn. "You never noticed the resemblance before?"

Annabelle shook her head.

"You?" said Kathryn. "The Lennon freak? You never noticed the resemblance?"

"No," insisted Annabelle, "I never noticed."

"I wonder what else you may have failed to notice."

Annabelle frowned. "What do you mean?"

Kathryn shook her head. "All I'm saying is that love is blind. You haven't known him very long."

"You're ruining the TV reception," said Sarah that night, while Annabelle was working on the computer in the living room.

"I absolutely have to get this done," fumed Annabelle, "or else I can't get married."

"What?" said Sarah, turning away from the TV set.

"If I don't get this done and all the other stuff that's due by October 5th then I won't be able to take any time off that weekend to get married."

"Mom, you're going crazy!"

"Stop bothering me!"

"You don't even care about your wedding!"

Annabelle stopped typing and whispered, "Be quiet. Someone might hear you."

"Now my mother is going crazy too, just like my father," mumbled Sarah, turning off the TV, wandering towards her bedroom.

Joanne sent Annabelle a postcard on which she'd drawn a picture of a wedding cake with a description and the annotation: "Would something like this be OK? Gold with white icing, pink roses? Let me know."

1. What if Dennis has been going through my mailbox?
2. What if Dennis knows the mailman who might have read the postcard?
3. Why does Joanne care so much about that cake?!

Annabelle immediately phoned Joanne and told her that gold cake with white icing was a very good idea.

On the Sunday before the wedding, Annabelle went shopping with Sarah. Eddie and Joanne had decided that Danny shouldn't come to the wedding, so Eddie was devoting his entire weekend to him. Annabelle had taken Sarah to visit Mary earlier in the day, not daring to mention the upcoming wedding, certain that Mary wouldn't understand anyway.

Annabelle and Sarah walked around Salem, searching each tiny shop for a shawl, but it was autumn, nobody was selling white shawls. In one store she stood a while, inspecting a necklace to give Kathryn as a maid-of-honour gift, when she heard a voice say, "Hi Annie!"

She looked up in confusion, recognizing the face but unable to place the person. Then she realized it was one of Dennis's cousins, someone she had seen infrequently at his family's events over the years.

"Hi," said Annabelle, cautiously.

"How are you?" said the woman. "I haven't seen Dennis in so long. How's he doing?"

Annabelle lowered her left hand, hoping the ornate glass jewellery counter would conceal her engagement ring.

"Dennis and I are divorced," said Annabelle.

The woman continued to smile but confusion clouded her eyes.

"Oh, I'm so sorry to hear that. I didn't know that."

"Yes. We've been divorced for a little while now."

The woman paused, peeking from behind her wide glasses, her grey hair just brushing the lenses. "Well, so how's he doing?" she asked, awkwardness grazing her voice.

Annabelle became impatient, expecting Dennis himself to appear any moment. Sarah walked over, stood next to Annabelle, and stared at the woman.

"Hi," the woman said to Sarah. "You look just like your father. The last time I saw you, you were just a baby!"

"I really don't know how he's doing," Annabelle said tersely, "we're divorced now. So I don't know how he is."

The woman nodded and stiffened. "Well," she said, walking away, "it was good to see you."

On the way to the car, Sarah quizzed Annabelle about the woman.

"She's your father's cousin," said Annabelle, "I don't even remember her name."

"Did you tell her that you're getting married?" asked Sarah.

"No!" snapped Annabelle, looking around to see if anyone had heard what Sarah had just said.

To: EWRIGHT
From: ABonney

> Yesterday I ran into one of Dennis's cousins. It made me extremely nervous. I tried to call you last night but I guess you were out late driving Danny home.
>
> Just before I woke up this morning I had a terrible nightmare. I dreamt I would give Dennis one more chance, so I called off the

wedding and went to live with him again. It was just horrible. I was paralyzed with misery. He kept saying things would be different this time.

    I'm so glad I woke up.

    Annabelle

To: ABonney
From: EWRIGHT

I also had a nightmare last night in which you said you couldn't marry me because you were still married to Dennis and you had to give him one more chance!

    And so I became a hermit, living in the woods like a wild man, piling stone on top of stone, erecting an impenetrable wall in the forest.

    Great minds dream alike.

    I love you with all my heart.

    Eddie

"I ordered the bed this morning," said Eddie at lunch the next day. "I'm going to have them deliver it on Thursday so it should be waiting for us when we come home from the closing."

He sat back and stared at her. "I can't wait to try it out."

She looked away.

The following afternoon Annabelle sat at her computer, writing steps for handling a corrupted database.

    The telephone rang. She stared at her monitor, wondering how many users would actually be able to follow the twelve-step procedure without calling customer support.

    "Hello, Annabelle Bonney," she said, still looking at the terminal screen.

    "Hello Annabelle," said a man with a friendly voice, "this is Fred from after-school. Listen, Sarah's Dad came by to pick her up while we were walking all the kids over here from school. I thought it was OK but then I figured I ought to double-check with you."

    Annabelle froze. "Dennis took her?" she said.

"Is that not all right?" said Fred, his voice suddenly full of concern.

"It's not all right," said Annabelle, her voice breaking. "The school knew that. He's had a lot of problems. I made it very clear to the school that he's not to pick her up without my permission."

"Oh gee," said Fred, his voice wavering, "I wasn't aware of that."

"What happened?"

"Well he drove up along next to us while we were walking over here. If we'd been here I probably would have called you first but she wasn't really at school and she wasn't here yet. I really didn't know. He said he'd bring her back by five."

Annabelle stood up, stressing the phone cord.

"I don't know what to do," she stammered.

"Gee," continued Fred, "I really didn't know this was a critical situation. Do you want me to call the police?"

Annabelle paused. "Let me call you back before we do anything, OK? You see, we have joint custody but I have physical custody, which means that he can't see her without first receiving my permission."

Fred paused, then said, "I'll call the police if you think I should."

"Well let me just think for a minute and I'll call you back, OK?"

"I'm really sorry."

"Well you didn't know," she said, her voice cracking. "Bye."

Tears ran from her fatigued eyes.

She dialled Eddie's extension.

"Ed Wright," he said.

"Dennis took Sarah."

"I'm coming up."

Three minutes later Eddie appeared at her office and embraced her, without closing the door first. Annabelle squirmed out of his arms, pushing the door shut.

"What happened?" said Eddie.

"Fred at the after-school programme called; he said Dennis just picked her up—"

"Why did they let him?"

"He said he didn't know he wasn't allowed to. Dennis told them he'd bring her back by five. Fred said he'd call the police if I wanted. I don't know what to do!"

"First you have to breathe," said Eddie. "Take a long deep breath."

Annabelle stood still, closed her red eyes and breathed deeply. She looked at Eddie.

"Take another one," he said.

"No!" she shouted. "I have to do something!"

"If you're relaxed you'll be able to think more clearly."

"How can I possibly relax?! My daughter's been kidnapped!"

"We don't know that," Eddie calmly said, "we don't know that that's happened."

"Are you crazy?! What do you mean we don't know?! Dennis just came along and took her!"

"But he said he'll bring her back—"

"And you believe him?"

"Sweetheart, it won't do anyone any good for you to get all upset about this."

Annabelle covered her face with her hands, then spoke through clenched teeth.

"Eddie, please do not patronize me. My child has been abducted. I am upset. I have every right to be upset."

"Then call the police."

"But if he actually does bring her back she'll be all upset if I call the police. I don't want another scene with him. Shit."

"Let me know what I can do to help," said Eddie.

"You can't help."

He reached for her, tried to hug her. She pulled away.

1. *I could call the police but if they left Gardenia they could be on any number of highways by now.*
2. *He trashed the car that was registered in my name. I don't even know what kind of car he's driving now! I don't even know if it's legally registered. What did it look like? What was the model? Blue? Dark green? An old, dented two-door subcompact; it was something like that. I wish I knew the licence plate. I could call Ellen and ask but she probably wouldn't know much more than I do.*

"I'll call Fred and have him call the police," Annabelle finally said. "Maybe he can give a description of the car."

Eddie nodded. They both sat down while Annabelle opened her day planner and found the number to Sarah's after-school centre.

"Hello, Fred Winslow please," Annabelle said to the person answering the phone.

A moment later Fred said, "Hello?"

"Fred, this is Annabelle, Sarah's mother—"

"Annabelle – I was just going to call you. Sarah just got back. She's walking in the door right now. Her father dropped her off at the kerb. Do you want to talk to her?"

"Yes," sighed Annabelle, motioning to Eddie.

"She's back!" she said while waiting for Sarah to take the phone.

"Hello Momma?" said Sarah.

"Sarah! Are you OK?"

"Yeah," whispered Sarah, her voice tired and weepy, "I'm sorry you were worried."

"What happened?"

"I'll tell you later," she whispered, "I'll tell you when I see you. OK? Can you come and get me right now? OK?"

"OK, sweetie. I'll be right there."

Annabelle hung up and Eddie smiled.

"See?" he said. "Nothing is accomplished by getting all upset. You would be so much happier if you could learn to meditate, if you would study Zen, really learn and practise the Tao."

Annabelle stared at him, then turned away without a word and started putting on her coat.

"Why are you angry at me?" he asked, confused.

She paused then said, "You didn't care at all about what happened to Sarah. You couldn't have cared less."

"I love Sarah. I do care, very much. I just know that it's easier to handle stressful situations when you're calm. That's all. I was just trying to help you."

"I told you, you couldn't help. You didn't help."

"If you'd just listened to me you wouldn't be so upset right now," said Eddie, softly, still sitting, his legs crossed. "I wish you could learn how to breathe. I wish you could learn how to relax."

"I'm going to get Sarah," said Annabelle, grabbing her purse from her desk drawer, locking it after her.

"OK," he said.

Annabelle paused and stared at Eddie. They were frowning at each other.

"Things just aren't working out," she said.

"What do you mean?"

"Things are a mess. They're just crazy. Dennis tried to kidnap Sarah. We're supposed to buy a house in two days. We're supposed to get married in four days. Your son hates me. I've been so immersed in work that I haven't had time to plan my own wedding, I'm not even sure what my vows will be. I can't handle this stress."

"If you stack up all your problems like that they'll seem overwhelming," said Eddie. "I'd like it if you would take a yoga class."

"Is that your answer to everything?"

"What do you mean?"

"Yoga. Meditation. Does that solve all your problems for you?"

"Once you realize that you create most of your problems yourself, it becomes easier to solve them," he said, calmly, "I solve my problems through meditation. I never get stressed out."

Annabelle was shifting her weight from foot to foot, getting ready to bolt out the door.

"I don't think it's that simple."

"Actually, it is simple," he said. "It's very simple. I just don't understand why you like to punish yourself so much."

She paused again.

"I can't marry you," she finally said.

"OK," he nodded.

She shook her head and left her office, closing the door hard.

After Sarah stumbled to the car and was buckled in, Annabelle said, "Exactly what happened?"

"Well, while we were walking to after-school, Daddy drove up next to us and told me to get in the car."

"Didn't you know—"

"I knew I wasn't supposed to go with him without your permission but I didn't want him to get mad at me. He promised he would take me right back so I said OK."

"What happened? Where did he take you?"

"We drove down to the beach and walked around."

"He picked you up to take you for a walk on the beach?" asked Annabelle, confused.

"I think he thinks you're getting married," said Sarah, after pausing for a minute.

"Why?"

"He said, 'Is your mother getting married?'"

They had arrived at their apartment. Annabelle shook her head, unlocked the front door, and said, "What did you say?"

"I told him I don't know."

"You told him you don't know?"

Sarah started to cry. "I didn't want to lie! But I don't want him to stop you from getting married! So I told him that."

"What did he say when you said you didn't know?" asked Annabelle, hugging Sarah, stroking her thick, blonde curls.

"He said, 'Is she buying a house?'"

Annabelle paused and sighed. *It's a small town.*

"What did you say then?"

"I said I don't know."

"I see."

"I hated to lie! I hate to lie!"

"You didn't have to lie, sweetie."

"Yes I did! He would have gone crazy again if I didn't!"

"Well it's not our problem if he goes crazy."

"Are you sure you're allowed to marry Eddie?"

Annabelle paused, tilting her head; the nightmarish events of the past few hours now required explanation: "I'm allowed to but I'm not going to. I realized that it just wouldn't work out."

She attempted a smile. Sarah stared at her, her eyes widening.

"Are you crazy?!" Sarah suddenly shouted. "What do you mean, Mom? What do you mean? What do you mean?"

"We decided not to get married. I think that Eddie and I love each other very much, but we have very, very different ways of handling problems. I just realized that if we were to get married we'd just make each other miserable. So I called it off."

"When? When did you do that?!" shouted Sarah.

"Today. This afternoon."

"You idiot!" screamed Sarah. "We were going to be happy! We were going to live in a house and be a family! We were going to be a happy family!"

"Sarah," said Annabelle, "you are not to speak to me that way. Go to your room please."

Sarah stood still, arms locked across her chest. "I'm not doing anything you say. I hate you."

"Sarah," pleaded Annabelle, "we are a family. You and me. We are a happy family."

"You are a crazy stupid head. Both of my parents are crazy stupid heads. I was going to be happy." Sarah started to cry again. "Now I'll never be happy," she sobbed, "I'll never be a happy person."

Annabelle tried to hug her. Sarah pushed her away and ran to her room, fell on her bed, and wept uncontrollably.

Sarah refused to speak to Annabelle for the rest of the day and into the night.

The apartment was a sea of packed bags and recycled liquor-store boxes, carefully organized for the trip to Vermont and the move to the house. Annabelle knelt by a box and began placing its contents back on one of the kitchen shelves. She carefully dusted spice jars, working slowly, accomplishing little.

After Sarah was asleep, Annabelle called Eddie.

"Hi," he said, "what's up?"

"I was just wondering if you'd like to call the realtor and cancel the house deal, or if I should."

"Whatever you prefer," he said.

She looked at the ceiling, held the phone before her, and shook her left hand in exasperation.

"Why don't you?" she finally said. "I mean since you made all the arrangements it might make sense for you to cancel them."

"OK. Is that all?"

"Yes, that's all."

"OK," he said. "See you later."

They hung up together.

She dialled Kathryn's number and listened to the answering machine ask her to leave a message.

"Hello, Kathryn?" she said. "This is Annabelle. Please call me as soon as you can. There's been a change in plans. Bye."

She decided she would call her friend Diane the following evening, when she'd be calmer. She would call her landlord later; staying shouldn't be a problem, he hadn't found a new tenant yet.

She sucked on an Aconite pellet, a homeopathic remedy for shock and fear and fever. She wasn't sure what drove her to it; she wanted something to calm her. She lay down to sleep, then got up and started putting away more of the kitchen equipment that had been packed.

1. I thought I loved him unconditionally. I thought we'd get married and live in that house and everything would be happy.
2. I was playing that same absurd happy tape in my head that Sarah's got in hers.
3. I can't believe I've done this to Sarah. Whatever made me think there could be a man out there who'd really be compatible with me?
4. It's like I'm addicted to failure. It's like there's something that stops me whenever I'm about to feel happy.
5. Eddie said I like to punish myself. Maybe I do punish myself, but I don't like to. That's the problem, he thinks I like it. That's why I could never marry him. He insults me.

Finally she got up. After drinking three large glasses of burgundy, she slept fitfully with long strange dreams.

She was sanding something, some kind of frame, a windowsill, a picture frame, she wasn't sure. Shake... baby... shake... shout... Some mysteriously familiar song kept playing; kept playing the same thing. She was working hard, using muscle grease, sanding away. Suddenly a long splinter penetrated her palm, thick and long and painful. She squeezed her hand and pushed it out, was about to throw it away, but stopped. It was solid gold, some ancient Goddess artifact, priceless. She clasped it in her injured palm, not wanting to disclose it, not wanting anyone to know about it.

Then she woke up.

Her head pounded. Sarah refused to speak to her as they attempted to eat breakfast.

"Sarah," said Annabelle, "I know it sounds crazy but it really is for the best. You wouldn't want me to get married, then get divorced again, would you?"

Sarah stuck her fingers in her ears.

Annabelle sped to work, attempting to avoid the meditative mode that driving induced. She developed a mantra for the fast commute: it's over, it's over; it is good that it is over.

All morning she waited for the telephone to ring. She wouldn't change her mind. Eddie didn't even bother to call. His silence affirmed her decision.

1. *He doesn't love me.*
2. *If he loved me, he wouldn't give up this easily.*

She ventured down the hall, to Daryl's office. A note on his door said he had a dentist's appointment and would be back by two. Patty was in but every time Annabelle walked by her office she was busy – on the phone or heading to a production meeting.

1. *I shouldn't bother my colleagues.*
2. *I should keep my problems to myself.*
3. *They'll find out about it soon enough.*
4. *This weekend I'll start looking for another job.*

She ended up at her computer, which was a solace: it was the only thing receptive to her thoughts. Instead of eating lunch, she worked diligently, completing the trouble-shooting section by early afternoon.

1. *I should probably at least tell Daryl that we've cancelled our plans.*
2. *He's probably back from the dentist's by now.*
3. *I wish I had my homeopathy kit here. I need some Natrum Muriaticum for this headache.*

Her telephone rang – an outside call that she answered.

"Hi, it's Joanne," said the voice.

Annabelle caught her breath.

"Hi Joanne."

"Listen, I was just thinking it would nice to have some edible flowers on your wedding cake. Well, not exactly edible, but fresh, real, you know what I mean. We could use roses but those are so expensive up here this time of year. Or we could use marigolds, see. I rather like that idea. How would marigolds be?"

"Joanne, have you talked to Eddie lately?"

"Yes. Just a few minutes ago."

"Did he tell you that we've cancelled our wedding plans?" asked Annabelle, softly.

"Oh, well he said something about that but I figure you just have cold feet, see. I had cold feet before I married Don, see. We got to the city hall and I told Don I just couldn't do it but he said I had to. Well, what was I going to do? We had planned it, so we did it. That was all."

"This isn't just a case of cold feet. This is a little more serious than that. I'm sorry."

"Well, what's the problem?" said Joanne, her voice emotionless. Annabelle rolled her eyes.

"OK," she said, shaking her head, "the problem is that it won't work. We aren't compatible."

"What do you mean by that?"

"My ex-husband tried to kidnap Sarah yesterday and Eddie acted like nothing was wrong. He just told me to relax and breathe. How could I relax?"

"Well, Eddie told me all about that and it wasn't such a catastrophe, was it? Sarah's fine, isn't she?"

"That's not the point!"

"Annabelle, you have to learn to stop borrowing trouble! If you were a smart girl, you'd get that through your head! Sarah is fine. Eddie was right not to get all upset about it. You need someone whose feathers don't get ruffled, see. Otherwise, there'd be two of you running around like chickens with their heads cut off and what good would that be?"

Annabelle held her breath, insulted once more.

"Well, it really was a very serious situation and Eddie obviously didn't care."

"You know that's ridiculous," said Joanne. "Eddie cares very deeply for Sarah and so do I, so does Don, we all do. She's part of our family, see. She fits right in. Now what you need to understand is that strong women don't give up this easily. If you were a strong woman you'd recognize that of course there are going to be conflicts. Every relationship has conflicts."

"Joanne, I've supported Sarah for years. I took care of my mother for years too. I've successfully survived quite a lot, more than you know. I do think that I am strong." Annabelle's words were clipped, controlled and angry.

"Well, I don't know about that," said Joanne, "You're certainly brave, taking on all that responsibility. I mean you need to be strong-minded. If a woman has a strong mind, she'll recognize that problems are inevitable, and she'll just go on, she'll persevere. It's silly just to throw in the towel when one thing goes wrong. Now let me just say this. If you are serious about cancelling this wedding, you should know that we have already paid a deposit for the caterers. We'll lose a lot of money if we cancel now."

Annabelle took a deep breath. "I'm sorry. I really do appreciate all the energy and money you've spent but Eddie and I are not compatible. Isn't it better that we recognize that now? Isn't that better for everyone?"

"Well, what's wrong with him?" demanded Joanne.

"Couldn't you just have a catered party there anyway? Without us?" Annabelle was trying to rub her aching temples with her right hand while holding the phone in her left.

"What's wrong with him?" repeated Joanne.

"He never gets upset! He never argues. If there's a problem, he meditates, he just breathes. It's like he's too perfect, so I end up feeling like his inferior."

"What a selfish girl!" said Joanne, authoritatively. "You're saying his only fault is perfection. You won't allow him to have any faults so you criticize his perfection? You're a very selfish girl, Annabelle, that's all I can say."

Annabelle's face became flushed and feverish.

1. *She says I'm not smart.*
2. *She says I'm not strong.*

3. *She says I'm stupid.*
4. *She says I'm selfish.*
5. *God, am I glad I'm not marrying that man!*

There was a knock at the office door.

Annabelle turned around and shouted, "Come in!"

Daryl opened the door and pointed to his watch.

"We have to get to that mandatory meeting," he said, his face drawn and serious. Annabelle had received e-mail about it that morning and had heard hushed rumours of layoffs in the halls and at the water cooler. Normally she would have obsessed about it, but today she ignored it, it was insignificant.

"I have to go now," Annabelle said into the phone, "I have to go to an important meeting."

"Well wait a minute. What do you think of fresh flowers? Do you like marigolds? Do you like that idea or not?"

Annabelle exhaled deeply. "I'm sorry but I have to go!"

"Well go then," said Joanne, briskly. "Just go. Don't let me stop you." She hung up the phone.

Annabelle found Daryl in the hall, waiting for her.

"What's this meeting about?"

"I'm not certain," said Daryl, "But I don't think it's good news. Stocks are down and Zimman hasn't seemed too pleased lately."

"Do you have a minute, after the meeting?"

"If we're both still employed here," quipped Daryl.

They walked down the silent hall, towards the executive briefing room.

1. *I'll probably get laid off.*
2. *At least I won't have to work with Eddie any more.*
3. *If I don't get laid off I'll definitely have to find another job somewhere else.*

The large room was crowded and quiet as they entered. The folding chairs were missing; everyone was standing around. Then Annabelle saw beer bottles in people's hands. An enormous white cake was placed on a table in the centre of the room, surrounded by several boxes wrapped in shiny white paper.

Annabelle looked at the cake, and then looked at Daryl. He smiled. She frowned and glanced around the room.

Frank Marks stood by the door and announced, "Well I'd say she's surprised!" He had shouted into his beer bottle, as though it were a microphone.

The room filled with laughter. Eddie was leaning against a wall, staring at her. She stared back. He came towards her, and knelt before her.

"Will you marry me?" he said.

"A dramatic re-enactment, ladies and gentlemen," announced Frank. Everyone laughed again.

Annabelle held her breath, attempting to contain her splitting head. Eddie clasped his hands in front of him, as though in prayer.

"A pregnant pause," boomed Frank. There were chuckles here and there. Annabelle was compelled to respond.

1. *Jesus, Eddie, why are you doing this to me?!*
2. *Don't you take anything seriously? Am I really nothing but a big joke to you?*

Her eyes filled with tears. The room was hushed.

"What do you think?" she finally said, loudly, sarcastically. More laughter. Eddie smiled and stood up. People began milling about, grabbing her arm, and congratulating her. A beer was thrust in her hand, then a package.

"Come on," said Patty, "open these."

"Oh, you really shouldn't have done this," said Annabelle, earnestly, glancing around, reluctantly pulling apart the paper. The boxes contained delicate white china with a matching tea service, a soup tureen and a platter.

"Thank you very much," she mumbled, "but you really shouldn't have. This is so lovely. I never had a soup tureen before…"

Eddie whispered in her ear, "I wanted you to have a party. Even if you won't marry me. Just enjoy it. Just enjoy the moment."

He wandered over to a group of engineers and laughed at their jokes, remaining perfectly relaxed.

Daryl and Patty started quizzing Annabelle about the new house and the wedding plans.

"So you're closing on the house tomorrow, eh?" said Daryl.

Before she could answer, Patty said, "You must be so excited. I remember when Paul and I bought our house. But we'd been married for a while then. How does Sarah like the house?"

Annabelle paused, then said, "She likes it."

"Is everything all set for the wedding?" asked Patty.

"No," said Annabelle.

"It never is," said Daryl.

"I know," said Patty, "you can plan those things for ever and you'll never finish all the details."

Patty started mingling with the crowd. Annabelle stared into space.

"A little too overwhelming?" asked Daryl.

Annabelle nodded and was soon standing alone, watching Eddie study her across the crowded room, the way he had before they'd met.

1. *It's like a nightmare that should have been happy.*
2. *Eddie, what are you looking at? Why do you have to be so good looking? Why do you have to be so horribly perfect?*
3. *God Eddie, why do I still want you? Why do I keep punishing myself?*

She remained motionless, beside the cake. Eddie returned, and stood beside her. Her cerebrum was beating to the rhythm of chattering voices – a painful beating. They said nothing.

Frank Marks' left hand slapped Eddie's shoulder.

"Well I just want first dibs on your kid's basketball contract!" he boomed, heading for another drink.

Annabelle took a long sip of beer and allowed her head to swim, closing her eyes.

"I have a headache. My head hurts a lot," she said, not bothering to whisper, her voice barely audible in the loud, packed room.

"Would you like me to massage it?" Eddie offered, taking her hand. His touch shocked her, the way it had the first time, moist warmth, huge palm. She remembered her dream that morning and opened her eyes.

"Did you call the realtor?" she asked at last.

"No."

"Why not?"

"I couldn't."

"What do you mean?"

He shook his head. "Did my mother call you?"

She nodded. "Did you ask her to?"

"Aren't you guys going to cut the cake?" called Patty, above the din.

Annabelle paused, and then obediently started slicing big pieces for the party participants.

"It's just that you insulted me," Annabelle said to Eddie, suddenly, privately, her voice hushed, the cake cut.

He shook his head. "How? How did I do that?"

"You said I like to punish myself," she whispered. "Maybe I do punish myself, but I don't mean to. I don't like it."

"I'm sorry I said that. I didn't mean to insult you. I worship you."

"And then your mother called and insulted me," she said, still hushed.

"Oh no," he said, looking up, shaking his head. "What did she say?"

"She said I'm stupid, weak and selfish."

The party was still loud but Eddie and Annabelle had drifted to a quieter corner of the room.

"I asked her to help me," he whispered. "I asked her to call you and see if she could somehow change your mind. I never thought she'd insult you!"

Annabelle stared at him.

"I asked her to help me," he repeated. "I'm sorry, but I need you. What else could I do?"

Annabelle said nothing.

"I need you. I'm awfully sorry about that."

She looked away.

"Did my mother say anything that wasn't insulting?"

"Well, she said she was calling to find out whether or not I'd like fresh flowers on the wedding cake."

They were both silent.

Eventually Eddie said, "Would you?"

"No! I do not want a wedding cake. I cannot marry you. I want you to start taking me seriously. I want you to stop insulting me."

"I'll never leave you," he said, "I will never leave you. You have to marry me."

Annabelle scowled. "What about our first by-law?"

"It was stupid."

She huffed. "We agreed that if you wanted to leave, I wouldn't stop you and if I wanted to leave, you wouldn't stop me. You agreed to that."

"I wasn't being serious then. Now I am."

She breathed a deep, exasperated sigh.

"I'm going now," she said, turning her back. He grabbed her arm. She turned to face him.

"Eddie, if I marry you I'll become just as fake and frigid as your first wife. Because if I marry you I won't be able to have feelings any more. I'll have to eat all my feelings and that will make me sick and cold and dead."

Eddie shook his head. "You're saying I don't have feelings? How can you say that? How can you possibly say that?"

Tears filled his huge eyes.

"When I first met you," explained Annabelle, "you gave me all those poems about feeling your pain and you told me how I shouldn't deny the pain in my divorce. But you deny all of your pain! And you refuse to see the way you tune out every single thing that hints at unpleasantness. You have a Baba Yaga mother who fed you so many chicken bones that you grew up tuning her out. You learnt how to do that in order to survive but you don't see it. You don't see how you tune me out! You tune out anyone who presents you with conflict – including your son – but Danny needs you to fend off his own Baba Yaga! But you're too nice to hate – plus you're his father and so you're not safe to hate – so he transfers his hatred to everyone else and you don't see it. If I marry you it would be like having a fair-weather husband. Because the moment I need you – just when I need you the most – you tune me out. You don't see the problems. You pretend they don't exist."

Annabelle stopped speaking and looked around. The room had emptied, the party was over; her words were louder than she'd intended, streaming from loose beer lips and insights she hadn't been aware of before. She held her hand over her mouth and stared, wide-eyed, at Eddie.

"I'll never leave you," he whispered, "I own you."

Annabelle imagined curious ears lurking outside the door.

"I can't believe this," she said, sighing, covering her face with her hands.

"Love isn't something you can put on your list, Annabelle. You don't make plans for it. Your brain doesn't control it."

She shook her head.

"Love lives inside your body," he moaned. "It's the spirit inside you that gives even when you can't, even when the person you love sickens you."

She shook her head again.

"You asked me to rape you!" he screamed, his voice echoing in the wide corporate spaces surrounding them. He grabbed her waist and picked her up, shaking her.

"So I did it! I raped you! I own you! I will never leave you." He stared in her eyes. She began to cry.

"Let me go." He set her down. She ran to the door and peered out. No one was waiting outside. No one was listening.

She glanced back at Eddie's huge form, seated against a wall, his head erect, sobbing. She paused.

"You own me," he finally said. "You raped me too. Do you remember that? You have to commit to this. You can't have by-laws that say you can leave when things screw up. That's utter bullshit. You forced me to be a wild man. And now you can't control him. You can't make him go away. I worship everything about you, including all your petty insecurities. Override that fucking by-law. You may be right about me but it doesn't matter. You need to surrender."

Annabelle stared at him and waited.

"I'll go live in the woods if you leave me," he sighed. "I'll build a cross and tie myself to it in the rain. I'll live like Thoreau, alone. I'll become a hermit. I'll become a human sacrifice to your need for perfection."

She slowly wandered to the table, picked up the cake knife, and began carving the remaining block of cake, in half, then in half again. She licked white icing off her fingers.

"Eddie. I don't know."

He stood up and joined her at the table, covered his fingers with icing and held them to her lips. She pushed his hand away.

"You are just trying to manipulate me... with all that hermit talk," she said finally.

"Yes!" he shouted, grabbing the remaining block of cake. His shoulders widened to immense proportions as his right arm loomed back, preparing to heave the cake to the floor, at her feet. "I can't make you want the wedding or the family or the house," he screamed, "I can't fight with your mind!"

Annabelle remained motionless, her eyes wide.

Then he paused and steadied himself, lowering his hands and his voice. "But Annabelle, my love for you is pure. My love for you is true."

She drew a deep sigh.

Eddie began to smile, holding the cake before her. "I want you to have this," he whispered, his voice solemn, unwavering, "I want you to have this cake and eat it, too."

17

Sunbeams woke Annabelle at dawn. She found a poem on the pillow next to her, on the new bed.

    Asking

I looked for you
deep in August water
where peace abounded
amid stormy white caps

I looked for you
in reading class
when they decided I couldn't read
and forced my eyes
with a machine
to move them very fast

when all I really wanted
was to hold your warm breast.

I looked for you
in the woods
which smelt of leaves
bark and rock
wet with time

but you were not there.

Your path was deep
In Maya time
in a dream so dark
its remembering made you bleed

deep but waking to the thought
of your own wild perfection.

She crept down the unfamiliar staircase and found Eddie sitting cross-legged in meditation on the living-room floor.

"Thank you for the poem," she whispered.

She stumbled around the new kitchen, preparing tea and cold cereal.

"How's the baby today?" asked Eddie, joining her at the kitchen counter.

She sighed. "Did we really do that?"

He nodded. "It's for real."

They packed the car while the sun rose. Annabelle had written her letter to advise Dennis of the marriage.

"I'll mail it in Vermont," she said, "that way he'll get it on Monday. He doesn't need to know before then."

Sarah wanted to eat the candy Eddie had brought but Annabelle told her to wait until after lunch. They sang Christmas carols. After stopping for fast food midway up Route 93, Sarah fell asleep. They drove through the silent notch, surrounded by intense foliage.

"It's good we left in the morning," said Eddie, "we're missing a lot of traffic; this will be the peak leaf-peeping weekend."

Annabelle remained silent.

"What are you thinking about?" he asked.

"How am I ever going to face everyone at MVI again, after that scene we had? They're going to think we are both completely crazy."

"No," said Eddie shaking his head, "we cleaned everything up. And we're taking off next week to move into the house. By the time we get back, it will be old news. And I'm sure they're all laughing about it right now. Most people have a good row just before they get married."

"Maybe. But I'm still worried."

"Yesterday you woke up worrying about the house closing. Now that that's over with you have time to worry about your colleague's opinions of you? Why not worry about our wedding tomorrow?"

"No, it's not all that," sighed Annabelle. "I'm mostly worrying about what Dennis will do when he gets the letter. He probably will start acting out again."

"But this time you have me to protect you."

Annabelle sighed again.

"It really doesn't matter what he does," said Eddie, "you're not responsible for him."

"I know. I can't help it. I'm just worried. And I'm still upset about Danny. He'll probably always resent me. That makes me sad. I'm sad for him too."

"Let Danny be Danny. You're not responsible for his feelings either. Someday he'll understand why I left his mother. Someday he'll leave her too. Just give it time."

"Well, it's just hard knowing that Dennis might go nuts and Danny will always hate me."

Eddie paused. "Do you realize that now we own a house together? Do you realize that tomorrow at this time we'll be married? You have a healthy, beautiful daughter. You're a healthy, beautiful woman and you're marrying a man who adores you. And after what we did last night, you might even be pregnant right now, and one of your biggest wishes is to have another baby! Isn't that enough?"

Annabelle smiled. "I'm sorry," she said. "You know that I worry."

"When will it be enough? When will you have enough?"

"I'm sorry," she repeated, "don't you ever worry?"

"No, but I think I know why you do, I know what your problem is. No one ever gave you permission to be happy."

Annabelle looked at him.

"You have my permission," he said.

She leant back, gazing out the window. The mountains were rolling jewels ablaze in the sun, bodies of pregnant women peacefully sleeping, nipple peaks, amber thighs, soft and brazen faces staring at the sky.

She had everything she'd ever wanted and no more excuses.

Eddie broke her reverie, saying, "Dennis might go crazy, that's true. That's possible. He might even have found out about the wedding and he might come up to Vermont and try to ruin it, he might cause a scene! Danny might resent you forever. And up a few miles ahead of us, we could get in a terrible car accident and we could all die. Or next week we could discover that I have incurable cancer. The world might even blow up tonight. So… I don't think we should worry about any of it. Look at all the special things. Look at all you have. It doesn't get any better than this. All you have to do in order to be happy is just decide to be happy, that's all you have to do."

"It really isn't that simple," she said.

She looked at Eddie. He was smiling and nodding. "I know," he whispered.

The car suddenly lurched and swerved along the highway. Eddie skidded and pulled over.

"I don't believe this," he moaned, "we blew a frigging tyre!"

He jumped out and began pushing aside luggage, searching for the buried jack. Annabelle got out of the car and stood beside him while he slipped the jack under the car and pumped.

Sarah was still sleeping peacefully.

Annabelle sighed, watching Eddie's large hands patiently persevere.

Then she closed her eyes in the bright sunlight. The mountain images lingered, like photograph negatives, impressed before her.

In the crisp autumn air, in the slow passage of time, she began breathing deeply, imagining life without fear; imagining joy.

Leda Joandaughter is a novelist and poet whose work has been published in the USA, Iceland, and Greece. She has worked as a professional writer in the computer industry, and for humanitarian and educational organizations. A mother of three, she currently lives in Western Massachusetts with her husband and two younger daughters.